The Devil's Own

Also by R. A. Scotti
The Kiss of Judas

The Devil's Own

by R. A. Scotti

DONALD I. FINE, INC. · New York

The Devil's Own is a work of fiction and should be read as such. Any resemblance to persons living or dead is simply that, and nothing more.

—R. A. Scotti

For Evans:
   "high Asia is not so high nor the Nile so long"

"*Thus spake the devil unto me, once a time: 'Even God hath his hell; it is his love for man.'*"

—NIETZSCHE

The
Gathering

IMMACOLATA CARLATTI was laid to rest as she had lived, in a homespun black dress and stockings. But her glass-enclosed coffin, set atop a mountain of floral wreaths, was edged with gold. The sweet fragrance of azaleas, mingled with the aroma of sweat and death, hung shroudlike over the mourners. The falsetto chant of the old Archbishop committing her soul to paradise rose above the unrestrained crying of Stefano Carlatti. Supported by his son and daughter, he bent over the open grave and reached out for his grandmother, impotent before her mortal remains. His wife Donna stood behind him dry-eyed and pale.

Although the funeral was a private affair for the immediate family, four other mourners had chosen to attend. They stood in a solemn row behind the family, like theatergoers with seats in the mezzanine. Elena Maria Torre in a gray silk suit, aloof and watchful. Bishop Joseph Desmond, the trappings of office exchanged for a plain black suit, head bowed in silent prayer. Bruno Parente, shifting uneasily from one foot to the other, hands clasped in front of him. And Gaetano Badalamenti, hat in hand, scuffing at the grass with the toe of a polished boot. Marco Boni recognized them all: three bank presidents and a local businessman—yet each was a representative of so much more.

He leaned against a gravestone obelisk, screened from view by a spray of juniper trees, feeling like a voyeur before a grief so intense that even his presence could not intrude. The cemetery, dug into a slope of the Monti Peloritani, hung over the port of Messina. Ferries and fishing skiffs slid in and out of the harbor below, combing the deep Strait of Messina. Boni started back, wondering why he had made the long trip to this Sicilian hillside. What had he expected to discover at the funeral of an old peasant woman?

Although he looked like a soccer star with his barrel chest and dark curly hair, Marco Boni was a lawyer appointed by the central bank of Italy to investigate the most spectacular fraud perpetrated since Ponzi: the case of Stefano Carlatti, devoted grandson of Immacolata and financial wizard who had come within a hair of creating the largest conglomerate in Europe and who, in the process, had brought not only himself but his country to the brink of bankruptcy. Boni had a reputation as a rapacious investigator, single-minded and compulsive, but this case was putting his skills to the test. After five months he was still trying to cut through the jungle of holding companies, shell companies and subsidiaries that Carlatti had built on two continents.

ELENA TORRE, president of Banco di Milano, was the first mourner to turn away. Her heels sank into the dark earth as she walked toward the hired limousine that would take her back to the airport in Palermo. Her briefcase lay open on the back seat. She'd used the time well on the trip down and she planned to get even more done on the return flight to Milan. Annoyance flickered across her face like a caution light as she reached the car. The chauffeur was seated across the road, having a cigarette with the other drivers. If she had been anywhere but in a cemetery she would have leaned on the horn to get his attention. Instead, her dissatisfaction would be reflected in his payment. Elena opened the door herself and slid in the back seat. Marco Boni was waiting for her.

"What are you doing here?"

"I wanted to ask you the same question. I distinctly recall you saying that your business with Stefano Carlatti was over." Boni offered her a cigarette, she ignored the gesture.

"I can imagine what you're doing at Immacolata Carlatti's funeral. I want to know what you're doing in my limousine."

"I was hoping you'd give me a lift to the airport." He lit a cigarette for himself.

"Why not ask one of the others . . . Bishop Desmond or Parente?"

"I thought I might enjoy your company more." He snapped her briefcase shut and put it on the floor in front of him.

"Sometimes second thoughts are advisable, Signor Boni. And what did you expect to see here anyway? Haven't you any sense of decency? Spying on a man burying his grandmother."

"Everything about Stefano Carlatti interests me."

"Obsesses you would be more accurate."

He didn't deny it. "The guests alone are instructive. God, Satan, and the moneylenders. Why were you there, for instance? Were you invited or were you paying a debt?"

"I want you out of this car, Boni."

"I can't. I'd have to walk all the way back to the airport and it's too hot. Anyway, you haven't answered my question."

"I owe Carlatti that much."

"For services rendered?"

She stared at him. "If you like."

"By him or by you?"

His hand closed over hers and held it before she could lift it across his face. A strand of emeralds dipped below the cleavage of her gray silk jacket. The skin beneath them was golden brown and moist with sweat. The pressure of his hand over hers tightened.

Elena shuddered. "I hate funerals."

He wanted to taste her sweat—test it for saltiness and perfume. He pictured her spraying herself with scent—a halo of mist around her hair, a fine dew over her breasts and thighs.

"Where do you want to go?" She was staring at him. Her eyes like green glass matched the stones around her throat.

"To the airport in Palermo."

"You're a liar as well as a spy, Boni. You want to go to bed with me."

He opened the door and flicked out the cigarette. "Either way. You lead, I'll tag along."

The driver came up gushing. Elena cut off his apologies with a word and closed the window between them. The air conditioner went on with the engine, drying the moisture on her skin. Boni let go of her hand and she turned to the window, staring out all the way to the airport.

Limestone cliffs studded the road from Messina to Palermo. To the right a profusion of wildflowers, myrtle and lavender, anemones and bee orchids tumbled to the sea. Boni wanted to fill her lap with them and make love to her through the fragrant blanket. The limo hugged the road, climbing the steep, winding path, effortlessly mounting the foothills of the Monti Peloritani. At the crest the view was stunning. Coastal shores stretched on either side of them, and beyond, east and west, was the infinite sea. As they hurtled down he glimpsed the Lipari Islands and the conical mouth of Stromboli in the distance. Snatches of Greek temples and Roman baths shot past; the car never paused. Light eclipsed as they dove into the tunnel that burrowed through Capo Calava, then they were crossing the Fiume Grande, covering the final kilometers to Palermo. Traffic thickened as they approached the gulf through groves of citrus and carob trees heavy with fruit, on through the crust of poverty and decay that skirted the main city of Palermo to the Punta Raisi airport. A silver Lear jet bearing the crest of Banco di Milano waited on the runway. They went directly to it. . . .

* * *

"POUR SOME wine, then we won't have to call the steward." Elena pointed to a refrigerator at one end of the cabin. "I only have champagne, I don't drink anything else." She unbuttoned her jacket as she talked and tossed it over a chair, then reached back and unfastened her bra.

When he'd first interviewed her behind her Renaissance desk in Banco di Milano, her hair subdued in a bun, her ripeness camouflaged by a tailored suit, she had appeared remote, unattainable. Now, though, she appeared almost wanton—slanting green eyes, high jutting cheekbones, thick toffee hair. A Botticelli Venus, he thought extravagantly. Every seductress of myth and history seemed contained in her. Lorelei on her rock in the Rhine, Jezebel, Delilah, Cleopatra, Madame du Barry; queens, mistresses and fornicators of every hue and tongue. No question, he was carried away. Elena unzipped her skirt and stepped out of it. The engines fired. The Lear cleared the runway. Boni lurched forward and grabbed for her to regain his balance. She was naked except for a garter belt.

"What are you waiting for? If you don't want the champagne, then get undressed."

Disinterested in the way he shed his clothes, Elena turned away and bent to peer out the window. They were flying over Messina, five thousand feet above the spot where Immacolata Carlatti lay in eternal peace. From the air the town looked like the white crest of a wave dashed to shore at the mouth of the Strait. Behind them the fulminating crater of Mount Etna steamed and just ahead lay Scylla and Charybdis, lethal rock and churning whirlpool, twin terrors of ancient mariners. Boni's attention was concentrated on a different geography. The round curve of her behind gleamed like an offering, tanned except for a white bikini line that ran vertically along the breach. Midway up it crossed horizontally, an *autostrada del sole*. He came up behind her and pressed himself against her. Shivering at the first touch of a new body, she turned in his arms.

"What do you like best?" He said the words against her lips.

"Everything." She moved against him. The jet soared into a billow of clouds. He lifted her onto himself. She wrapped her legs around his waist as he carried her through the sitting room into the bedroom. They hadn't even kissed, he thought. Elena didn't seem to care. She was taking him inside herself, every fluid stroke expert, every touch a joy. He wanted to be good, to show her that he was the equal of any man she'd had. At least here he could be as powerful as she. She laughed as if she was a mind reader as well as a sorceress and arched her hips high, anticipating the force of his drive. He could have been anyone, it didn't matter to her now. What a pleasurable way, she thought briefly, to work off a disagreeable debt. . . .

LIKE THE sitting room of the Banco di Milano jet, the bedroom was decorated with suede walls and Saporiti furnishings. A Paul Klee oil hung on one wall, a medieval tryptich on another. Boni lit a cigarette and let his eyes wander around the room, trying to decide if what he was feeling was caused by the condition of being airborne or by the Botticelli beside him.

"What have you found out about Carlatti?" Elena's question was casual.

Boni turned over on an elbow and studied her stretched out at his side. She'd made no move to cover herself when they finished. Her breasts were still flushed from their lovemaking. "Is that why you took me to bed? To pump me for information?"

"That might have been true the first time." She laughed and reached down for him again. "Is it too soon for you?"

Elena didn't have to wait for an answer. Maybe it was the freedom of flight, the sensation of weightlessness, or the fact that they were suspended, encapsulated, joined inescapably as long as the jet was in motion, but Boni had never wanted a woman more. He ground out the cigarette and pulled her under him, aroused by her touch. "How would you like to do it? Dangling from the wing? Floating on a cloud—?"

"Shut up." She laughed once again, showing him the way.

As he entered her the second time, Boni found himself wondering if Stefano Carlatti had been there before him. . . .

Boni realized that on every level Elena Torre was the antithesis of Stefano Carlatti. She was the scion of one of the oldest families in Italy, president of the prestigious Banco di Milano, arbiter of Milanese society. Yet on more than one occasion she had conspired with him and Bruno Parente, lending the prestige of the Torre name to their questionable ventures. Boni didn't yet have all the facts, or explanations, but he had enough to make him curious. Very curious.

Stefano Carlatti had built a giant industrial and financial consortium by an adroit rendering of services. It was a talent he had begun to perfect some twenty years earlier. . . .

Book One

Chapter One

MARBLE SPIRES reached up like tapering fingers to the celestial realm, five hundred years of incontrovertible testimony to the builders' faith that somewhere in the vast heavens the eye of God gazed down. Wisps of clouds as fine as gauze blew in from Lake Como, marring the clarity of the evening. Inside the Gothic cathedral where the Archbishop of Milan waited for Stefano Carlatti, roseate light filtered through the stained glass windows, casting mystical shadows along the five great aisles.

The Archbishop watched Carlatti walk the length of the center aisle to the high marble altar, grateful that the Lord had sent this disciple north to help him in his new apostolic see of resentment and discontent. It was a difficult mission. The Italian postwar miracle had transformed Milan into the industrial heart of the nation, and burdened it with all the problems of urbanization. The factory workers might come home to their Holy Mother to die, but in the here and now they were turning increasingly to the Communists for answers. And this in spite of the church's most dire warnings. Equally distressing, family unity, for centuries the staple of Italy, was dissolving in the sacred name of progress. There was no room in the crowded city apartments for grandparents, maiden aunts or lonely uncles. The Archbishop visited the factories like St. Paul proselytizing among the Ephesians, but the plight of the elderly was dearest to his heart.

Stefano Carlatti knelt and kissed the jeweled hand.

"Come," the Archbishop said, inclining his head to one side to acknowledge the homage. "We will pray together and ask God's blessing for our mission."

Beneath the elaborate canopy the altar was an empty table offering nothing, not even a flicker of light, to the two men who knelt before it. The Archbishop crossed himself. "*Pater noster . . .*" Carlatti copied the gesture, thinking how cold the stone was against his knees.

The Duomo of Milan, third largest church in the world, fourteen thousand square yards of granite and marble, twenty thousand people able to worship together in the cruciform . . . the Archbishop followed the Lord's Prayer with an *Ave Maria*. Above them massive pillars soared uninterrupted to the very top of the vault. In the crypt beneath them the body of St. Charles Borromeo, dressed in finery, reposed in a rock-crystal casket.

Satisfied, the Archbishop made the sign of the cross again and led the way to a pew. Although Carlatti had been commended to him by the aging Bishop of Palermo, he hadn't relied on anyone's word alone. The Archbishop was by instinct cautious, and he had done his homework. After the war when Milan was a wasteland, Stefano Carlatti had come north from his native Sicily, a young tax lawyer with nothing but his wits and a single dark blue suit. By shrewdness and audacity he had insinuated his way into the closed world of Milanese finance, manipulating the tax problems of the new industrialists and accepting payment in stocks as often as cash. From such a humble beginning he was on his way to creating a multinational conglomerate. Socially, Carlatti remained the outsider, his face pressed, so to speak, against the plate glass pane, but the world of business was more pragmatic.

The Archbishop clasped his hands in the folds of his crimson cassock and leaned closer to the Sicilian. "I am worried for my people," he confided. The vast cathedral was hushed. The few faithful who had come to pray or to steal a moment's rest were out of earshot. "They see only the glittering promises of materialism and are blind to the subtle, mortal dangers that threaten their eternal souls."

"One never perishes through anybody's fault but one's own . . . Nietzsche, Eminenza," Carlatti murmured.

The prelate looked at him. *"The Twilight of the Idols,* isn't it? I've been told that he is a favorite of yours. For me, Nietzsche is a philosopher of mortality; my concern is eternal life. And immortality is threatened when the veritudes of faith and family are forgotten. Look around our city today. In the rush for prosperity the old people are left to fall by the wayside, like the unfortunate man in the Scriptures on his way from Jerusalem to Jericho." The Archbishop paused and smoothed his skirts. "We would like to build a home for them, my friend, but it is very costly. . . ."

"You have an estimate, Eminenza?"

The Archbishop nodded. "Two million dollars."

"Two million dollars." Carlatti exaggerated each syllable. "A large sum."

"It is," the Archbishop agreed, "but perhaps it would be wise to meditate on the parable of the Good Samaritan. Do you recall the story? A certain traveler on his way from Jerusalem to Jericho was attacked by robbers, stripped, beaten and left half-dead. A priest and a Levite passed by without stopping. But a Samaritan saw the man and was moved by compassion. He bound his wounds and brought him to an inn to be cared for, promising the innkeeper, 'Whatever more thou spendest, I, on my way back, will repay you.' And Jesus said, 'Go and do thou also in like manner. Love thy neighbor as thyself and thou shalt live and gain eternal life.' Luke, chapter ten." The Archbishop leaned closer. "The Church of Milan is like that poor soul. We need a good Samaritan to help us raise the funds."

Carlatti met the intense eyes of the prelate and smiled. "I won't disappoint you," he promised.

Chapter Two

"PRINCESSES! SKELETONS!" The shouts of the vendors sounded in the curtained suite like distant echoes. In the square below, children clambored around the painted carts grasping for the sweet foot-high cookies, knights for the boys and princesses for the girls, elaborately decorated with red, white and green sugar icing. Others gobbled up spines and femurs, ribs and tibias, the chocolate and sugar cookies shaped like skeleton bones that were a holiday specialty in Palermo.

It was November 2nd. From the Dolomites to Calabria—the length of the boot—Italians were commemorating the Feast of All Souls with somber prayers for the repose of the souls of the faithful departed. Fresh flowers were placed on graves, masses were offered to speed a dear one's ascent out of purgatory. But in Palermo the holiday had a macabre tone. Only Sicilians still dared to celebrate the Feast of the Bones of the Dead, the ancient pagan counterpart to All Souls' Day.

Stefano Carlatti elbowed his way through the thronged *Vucciria*. It was his first visit back to Sicily and the profusion of colors and smells in the marketplace was tempting, but he paused only once in front of a puppet theater. Marionettes had intrigued him since he was a boy watching them for the first time from the security of his grandmother's skirts, and he stayed longer than he'd intended, admiring the invisible hands imposing their will on the characters, controlling every movement, their identity never revealed. The play was the fable *Petrosinella*. A wicked ogress had just imprisoned the innocent, golden-haired beauty in a high tower when Carlatti turned away and pushed through the crowd, making up with quick feints and unexpected movements what he lacked in physical force. Piazza San Domenico opened ahead of him, and he made his way more easily past the *colonna* to the Immaculate Virgin, along Via di Roma to the Grande Albergo e delle Palme. The venerable hotel where Wagner completed *Parsifal* was hushed. Carlatti ran both hands over his thinning hair, then went upstairs to Suite 301. His suit, a conservative blue pinstripe, distinguished him from the eight men who had proceeded him . . . thin-faced or jowled, with bald pates or ample stomachs, they wore their black suits and white shirts with short spreading collars like a uniform.

Carlatti knocked once and waited for the door to be opened. Though quieter than the *festa*, the mood in the suite was welcoming. It might have been a lodge meeting or a family gathering. Nothing distinguished the eight from the men in the marketplace below, except their membership in a most elite fraternal society—the Commission. Deferentially, Carlatti approached each don and greeted him formally with a kiss on each cheek: the Signori Bonanno, Genovese and Gambino from New York; the Sicilian overlords Ignizio Inzerillo, Stefano Bontade and Michele Greco; and, to Carlatti, two newcomers, Gaetano Badalamenti and Tommaso Buscetta. It was not coincidence that the unusual meeting of the Commission was being held on the Feast of the Bones. The crush of revelers in the streets provided a useful camouflage for the members' arrivals and departures.

When the circle of greeting was complete, Carlatti took the place of honor at the right hand of Joseph Bonanno. In the marketplace below at the puppet theater Petrosinella was letting down her long golden hair so the prince could climb up to her tower window.

"You have done well in the north . . . your grandmother has kept us informed," Bonanno began. "We have watched your career with interest and pride."

Carlatti knitted his fingers nervously in his lap. The table, he was sorry to see, was bare, not a single sheet of paper for him to fold. The first woman he had taken as a lover at the university had taught him origami. He remembered little about her, but he'd become expert at the intricate art and now his hands needed to be busy to quiet him. "I have much to be grateful for. I have not forgotten my first business venture . . . exchanging the citrus fruits of Messina for fresh produce from the interior after the Allied invasion. I bought a truck from the GIs, but the trip was dangerous. My grandmother went to the bishop, who interceded with you."

"Your grandmother Immacolata Carlatti. She raised you well. You understand respect. Even though you are an important and honored businessman you have not forgotten who your friends are. That is good." The others added their silent benediction. "The time has come to reward her fine teaching."

Bonanno cleared his throat. The courtesies were concluded. It was time to talk business. Outside, the crowd cheered as Petrosinella and her prince slid down the ladder of silken hair and escaped from the tower. "Narcotics is a dirty business. For many years and for many reasons we've left it to others—mostly because it offended our scruples." Bonanno pointed across the table. "Tommaso Buscetta and Gaetano Badalamenti have shown us how expensive our scruples have become. Who can afford them today? We must move with the times or else we will weaken ourselves." The gravel in his voice had thickened as he talked. "The Commission has decided to make the business of drugs our own. We have the suppliers, the merchandisers, the importers, the distributors. We need a financier we can trust."

Carlatti understood that Bonanno was talking for all of them. He didn't ask where the drugs were coming from, how they were handled or where they were going. There was only one detail that interested him. The profits from the drug trafficking would be enormous, putting billions of dollars into his banker's hands. He looked around the table, including each don individually in his expression of gratitude. "You honor me—and my grandmother."

The wicked ogress was pursuing Petrosinella and her prince through the forest in the puppet theater below.

"I won't disappoint you."

CARLATTI BENT over the sleeping woman and kissed her forehead just below the black scarf that was as familiar a part of her face as the canny peasant eyes. He had never seen his grandmother in anything except black—black scarf shrouding her face, black dress enveloping her thickened body, black stockings covering her clotted veins, black shoes constraining her calloused feet. His grandfather had died before he was born.

"Wake up, *nonna*. It's Stefano. I've come back." He shook her shoulder and a half-peeled onion rolled out of her lap. Carlatti picked up the onion and returned it to the basket that tilted in the folds of her skirt. She must have fallen asleep preparing dinner, he thought, stroking her cheek. "*Nonna, alzati,*" he called again.

Immacolata reached out and took hold of her grandson's hand. "Stefano. Is it really you?"

He kissed the fingers that held onto his. "You're not dreaming, *nonna*. Open your eyes and see for yourself."

Immacolata's eyes were like pitch. She raised them, blinking up to her grandson. "Is it good for you in Milan, *carino?*"

Carlatti beamed. Three months before he had delivered a check for two million dollars to the Archbishop of Milan, and this morning he had been consecrated the most powerful banker in the world. God and Lucifer—it seemed he would own them both. Instead of organizing a fundraising drive and launching it with a substantial gift to demonstrate his dedication, he had handed the Archbishop a single check large enough to build a magnificent home for Milan's elderly. He had shrugged off the gift and the prelate's gratitude, confident that his generosity would be repaid many times over. "Have you forgotten the Gospel, Eminenza," he had said. "Ask and you shall receive."

The Archbishop had studied him briefly. "I do remember. 'Ask and you shall receive, knock and it shall be opened to you.' "

Carlatti knelt beside the old woman now and rested his head against her breast. "It is good, very good. Soon I will be the richest man in Italy. I will make you proud. Men will cross themselves when they speak the name of Carlatti."

Immacolata nodded. Her faith in her favored grandson was absolute. She had raised him, and he would not disappoint her. Once before the name of Carlatti had been honored. Their house had been the largest in town, their animals the fattest, their table the heaviest. Women had bowed when she passed in the street. Men had come to her husband to receive the counsel and gifts that he liberally dispensed. Then there was the earthquake; the ground beneath their feet erupted as if the souls in hell were rising up in rebellion. Immacolata had fled with her infant grandson but her husband had stayed to try to save their village and their neighbors. The next morning she went back. The day was glorious. But a pagan sun, like the devil's eye, she said, glinted on the devastation. There was no movement, no house, no possessions except the child whimpering in her arms. Immacolata had come back to nothingness. Homes had become lethal, crushing the families they'd once sheltered with beams and stucco, burying them alive under the rubble of their own lives. Her husband had been killed, along with two-thirds of the people of Messina.

In time the city was rebuilt with broader streets and lower buildings to minimize the danger of a second quake, but the Carlattis never recovered. Through those barren years pride had sustained Immacolata and the promise that her grandson, fragile yet brilliant, embodied. She nursed him through a sickly childhood, filled his mind with vengeance and glory and fed his dreams until he became a glutton. Her husband Stefano Carlatti had been a man of honor. Her grandson, who bore his name, would be a man of property and power.

She touched his cheek. "Have you come home, Stefano?"

"I've come to bring you back to Milan with me. You will live with Donna and the children . . . in your own suite. We have a flat with many rooms. . . ."

"You go back, I belong here."

Carlatti felt the disappointment like a pain in the pit of his stomach. With her beside him he felt unbeatable, he could do anything, be anything. He needed her love, her judgment, her imprimatur. His own mother had been limpid, but Immacolata was like Persephone, the supreme mother, giver of life and, more important, promise.

"*Nonna, ti prego,*" he begged.

Immacolata shook her head. "I am too old to move."

His victories soured. "I lied, *nonna,*" he said. "I am not good, not good at all. I have headaches, I can't sleep at night. If I eat I am nauseous. Donna is a good wife and a good mother. She washes, she cooks, she cares for her family but I can pay a servant to do that. She is a simple woman and the children are too young. I need you near me."

The old woman took his upturned face in her hands and shook him. He felt the passion in her grasp and the fierceness entering his own body. "Look at me, Stefano. Count the wrinkles in my cheeks. Look down to where these breasts hang. I am too old to move. Too old for everything. I can only remember and wait for death, or for glory. Which will come first? It is up to you, Stefano."

Chapter Three

CARLATTI TOOK his visitor by the arm and led him to the office window. "Do you see those steel girders going up over there?" He pointed south toward the distant site where the new diocesan home for the elderly was rising. "I am waiting for the Archbishop to repay a kindness. He's not the sort of man who has a short memory."

Bruno Parente nodded his agreement. Everyone in the city was gossiping that Carlatti had paid for the building out of his own pocket. Generosity like that deserved something more temporal than the promise of the beatific vision. Still. . . . "The Archbishop is a very holy man. He may believe that goodness is its own reward," Parente cautioned.

Carlatti squeezed his arm as if he were a younger brother. "We should work together, my friend. The benefits would be great . . . who can say how great . . . for both of us. We will be richer than your dreams. Croesus would be envious to see us. I am looking for an associate, someone with financial assets of his own."

The steel girders turned to gold as Parente stared at them. "I am just the manager of Banco Bartolomeo—"

"Now you are, but I understand the president of your bank is in poor health. He will step aside soon and you will be there. We will use each other, Parente. It is the safest way. Have you read Nietzsche? 'Distrust is the touchstone for the gold of certainty.' "

Parente was uncomfortable with philosophical talk. All he knew was a kind of economics. War had robbed him of the self-confidence of schooling. His university had been the Russian front, and the lessons he'd learned in the red snows of Stalingrad had taught him survival at any cost. He had to be better, cleverer, smarter, more successful than the next man. With Carlatti for a partner he would be all that, and more. . . .

Parente's decision proved a good one. By the time the cornerstone of the new diocesan home was in place, the Archbishop had been elected to the Holy See. And soon after that, Stefano Carlatti was called to Rome.

IN THE fifteenth century Pope Julius II called on Agostino Chigi to come to the aid of the Church. Agostino "il Magnifico," merchant prince, patron of the arts, creator of one of the wealthiest business houses in Europe, turned his financial genius to administering the revenues of the Church. Now the Vatican was in need of secular help again.

The gray Mercedes slipped through the Gate of St. Ann, the back door of Vatican City. The one-hundred-eight acre sovereign state was as silent as a catacomb. The Annona, the Vatican store, was closed for the night. The post office and the railroad station, which had never sheltered a single passenger, were closed too. The car turned into a small courtyard enclosed by high walls and the dust of decades.

Stefano Carlatti did not wait for the chauffeur to come around. Since no one was watching he opened the door himself and walked toward the rugged tower constructed by Pope Nicholas V five centuries before. Bishop Joseph Desmond waited for him upstairs in the Istituto per le Opere di Religione (IOR), also known as the Vatican Bank.

Although Carlatti was a tall man, the Bishop's monumental presence seemed to reduce him. In a different uniform, the blue and white of Penn State, Joe Desmond had been a star blocking back. When he was graduated he had been torn between two careers—pro football or the seminary—and after considerable soul searching had chosen the latter. He was still, though, running interference.

Desmond crushed Carlatti in an ursine embrace. "Any friend of his Holiness is a friend of mine." His voice was as big as the rest of him.

The Vatican Bank's substantial assets were not evidenced in the old-fashioned hall with its marble floors, glass partitions and outmoded tellers' cages now unoccupied by the priests who worked behind them. Nor were they evidenced in the modest office of its president. Carlatti's own office was as austere as a monk's cell, but each object in it— the hand-carved medieval desk, the Venetian seascape, the Renaissance crucifixion—had been carefully selected. In fact everything about him had been calculated to achieve a specific effect. Desmond's office, by contrast, had the feel of a comfortable den, a bear's winter lair in which everything was crammed for hibernation.

Carlatti shifted his attention from the office to the man. Everything about Desmond, his person as well as his surroundings, appeared unstructured. But Carlatti had no doubt that the impression was deliberate. Few Americans served in the Vatican, and fewer still achieved such high rank. Joseph Desmond had not stormed the bastion of the Roman Curia by being naive or haphazard.

Desmond motioned Carlatti into a chair, wiped a stack of magazines off the seat beside him, sat down, stretched out his long legs and offered his guest a Havana cigar. Carlatti declined and waited while the Bishop proceeded with the elaborate task of choosing a smoke.

Desmond bit off the tip of the cigar and spat it in the direction of the ashtray, just catching the rim. "I'm new to this job . . . new to this whole world really. Everybody thinks Americans know about money, but when I came over here, still wet behind the ears, I thought I was going to be working in the Holy Office. So you see, I can use all the help I can get from experts like yourself."

"Expert is a word used too loosely. I prefer to be thought of as a merchant banker who knows his business," Carlatti replied.

Desmond laughed and lit the cigar. "Wizard wouldn't be too modest a description," he said between draughts, "if the tales I've heard about you are true. The Holy Father holds you in high esteem, and that's good enough for me."

Carlatti reached in his pocket for a cube of sugar. "I could say the same about you, judging from the position you have been given."

"It is a delicate job, especially now when the Socialists and Communists are making such serious inroads in your government. Their gains are dangerous to the Church . . . and to the IOR." The Bishop rested an elbow on the arm of the chair and leaned forward. "After the war, to help Italy rebuild, the Vatican invested heavily in Italian industry. The motive was generosity, not greed or self-interest. Pius XII wanted to help his beat-up country. Today that history's forgotten. No one is interested in the causes, only in their effects . . . and I can't deny that the Church has profited from those investments. The upshot is we find ourselves in a delicate position."

A thick ash had formed on the cigar as he talked and beneath it Carlatti could see the tip burning orange.

"To put it in a nutshell, the Church's profile is too high. Our enemies on the left are trying to brand us as the world's biggest businessman and put a tax on all our Italian investments. We're a sovereign state but they would just overlook that fact. They sweep everything under the carpet that gets in the way of their new ideas. So . . . the time has come for the Vatican Bank to diversify—to put distance between itself and its political enemies, not to mention any special economic philosophy. It seems good old capitalism is beginning to weigh on the Church like . . . like a crown of thorns." He smiled. "Between you and me, I think capitalism is a lot better than any other system anyone's been able to dream up. But that's my private opinion. Capitalism is a dirty word in lots of places, particularly in the Third World. The Church has lots of work to do there. On top of all that the national government is making noises about assessing the Vatican's investments in Italy for tax purposes."

Desmond paused to flick the ash from his cigar. A bishop's miter and the date of his investiture were inscribed in the bowl of the leaded crystal ashtray, a gift from the Cardinal of Philadelphia. "A decision has been made at the highest level to move the bulk of our resources out of the country . . . if our investments aren't so concentrated we'll be a more difficult target."

"A wise move," Carlatti agreed. The sugar had melted in his mouth, and the sweet taste of it, of his own power, made him smile. "As I'm sure you know, the opportunities for foreign investment are huge, and not just in your United States. But to dispose of such substantial holdings in Italy will require the utmost discretion . . . unless you want to have the IOR's new policy debated in the daily press."

"The finances of the Church are as private as any man's checkbook, and as long as I'm sitting in this office I intend to keep them that way."

"Very understandable, but perhaps not so easily implemented." Carlatti's voice was velvet smooth, a rose petal.

"That's why we need someone with skill and experience who would never betray our confidence." The Bishop considered his guest—his easy grace, his impeccable dress, his undistinguished face . . . the eyes too small, the lips too thin, the hairline receding. "You're a Catholic, of course, but do you believe?"

Carlatti laughed. Bishop Desmond possessed the kind of face that no doubt had looked cute when he was ten years old and had gained little with maturity. It would be easy to believe in his naïveté—and it would be damn foolish. "They say one man's vision is another man's blindness."

The Bishop dropped the question of faith. "An interesting evasion—we'll have to discuss it some other time. And I sincerely hope there will be other times." He dragged on the cigar. "We would like you to be the financial adviser to the Church, responsible for our new foreign investment policy. If you accept we are prepared to give you whatever authority you need to buy and sell, invest or withdraw."

He went on, explaining the operations of the Vatican Bank, but Carlatti had leaped ahead. The reward for his generous contribution to the Archbishop of Milan was proving to be far greater than even he had anticipated. The IOR was as free of regulations as any off-shore bank in the financial havens of the Caribbean. Because the Vatican was a sovereign state, it was not subject to exchange controls and it did not have to report its transactions to any government.

"I will serve you and the Church to the best of my ability." Carlatti couldn't possibly have devised a more ideal way to launder money if he had created it himself. It would be a godsend to the Commission.

Chapter Four

THE HOUSE that Carlatti had built for his grandmother was cut into the hillside a mile above the humble home where he had been born—a rhomboid of glass and limestone that blurred the distinctions between inside and out. Immacolata lived in it alone. The profusion of glass created the illusion that the azaleas and anemones were spilling into the interior and to Immacolata it was like living in a flower shop window, but she bore the confusion because Stefano had designed it himself, a gift offered to her with pride.

She was la Signora Carlatti again in spite of her swollen ankles that spread over the tops of her shoes like dough with too much yeast. And she was well-protected. Each week Stefano's friends sent someone to inquire if there was anything she lacked. Since there was always the one thing they couldn't provide—her grandson's presence—she never asked for anything. When in the summers Donna came with the children for a month to escape the August heat of the city she was respectful and affectionate, but it meant nothing to her. She waited only for Stefano.

She wrote to him and told him that the women bowed to her in

the street again, and the men tipped their hats. It was a half-truth—
some did, some didn't, the times had changed—and it made no difference. He wasn't satisfied. She had taught him too well. He hired
two servants, a woman and her daughter, to cook and clean for her.
When he visited her now there would be no half-peeled onions rolling
out of her skirts. But he didn't come back.

When he wrote he always said how busy he was and asked about
the house. It gleamed like a diamond in his imagination, multifaceted,
unique, outshining all the others—a heraldic crest, symbol of all he
would create. His letters came from London, Paris, Hamburg, Geneva,
Rome. She saved the postmarks, cutting them off with her husband's
straight-edged razor and sliding them between the pages of the family
bible, a black book in which she marked off milestones.

In London Carlatti stayed at Claridge's, dined at the St. James
Club and prevailed on Chatton Bros. to invest in the holding company
he was forming in the Swiss financial haven of Lugano. The combination of a continual cash flow from the Commission and a personal
concordat with the Vatican proved irresistible, even to the venerable
British banking house. Carlatti was too well-connected to pass over.
With Chatton Bros. behind him, Paris fell easily. On a two-week
visit he stayed at the Crillon and flew home with the deed to that
cavernous grand hotel in his pocket.

With each year the victories multiplied. It was said that Carlatti
bought and sold companies the way other men changed underwear—
and almost as easily. His method was deceptively simple. He bought
a company, divided it and sold off the components, the total of the
smaller sales always exceeding the single purchase price he had paid.
The nature of the company didn't interest him. Manufacturing, insurance, finance—he treated them all the same. The key was the speed
with which he could turn them over before they floundered and
drained off potential profits. Riding high, in Germany he was persuaded to sit on the board of Mercedes Benz, Krupp and numerous
other companies. In Switzerland he began to establish a network of
small companies, secured through his new holding company, which

he called Dapro and financed through Bruno Parente, who, just as he had anticipated, had taken over as president of Banco Bartolomeo. Through his skillful and ingenious use of these small foreign shells, he was able to create the illusion that he could not fail, was impervious to failure.

His circuitous system was based on the fiduciary accounts favored by Swiss banks. With Parente installed in Banco Bartolomeo the strategy appeared foolproof. Using the fiduciary or trustee contract, Parente's Milan bank transferred funds for an unnamed client to a Swiss bank, which in turn would loan those funds. The recipient of the loan would be one of Carlatti's numerous shell companies, which in turn would be free to reinvest the funds in Italy. The strategy not only evaded the Italian investment-tax charged to local companies which could be as high as thirty percent, but gave Carlatti a near-monopoly on the Milan market.

At his word Parente would dump stocks held by clients on his bank. When the price of the shares fell, Carlatti would step in and buy. Conversely, if he wanted to sell, he would have Parente buy up stocks for his bank's customers, and when the price soared, Carlatti would sell at a considerable profit. The wider his conglomerate grew, the more conclusive his control over the Milan market became. His touch was golden—or so it appeared to envious businessmen, many of whom rushed to invest in his concerns. Carlatti's faith in the power of greed, without realizing his own, was as absolute as a saint's belief in the Nicene creed, and he willingly passed on shares at inflated profits to these eager investors. And so the system fed on itself.

Carlatti quickly learned the importance of impressions . . . he never vacillated; once a decision was made he carried it out and he tried not to settle for anything less than the best—not so much because he cared personally but because he understood that so much depended on the perception of others. As an example, even his olive oil was one hundred percent pure *and* the most expensive—the unique product of Pietro Lacrisso's Lombardy Import-Export of Milan.

Pietro Lacrisso, a fair man to deal with, controlled the Commission's interests in northern Italy—a one-man show, an entrepreneur. Because he had the laboratories, the trucks, the contracts in the judiciary and the customs department, his territory was inviolate. He took orders only and directly from the Commission, but even that was becoming uncertain. Rumblings of discontent over who was profiting and who was profiteering from the heroin business were increasing. The given factor in any equation was greed, Carlatti told himself. His arrangement with the Commission had grown more lucrative than his most extravagant estimates, but the danger was growing along with the profits. The larger the rewards, the greater the discontent. As long as the old dons held onto power he didn't worry, but he looked warily ahead to the day of succession. Their instincts had been right, they should have stayed out of the drug business, but once in, there was too much money at stake ever to turn back. Somewhere down the road, he felt certain, war among the families was inevitable. Carlatti assured himself that he would pull out before the eruption. Until then, he would rely on the professional instincts of Pietro Lacrisso.

The Roman country club existed beneath a canopy of umbrella pines and cypress trees just beyond the ancient walls between Via Appia Antica, where the early Christians fled to celebrate their sacrifice of the mass without interference from imperial Romans, and Via Appia Nuova, which was the new road leading south from Rome before the *autostrada* was built making all other avenues of exit back roads. Like most everything else in Rome the sacred and profane blurred. A prison was named Regina Coeli, Queen of Heaven. An undistinguished street was designated Porta Angelica, Gate of Angels. A country club was called Acqua Santa, Holy Water. Whether consciously accepted or rejected, Catholicism coursed in Roman blood intermingled with anticlericalism. And Desmond, still a foreigner, wasn't sure which of the two a Roman might consider sacred and which profane.

The Bishop was a familiar figure at the club, friendly and gregarious. He waved to patrons and slapped waiters on the back, engulfing them. He was a presence impossible to overlook—a democrat, drawing no distinctions between caddies and Roman princes. Parente was impressed . . . even Carlatti seemed to shrink a bit beside him. But Carlatti understood . . . having come to regard the Bishop as a clever showman, a performer rich in guile who—when it suited him—played the part of the American naïf. The Bishop's pose suited both their ambitions, also intermingled, and put them both beyond close scrutiny. It left Desmond free to be ignorant as long as his Vatican Bank was prospering, and it permitted Carlatti a license to operate without interference.

Carlatti had returned from Switzerland two days before. He'd stopped off in Milan, only staying long enough to unpack his bags and give them to Lacrisso to refill, before proceeding to Rome with Parente. As long as he kept going, he knew he could accomplish everything for Immacolata. But if he tried to rest, the headaches and nausea assailed him. He blinked, trying to block out the light that was beginning to dance in his eye. The indolence of the country club made him nervous.

"The Bishop needs another drink," he snapped at Parente. "And I want a fresh lemonade. This one has no sugar." He pushed the glass away so impatiently that the liquid spilled over the rim. "Now look." He pointed an accusing finger at the puddle spreading around the base of the glass as if somehow Parente were responsible.

The Bishop swirled the ice with his finger and watched the Chivas Regal slosh over it. After eighteen holes of golf it was refreshing to sit down with a Scotch on the rocks—more satisfying than holy water. He'd played well—two under par. Usually, he'd be celebrating, but now he was concentrating on his drink to avoid looking at either of the two men who had joined him.

Carlatti was impatient to conquer the world. Caesar must have been an impatient man, Desmond thought. By contrast, he and Parente too, he suspected, were willing to bide their time. They would never make things happen. But they would always be there, ready to pounce when the opportunity presented itself. More cautious, and ultimately shrewder? The Bishop wondered. Carlatti used Parente like an underpaid secretary. What Desmond couldn't understand was why the banker was so pliant. He absorbed each effacement as if his entire being were porous. Nothing showed. No trace of resentment, no residue of annoyance lingered around his edges, even though his were sharper than Carlatti's. The Sicilian's edges were smooth, as if the corners had been carefully rounded off with a buffer.

The Bishop watched Parente trot off on Carlatti's errands, and cringed for him. He understood courage, chastity, fortitude, even fear of the Lord. But humility was one virture he had no stomach for. It was a handmaiden to meekness. Both reeked of insincerity, and even worse, of weakness.

Carlatti sipped the ice water that had been served with Desmond's whiskey and watched the Bishop drink. "Parente will go back to the bank with you," Carlatti said, confident that his command would be carried out. "I've brought some funds to deposit in my special account. They're in the car. He'll take care of the transaction."

"Parente is a good man . . ." Desmond felt the need to put in a word for the banker.

"You don't approve of the way I treat him? It offends your egalitarian American nature?"

Desmond laughed it off. "Sometimes, Stefano, I wonder if you're as smart as we both think. I've seen animals bite the hand that fed them for less."

"Not when every meal is choice beef, Your Eminence."

LATER, RIDING across the city to the Vatican, Parente asked the Bishop to spend the next weekend in Cervino, at the foot of the Matterhorn, where he had a country house, and Desmond accepted. He didn't want to watch the man humbled again. Furthermore, it was always revealing to see a man in his own home. His own father had been a despot, his mother a saint—or so he had thought as a child. Thinking about them later he would wonder if perhaps the exact opposite had been true—his mother the despot, his father the saint . . . his mother knowing better how to manipulate her children's minds. Certainly they had believed her blindly, their faith and their trust absolute. He had once thought it was his mother's saintly influence that had led him to the priesthood. Perhaps it was more to appease her, and the guilt she engendered. Or to escape her and find a substitute in the Mother Church. Or both. The Bishop was never certain. Perhaps, he thought, a smile crossing his face as he entered the Vatican, he was more Roman than he'd thought.

Chapter Five

Lunch was at 2 p.m. sharp, as it was every weekday in the formal dining room of Milan's Hotel Pincipe e Savoia. Stefano Carlatti was enthroned at his usual table, positioned so as to be noticed, but with discretion. The circular table was set for three. Bruno Parente, president of Banco Bartolomeo, waited at his left hand. The place to his right was empty.

Twelve years had passed since Carlatti had been summoned to the Vatican for the first time. Now his hold on the Church's finances was all but absolute. Bishop Desmond accepted his advice without question. Physically Carlatti had changed little. The hollows in his cheeks were only a little deeper, the cheekbones a bit more pronounced, the forehead somewhat broader, the hair slightly grayer. But during the twelve years his holdings had quadrupled. With the IOR and Parente as partners he had invested in land development, agribusiness, insurance and pharmaceuticals. His Swiss holding company, Dapro, was the umbrella for his burgeoning empire.

Across the dining room the maitre d' was bowing formally to the woman who had just entered. Even if she had not been an historic power in the *haute monde* of Milanese finance, Carlatti would have noticed her. Everything about Elena Maria Torre was a contradiction in terms. She was a sensualist, an aristocrat, a most important banker. Her business suit, appropriately, was as severely tailored as a man's but was made of the softest chocolate brown suede. The silk blouse beneath was a shade lighter and closed at the throat with a cameo depicting a much earlier, equally beautiful Torre woman. The crisp, graceful movement of her body as she walked toward Carlatti's table revealed, inevitably, the hint of its promises. The two men stood up to receive her.

Elena hadn't expected Bruno Parente. *"Piacere,"* she murmured, and sat down at the vacant place without shaking hands. Her voice was a feline purr to disguise her antipathy. For centuries Banco di Milano had been the premier bank in the city, but in the seven years that she had been its president, Parente's Banco Bartolomeo had overtaken it. Their ambitions were different. Elena wanted only to maintain the position and integrity her family had enjoyed since the Sforzas. Parente was trying to create a merchant bank, like the French *banque d'affaires.* He had expanded his Milanese base to Luxembourg, Switzerland and the Caribbean, where the rules were more relaxed. Bruno Parente made Elena feel that she was failing again—and worse, that her father's faith had been misplaced.

Carlatti took a menu from the waiter and presented it to Elena. "May I suggest the scampi. It was flown in fresh this morning, you have my assurance."

Elena nodded. "And a salad, please." In the summer she had salad with every meal, even at breakfast, when the greens and tomatoes were freshly picked from the garden behind the Torre villa at Tremezzo.

Carlatti turned to Parente.

"The same will be fine with me." Parente's taut face never relaxed.

Carlatti turned to the waiter. "Scampi for my guests and the usual for me, Matteo."

Elena bestowed a smile on her host as if she were conferring a special honor. "And what is the usual, Signor Carlatti?"

"*Stracciatella* to start, followed by a plain *risotto.*"

Elena glanced down the menu. Neither the soup nor the rice was listed, but it didn't matter because Carlatti owned the hotel.

"The rice is quite good," he was saying, "but the soup never fails to disappoint me. My grandmother used to make it for me when I was a boy. I'd watch her dice the spinach, then beat the egg and cheese into the steaming broth. A simple enough dish. Very healthy, rich in protein. But no matter where I go it never tastes as good as hers."

Elena allowed a smile. "I wonder if somewhere in the world there is a grandmother who is a terrible cook . . . one as bad as I am. Or do you think your culinary talents improve miraculously when you become a grandmother?"

The salad was being served as she spoke, and Carlatti motioned to her to begin. "I am not interested in all grandmothers . . . I only speak of one. Immacolata Carlatti, who raised me. She is the wisest woman I have ever known."

Elena wondered if he was trying to compliment his grandmother or denigrate her. "I am sure your sentiment is sincere, Signor Carlatti. But I don't believe you invited me to lunch to discuss grandparents, wonderful though they may be."

Carlatti took two sips of the soup, then pushed the dish away and dabbed at his lips with a corner of the damask napkin. "Why do you think I asked you here?"

"Not to play guessing games with you, certainly." Although her bank had invested in several of their ventures she had never met privately with either Carlatti or Parente before. Which, of course, didn't mean she was unaware of them. No one in Milan was neutral about Carlatti. Publicly he was treated with respect, but in private he was still disdained as a clever Sicilian peasant. Fear and envy made men afraid to speak a word in criticism; every office in the city was open to him, and every aristocratic home was closed. "I assume I have something you want."

Carlatti allowed his eyes to travel over her. "You have something every man wants—stunning beauty and singular intelligence." He leaned back so that the waiter could clear away the offending soup. "And now please tell me why you accepted my invitation today, when so many times before you have declined."

Elena waited until the entrée was served before she answered. "Surely a man as clever as you can guess. Curiosity to meet the man who controls forty percent of the stocks traded on the Milanese market on any given day, whose capital appears limitless and whose confidence apparently inspires the Holy Father himself." She bissected a shrimp and tasted it. "The scampi is delicious. An excellent choice, don't you think, Signor Parente?"

Except to greet her, Parente had said nothing. The meeting, he understood, was between Torre and Carlatti. He was there to observe, like a second. "Very good. My compliments to the chef." His plate was almost cleaned. He had eaten mechanically. When Anna questioned him that evening, he wouldn't remember what he'd had but he would be able to repeat every word Elena Torre had said.

Carlatti turned to his rice with renewed gusto, pleased with her answer. Clearly he had made an impression on the Torres. "I don't like to boast, but a fact is a fact. I am the financial adviser to the Vatican, and Parente here is the banker. It is an honor to be so trusted—and one that brings its own rewards." He leaned closer to Elena as if he were sharing a confidence. "Because of my, shall we say, privileged position I can transfer funds through the IOR in and out of the country in absolute privacy, and I sit on the board of more than four hundred companies. If the Pope believes in me, then who can doubt me?"

Elena cut another shrimp. "I have been told that you are a shark like many others." Her voice was silken, almost casual. "The difference, it seems, is that your teeth are the longest and the sharpest."

Carlatti's laugh was tight. "Then you have been listening to petty, envious men, men who are jealous because I am building the biggest conglomerate in Europe while they stumble along, or worse—run and run just to stay in place." He pushed away the rice, his appetite suddenly diminished. For a second or two he had believed he would

be accepted at last by the oldest of the old monied families of Milan.
"I have quadrupled my empire in just a decade, I can travel to any
capital in Western Europe and be accommodated at one of my own
luxury hotels. I can borrow money in four countries from banks that
I control. I can take a morning espresso in Turin or Rome and read
my own newspaper. No wonder the men you know are envious. I
have accomplished so much and they so little . . . and it is just the
beginning, let me assure you."

Elena wiped her lips and dropped the napkin on the table. Her
curiosity was more than satisfied. "It's good you don't like to boast,
signor. Imagine what you might say if you did."

"Yes, let's imagine . . . to amuse ourselves." He was still smiling
as if her insult had missed its mark. "I might say, for instance, that
I have a plan that would reverse your bank's diminishing fortunes.
Banco de Milano *is* slipping, isn't it? I assume that's why you're
looking for a buyer for Finaria. Sale of your finance company could
provide a critical injection of funds into your bank. Well, I am prepared
to buy Finaria from you for double the highest offer you have received."

"That would be either very generous or very foolish of you—assum-
ing, of course, it's for sale." It was annoying to hear her family's
finances discussed by the likes of Stefano Carlatti, and even more
annoying because his assessment was so accurate.

"Come, *signora*," Parente said. "We all know you are looking for
a buyer for your company, and Signor Carlatti is making an excellent
offer—"

"Excellent for whom? What do you want with Finaria, Signor Carlatti? By your terms it is an old and modest company that would
add nothing to an empire as . . . as conspicuous as yours."

"I thought you understood. As you know I've done business with
the Church and the governments of every industrial nation in Europe."
He took a cube of sugar from the silver bowl in the center of the
table and unwrapped it, taking care not to rip the paper. "I would
consider it an even greater privilege to do business with the Torres
of Milan. The price," he added, popping the cube into his mouth,

"is incidental to a man with . . . how did you put it? . . . limitless capital. Would you like an espresso? Parente and I will join you." He motioned to the waiter, but Elena was already pushing back her chair.

She stood up and considered her host with an impressive show of imperial disdain. "The Torre family is not for sale . . . at any price, *signori.*"

IF SHE and Carlatti had been alone Elena might have been able to listen, but Parente's presence made it impossible. She would never concede that her bank was in trouble in front of him. It would be tantamount to betraying her father. Pride and loyalty superceded mundane considerations.

Seven years before, just after her annulment had become final, her father had given up the presidency of Banco di Milano in her favor. Although he was too much the gentleman to say so outright, she understood that his early retirement was a gesture to indicate that he attached no stigma to the failure of her marriage. The rest of Milanese society had not been so kind. For months the city had been titillated with lurid exposés of her disastrous union with Grand Prix winner Peter Jenkins. On the day she took over her new office Elena swore that she would never allow the Torre name to be dishonored again. Her new position made her the most influential woman in Milan—and the most eligible. But she never considered a second marriage. She had power, prestige, beauty, wealth . . . and the memory of Peter Jenkins. That was more than enough.

She had been eighteen when she met him, and he had been beautiful, the most beautiful man she had ever seen, more beautiful than she. He was a Welshman with a rolling voice that made every word he spoke a poem, the bluest eyes and the blackest hair that curled around an angelic face, and when he smiled his cheeks dimpled in his delight. Jenkins had given up race car driving when he turned thirty to become an entrepreneur. He spoke enthusiastically and at great length about a new venture he was developing to sell commodities to the Common Market and about his partner Malcolm During, a sculptor and a genius, very funny and very clever. Peter's mother had died giving birth to him, and his father was killed at Dunkirk. During had become a second father to him; now they were partners. Elena had listened only to his voice, not to the words he spoke.

She was radiant with love, her first and her last. Although she was the only heir to the Torre legacy she didn't think any more about family obligations or taking her place beside her father. Blinded by the intensity of her happiness, her father gave his blessing to the marriage. She was his only child, his miracle and joy, and he lavished immoderate love on her. Special dispensations were obtained because the groom wasn't a Catholic.

Elena Torre and Peter Jenkins were married at the Torres' villa in Tremezzo on the lip of Lake Como in June. Malcolm During came for the wedding and stayed through the summer. He was very charming, very amusing, and his presence made Peter even happier.

Elena went to her wedding bed eager and afraid, and woke up in the morning filled with wondrous pleasure. She wanted to be with him and make love forever. She couldn't stop touching him, holding him. He was tender, and apparently excited by her pleasure. They sailed on the lake and swam and made love anywhere at any time of day. By August she was pregnant.

Through the fall her father watched with pride as her belly swelled. Peter and Malcolm took frequent trips to Brussels to develop their new business, and because of the baby coming she stayed home. They still hadn't looked for a house that would be their own. Although Peter's trips grew longer, Elena didn't object, he was so loving when he came home. Once she'd started to gain weight he tended to desire her less and she didn't press him, embarrassed by the awkward size of her new body, but when they were together he stroked her belly and would lay his ear against her stomach and listen to the baby's movements. Elena thought it seemed even more intimate than love-making.

Just before Christmas Elena went to Milan with her mother to shop and returned alone a day earlier than she'd planned. She was too pregnant to enjoy the holiday parties in the city, and she wanted to be with Peter. The villa seemed too quiet when she returned. Or maybe she had only thought that in retrospect.

She had brushed by the maid and run upstairs, her arms filled with baby presents to show Peter. At the door of their room the layette spilled out of her arms. Booties, buntings and embroidered nightgowns scattered over the floor. Malcolm During was stretched out on her marriage bed and Peter was poised over the sculptor's corpulent body. If they'd been anyplace else, perhaps Elena might have been able to understand, maybe even one day forgive. . . .

Long after Peter Jenkins was a closed chapter in her life and their annulment was final, Elena refused to sleep in that room. The marriage was dissolved after Peter agreed to sign a paper swearing that he would not bring up his unborn child in the Catholic faith. Elena's father paid him an exorbitant sum for the signature. By the time the baby was born, Peter Jenkins had left Italy, and Elena had taken back her maiden name. The child was christened Lucco Maria Torre and, although he had never seen his father, by the time he was eighteen he seemed to be very much Peter Jenkins's son.

Elena's secret dread was that, all along, Peter had been mocking her love. In her son Lucco that dread seemed to have taken life.

Chapter Six

THE CROUPIER'S hair was bleached platinum and elaborately coiffed so that even when she bent over to gather in the chips with a sterling rake it didn't move. Her face was skillfully painted to soften the coarse features, and her dress, which matched the rake, was beaded and silver. Aggressive breasts pushed over the edge of the dress. She reached into the crevice between them, brought out a neat stack of five hundred dollar chips and placed them in front of Lucco Torre.

"They're on the house . . . this time. But if you lose them, too, you'll have to settle with Dante tonight. He's putting out the word not to accept any more of your IOUs." As she whispered her lips were drawn back in a toothy smile, like a ventriloquist, and she leaned over him so that his face was trapped between her silicone breasts.

Lucco pulled back. "Just spin the goddamn wheel and keep your cow tits out of my face." His voice was too soft for the nasty words. Unscrewing the gold amulet around his neck, he sniffed cocaine to clear the scent of her perfume from his nostrils and slid half the chips onto number nine. The wheel spun, a dizzying blur of color, gradually lost momentum and became inert between eight and nine.

"Nine," the croupier said, and gave the wheel an extra spin.

The man beside Lucco squeezed his shoulder and whispered something in his ear that made him laugh. The coke made him feel invincible. He couldn't lose until he broke the bank. Each play would be more brilliant than the next. He was Lucco Torre, crown prince of Milan, and tonight he would prove it.

"Whiskey, waiter." He waved his hand in the air like a maestro.

The waiter began to ask for payment in advance because Lucco's credit at the club had been cancelled. Still, the directors, all foresighted men, had stopped short of expelling him in consideration of his family. After all, Lucco was the last of the Torres, and one day the Torre position and fortune would be his. The man at his side slipped a bill into the waiter's hand, silencing him. For the rest of the evening Lucco could consume as much whiskey as he wanted. He saw the gesture, accepted it as his due. Ever since he was a boy he'd had generous benefactors. Sometimes they amused him, but mostly he went along because he craved the admiration. Up to now he had been discreet, he hadn't wanted to risk having his allowance cut off, but now he had nothing to lose. He could be as careless or outrageous as his whims dictated.

Lucco had gone through the extravagant trust his grandfather had established for him and was living off his name and the older men drawn by his appearance of boyish innocence. He knew he was beautiful, more beautiful than most women. His body was hairless and oyster-white with a toylike penis that surprised by suddenly trebling in size. It appeared even larger because he was as small and delicate as a pubescent boy. He possessed his mother's fine bones, her high cheekbones and slanting eyes, and his father's ruddy complexion, black curls and blue eyes.

Everything had been determined for Lucco at birth. His name conferred honor, wealth and power. His mother would step aside in time and turn Banco di Milano over to him. He was enrolled in the prestigious Luigi Bocconi Commercial University of Milan to study economics so that when the time came he would be ready. There were no decisions left for him to make—they had all been made for him—except what drug to ingest, what liquor to drink, what number to play, what partner to take into his bed.

Lucco let the men he chose buy him drinks and drugs and lavish him with presents if they liked, but he never accepted payment from them. He made it clear he was not beholden. No one could own him. It was in an evening's entertainment, and he gave them his beautiful body—a more than fair exchange.

The gaming room of the Club Caravallo was filling. The older men wore tuxedos or black suits with the conservative tailoring of Saville Row. The younger men's dress was as varied as gypsies. Beneath their jackets, a rule of the house, they wore suede bodyshirts, turtlenecks and silk shirts open to the navel. Lucco wore a white T-shirt under his double-breasted evening jacket. The amulet around his neck was 18-karat gold and shaped like a water pump. The top unscrewed and the pump handle flipped up to become a spoon.

The Club Caravallo occupied a former palazzo. It was a building of grandeur or vulgarity, depending on the sternness of one's taste. Each room was proportioned like a gallery with huge leaded windows and ornately carved paneling. Marble of a dozen different colors created intricate designs in the floors and pilasters. Naked cherubim cavorted around the ceilings on pink clouds. Blue damask drapes braided in gold protected the club from curious eyes.

Lucco snorted and drank and played roulette, becoming more voluble, more omnipotent as the evening lengthened. The stack of chips in front of him grew and diminished with reckless speed. He didn't seem to notice. No matter how few chips he had, he believed he was winning—a conqueror as glorious as Caesar. By 4 a.m., when the man beside him coaxed him out of the club, the last chip had been lost and the croupier's warning forgotten.

The spectacle of Lucco Torre was noted by the other members, but never mentioned. The Club Caravallo was an inviolate, all-male sanctuary. Membership dues were greater than the average Milanese worker brought home in a year. The price insured privacy. No acts forbidden by Church or state would ever go further than the frescoed walls of the rococo palazzo.

Waving away his companion, Lucco stumbled down the marble steps. Three men were waiting for him at the bottom. He recognized the man called Dante. The other two looked like strongmen. The croupier must have called as soon as he left the table. Lucco didn't blame her, a whore doing what she'd been told. If she disobeyed she'd probably face a beating or worse. He hadn't even been decent to her . . . he knew she liked him. Lucco, forever perverse, loved his enemies and hated his friends.

Lucco looked around for his friend, but the man seemed to have dissolved into the night at the first sign of trouble. Never mind. He swaggered forward, confident that he could crush Dante with a snap of his fingers . . . Dante had been with Pietro Lacrisso when Lucco had gone to borrow $50,000 at usurious rates. "My secretary," Lacrisso had said, waving aside Lucco's question before he had a chance to ask it. "My memory is terrible. I forget everything, but Dante here will remember if you forget to pay me back. You have my word on that." Lacrisso had, of course, smiled. Lucco knew whom he was dealing with. Ostensibly Lacrisso was an exporter. In fact he was one of the leading underworld figures in northern Italy. Some believed that the profits of all drugs and liquor sold in Milan went directly into his pockets. Lucco didn't worry . . . why should he? He'd always found a way to pay his loans before. He was Lucco Torre, and this bully was Dante nobody. . . .

"What's your name anyway? Alighieri?" He laughed aloud. The miasma of coke made the joke sound brilliant.

Dante ignored it; he'd shaken down plenty of dissolute rich boys. When the drug wore off, Torre would grovel like all the others. "Didn't the croupier deliver my message? You ran out of time three hours ago, Torre."

Lucco didn't let himself flinch. He wasn't a hero, but he was a Torre. The Torres didn't beg, for mercy or anything else. "You'll get what I owe you, you always have. Just give me a little more time." He tried to brush past, but Dante blocked his way.

"You may look like an angel but I'd say you're the devil's own. I won't give you one more day, not one more hour."

The two thugs moved as if on cue to either side of Lucco and grabbed him under the elbows. Lucco tried to reach up to wipe the clammy sweat from his forehead but he couldn't move his arms. "Where do you think I'm going to get $50,000 at four o'clock in the morning?"

"From your grandfather. We'll take your car so we won't disturb the guards."

"My grandparents are away . . . on holiday in London."

"Then we'll take you to your mother. I always wanted to get a crack at her—show her what a real man can do."

"You've no right to insult my mother just because I owe you money—"

"Insult?" Dante laughed. "I'd be doing her a favor."

Lucco tried to get to Dante but the two men held him tight. When he was a little boy his mother used to take him into her bath and cover him with soapsuds until his body was white and slippery. He would slide out of her arms and she'd laugh and splash him as she tried to hold on to him. Other times when she looked at him, her eyes got teary and she would turn away. His mother hadn't changed through the years. Lucco still couldn't expect her to give him what a mother was supposed to provide. He wasn't sure whether she loved him, hated him or was just plain indifferent. But, perversely, in his eyes every other woman still paled beside her.

"I'm looking forward to this little visit. I bet mamma can't refuse her pretty boy anything his heart desires." Dante laughed again. "You'd like a crack at her yourself. I can see it in your face. Maybe tonight we'll have a little fun."

"My mother's in London too . . . on holiday with my grandparents . . . ." Lucco didn't recognize his own voice. It sounded too high and reedy.

"You're lying, Torre."

"No." The T-shirt stuck to his body like skin. "I swear." The effect of the coke had dissipated, leaving him terrified and impotent. Whiskey and fear made his bladder fill.

"I'm going to see for myself—and don't give me any trouble with the guards." Dante snapped open a knife and ran the blunt edge of the blade across Lucco's cheek. "Next time I'll use the other side. You won't be your mamma's pretty baby then."

"And if I refuse to take you to my house?"

"Then we'll take you. Don't you think I know where the high and mighty Torres live?"

At his signal the thugs jerked Lucco toward his car. Their pressure and the effect of the alcohol made him stumble so that he lurched into the driver's seat when Dante opened the door. He proceeded to speed across the somnolent city, careening around corners on two wheels . . . an accident was better than bringing Dante home to Elena. He had lied, she wasn't in London. Business concerns had forced her to cancel her planned holiday at the last moment. He thought now of her body as he had seen it in the summer at Tremezzo, clothed only in the barest string bikini, golden from the sun and shimmering with lake water. His mother . . . the only woman he had ever really desired.

He pushed the Jaguar harder until he felt the point of Dante's blade prick his ribs. "I thought you didn't want to go home. Just get us there in one piece."

One block from the apartment Dante ordered him to stop and the other two men got out. The knife was still pressed against his ribs. "Don't try to do anything smart with the guards," Dante told him again.

Lucco hoped for a chance to alert them, but as he drove up to the underground garage the attendant opened one eye and waved them through. Ordinarily he would park a car himself, but he knew Lucco Torre wouldn't allow anyone else to drive his custom Jaguar. Spoiled brat, the attendant thought.

Lucco pulled into his assigned space. The spot beside his where his mother's limo was kept was empty. He leaned against the steering wheel and felt the tension pour from his body like sweat. Usually he resented his mother's affairs, though they were always conducted with exemplary discretion. Tonight, he was thankful for them. No matter who her lover of the moment was, he had to be better than Dante.

"There's nothing for you to gain here. I told you my mother is away. You can see for yourself, her car is gone. So why don't you go back to Lacrisso and tell him you'll see me again . . . when I'm ready for you."

Dante's empty hand skimmed across the boy's face, snapping his head back. "Let's go. You must have something in there worth at least $50,000."

Lucco felt warm liquid on his tongue and tasted blood. He led Dante upstairs. The guard at the apartment looked up suspiciously as they approached, but Dante disarmed him with a pleasant smile. "Nothing to worry about, I just stopped on my way to Bari to spend a night with an old friend." Dante winked and patted Lucco on the shoulder. "You know how it is."

Lucco flushed at the suggestion, but the guard nodded knowingly and tipped his hat over his eyes.

Inside the apartment the domestic help was sleeping. Lucco hesitated in the foyer. He felt a renewed rush of fear, desperately needed a snort of coke to inflate him again. "I can't give you much except my gold cufflinks and studs . . . and my cigarette case—" He stopped himself. He didn't want to whine, damn it.

Dante rapped the side of his head with the knife handle. "Are you crazy? Lacrisso would spit at that stuff. Where's your mother's room?"

Lucco hesitated, but another slap convinced him. Wiping the blood from his mouth with the sleeve of his dinner jacket, he led the way to Elena's suite. Once in her bedroom Dante kicked the door shut and began to circle the room, opening drawers and closets, finding nothing to satisfy him.

"Okay, you show me," he demanded. "Where does she keep the good stuff?"

"My mother never keeps money in the house—"

"The jewels. Every picture I've ever seen of her she's wearing tons of them." Dante brought the point of the knife along the side of Lucco's nose to sharpen his memory.

"They're in a safe . . . behind that painting." He pointed in defeat to a Morandi still-life over the dresser.

"I should have known"—Dante nodded—"all rich bitches have safes behind pictures. Never fails. Open it."

He jerked Lucco over to the dresser and reached for the painting. It opened like a door, but Lucco didn't move.

"I don't know the combination, only my mother does. She doesn't trust me." He was fighting back tears.

Lucco had said nearly those very words to Elena just months before when she'd accused him of skipping his classes at the university. She'd suddenly grown very quiet, as if after eighteen years he'd finally touched her.

"I suppose I should trust you, Lucco. My father always trusted me, even when I didn't deserve it." She'd swung the Morandi and turned the combination of the safe behind it, saying the numbers aloud. "Left fifteen, right thirty-seven, left again three." The door had opened soundlessly, revealing a stack of jeweler's boxes; she'd shut it again and replaced the still-life. Lucco never moved a muscle.

"There, you see? No one knows except just the two of us." Elena had shrugged off the moment and picked up a crystal bottle of perfume, spraying it around her hair, a halo of fragrance. . . .

Lucco looked at an unyielding Dante, and gave in. His hand was shaking as he reached up and repeated his mother's motions with the dial to the lock. The door swung open, revealing only two jeweler's boxes. Elena had gone through with her planned trip at the last moment, but Lucco thought his mother had decided her one trust was misplaced. Two boxes instead of a stack . . . Dante pushed him aside and grabbed for the boxes. In one were two rings—a diamond solitaire and a wide gold band. Lucco had never seen them before. In the other was a magnificent necklace, too ornate to be worn on any but

the most formal occasions. Lucco recognized it instantly . . . a priceless heirloom of beaten gold with sapphire flowers, dating back to
the Renaissance. Dante pocketed it and closed the safe, replacing
the painting.

At the front door he made a point of stopping to tell the guard
they were going out again for a nightcap. Then, with his arm securely
around Lucco, they went downstairs. Lucco cringed from the contact,
but Dante held him in a painful grip until they were a block from
the building.

"*Buona notte, carino,*" he said as he released him. "*Ricordami a
mamma. . . .*"

Chapter Seven

THE YEARS passed and Stefano Carlatti had now made himself one of the wealthiest men in Europe. The Midas of Milan, some called him. Indeed, everything he touched seemed to turn to gold. His financial consortium was the most powerful in Europe. He wanted, of course, more. He especially wanted the name of Carlatti accepted and respected alongside the names of such as Agnelli, Torre, Pirelli. Immacolata had annointed him the Carlatti to reassert the family's rightful place. One day men would bless themselves again with respect when they spoke the name Carlatti. Now they only crossed themselves out of fear. A man with a mission, he devoured businesses, they said, the way vultures consumed corpses, plucking out the entrails until they were bare-boned. . . .

This day Carlatti leaned his elbows on the desk and pressed his eyes against the upturned palms of his hands, trying to ease the migraine headache he knew was coming. It always began the same way, with a light in his eyes—incandescent, blinding spots, then sharp slivers of pain above his eyes that thickened and intensified until the slightest movement of his head became a torture.

Only two things, he had decided, that money could not buy. Brains, an accident of birth . . . who, after all, were Neitzsche's parents, or DaVinci's or Galileo's? . . . and class, which was also a gift of birth, intangible, unmistakable yet impossible to define. Although it often came with wealth, no amount of money could acquire it, and those who had it carried it effortlessly, a droit de seigneur.

Elena Torre had it. It showed in her carriage, the cast of her face, the turn of her head, even the shape of her nails. She accepted that the world was hers, would bow to her wishes. Beside her, his wife would look like a maid. Donna had no pretensions and no interests other than her family. She fretted over every price as if they were still struggling in Sicily. It depressed him but, he knew, she couldn't change. She, like Elena Torre, was a product of her upbringing.

Donna was loyal, a good wife, but not an asset. She was uncomfortable with power, distrustful of wealth. Elena Torre took both in stride, as though they were her due. Carlatti still remembered how she had walked out of the hotel dining room as easily as if it were her own, her annoyance with him somehow patronizing him rather than exposing her. She had insulted him with style, indifferent that he was more powerful than she, unafraid of his vengeance. She had, damn her, reduced him to a plebeian. No question that she would make a formidable ally, and an equally formidable foe.

Carlatti reached for an origami paper and began to fold again— his nervous habit, as compulsive as smoking. These Milanese didn't realize that the Carlattis were once as patrician as they. They had, after all, been the leading family in Messina before the quake, but in the north Sicilian was a stigma, a curse word. He could control the most powerful conglomerate in Europe, but he remained the outsider, unaccepted and unacceptable. In Messina or Palermo he would have been a king. In Milan he was an upstart, envied but also disdained. From his office window he could see the giant signs of Motta and Dolcetta flashing in the morning sun like a challenge.

The two confectionery companies filled the air with the cloying smell of burnt sugar, and Carlatti began to salivate. He would buy a paper mill to supply himself with limitless origami paper, and Dolcetta to satisfy his glucose craving. Dolcetta was also old and established, a name recognized worldwide for the excellence of its confections. He would ask Bruno Parente to make a confidential report on the company, then he would move. He wanted his takeover bid to hit with the shock of a blitzkrieg. The element of surprise could not be exaggerated . . . if he could strike with Dolcetta off-guard there would be no time to block the move. . . .

But Carlatti underestimated the determination of his adversaries. For too long, it was decided, the first families of industry and finance had sat by and allowed the Sicilian newcomer to swallow up their businesses and manipulate the market for his own excessive gain. In the beginning his audacity had gone without challenge. They had expected him to burn himself out quickly or dissipate his energies like so many of his sort before him. They had even amused themselves by betting how long it would take. But Carlatti had been preempting their power for longer than any of them cared to remember, and he showed no sign of slowing down. Quite the contrary. The appetites of the patricians for new amusements, however bizarre or unnatural, didn't tempt him. He was as far from a libertine as St. Jerome isolated in the desert. No longer did he openly boast, as he had to Elena Torre that day at lunch. His manners had become silken, his methods devious. Every politician of influence was, to one degree or another, at one time or another, on his payroll.

Enough. The industrial aristocrats of Milan made Dolcetta their Rubicon. At the first hint that Carlatti was behind the hostile bid, they solidified to protect one of their own. And as he moved to take over the company, a cabal led by Elena Torre and her Banco di Milano commenced buying, driving the stock up to double and triple its true value.

They even dared to congratulate themselves that Stefano Carlatti had, at last, been stopped. Put in his place. And so it seemed.

* * *

IN MESSINA, Immacolata pulled the black shawl tighter around her head and turned away from the house that Stefano had built for her. A showcase, very modern with walls of glass so that one could see, envy and honor the Carlattis' riches. Although it was warm enough to swim in the turquoise gulf waters, she shivered as she began the steep descent to the house where Stefano had been born, her true home. It was a pink stucco oblong with tiled floors and arched doorways—pretty enough in its time, but it had been built above the barn and the stench from the henhouse and the rabbit coop and the goats had wafted up, pervading their lives. Though modest, it had been the most Immacolata could afford after her husband was killed. Stefano, a sensitive boy, had been embarrassed to live above a barn, no matter how pretty the house, and to carry the smell of the animals on his body every day. No wonder he had become a fastidious man, his dressing room containing every cologne created for men. . . .

Immacolata leaned heavily on the girl Pasqualina's arm and shuffled down toward the old home. The new house was beautiful, a marvel of architecture, but the glass walls made it feel too much like a coffin. She wasn't ready to die. She was waiting for her grandson to come back and take his place as *il grand signore,* as his grandfather and namesake had been. Then she would live in the glass house with him; for now she would wait at home, in the old but at least familiar embarrassment.

A sirocco blew across the sea from Africa and swirled through the trees. Immacolata shivered again, as if it were an Arctic blast.

"You can't be cold on a day like this." The girl stuck out her lower lip and blew her breath upward to clear a strand of hair off her face. "It's warm enough to wear nothing, and look at you. You must have four sweaters on." Pasqualina and her mother had been hired by Don Stefano to keep house for his grandmother, and they had the annoying habit of condescending to the old woman, as if she were a petulant child.

Another time Immacolata would have struck at the girl with her cane, but now she felt so weak that she contented herself with merely digging her nails beneath the back hairs that shadowed Pasqualina's arm.

Pasqualina shrieked, shoved the old woman away. "Witch, *nonna strega*, take yourself home."

Immacolata tried to keep her balance, but the push had disoriented her. She stumbled and fell forward, the impact of the fall carrying her thirty feet down the hill, hands and face grating against the loose gravel in the roadway. When the old woman tried to cry out her mouth filled with dust and dirt. She spat and shivered again, her helpless body buffeted by the chills that had begun three days before. A cold clamminess began in her left arm, then the sensations of chill and pain faded, and she lay still.

Pasqualina watched from a distance, waiting for Immacolata to get up or scream for help. When the old woman didn't move she inched forward, sure that the witch was just waiting until she got close enough to attack her. She crept closer. "Get up, *nonna*. Come on, I'll help you if you promise to behave yourself." When Immacolata didn't respond she moved closer and grimaced at the smell that reached her. The old woman had soiled herself. *"Porca, troia,"* she cursed, and yanked at Immacolata's arm, half raising her.

Immacolata's head jerked forward, but Pasqualina had seen enough—the scraped, bloodied face, the vacant eyes, the slack open mouth, a line of spittle drooling out. Terrified by what she had done, she dropped the old woman's arm and ran up the hill faster than she had moved since carefree childhood.

A farmer driving a wagon full of hay recognized Immacolata and drove her home to the house where the Carlattis had always lived, then went for the priest, who gave her the last rites of the Church, annointing her hands and feet with holy oil. The doctor he called prepared the death certificate, leaving out only the hour. But Immacolata was as stubborn and strong-willed as ever. After the fall her speech had become unintelligible, a babble of high-pitched noises, but her meaning was clear nonetheless. She would *not* go to the hospital, and she would *not* meet her maker until her grandson came home. . . .

Stefano Carlatti was meeting with the banker Bruno Parente and the Vatican's Bishop Desmond when the priest's telegram reached him. He had persuaded them to come in with him on the Dolcetta takeover—the Bishop was reassured of the propriety and profit for the Church—and the three were considering whether to raise their already large bid. Carlatti cut off the discussion and made the decision. They would double their last bid, which should end the matter. The details were left to Parente. . . .

Stefano and Donna were in Messina before the telegram announcing their arrival could be delivered to the priest. The doctor was summoned immediately to give his report.

"The Signora must have suffered a mild heart attack the day before. The shock of the fall had triggered a second, more serious one and left her confused and disoriented. A younger person probably would have escaped with surface abrasions, but the Signora is so elderly and already weakened. She may have been confused and started down the hill thinking she still lived in the old house."

Donna nodded—who were they to question the diagnosis of a physician and surgeon—but her husband turned away in disgust.

"My grandmother's mind is sharper than half of the ministers in Europe and two-thirds of the doctors. I want to know what happened to her. She is old, but she is not a fool—like you. Why was she alone, unattended? My grandmother has difficulty walking. You can see how swollen her feet are. She would never try to go so far by herself."

"I talked to the cook at the new house," the priest put in. "I didn't want her to be afraid when she found your mother missing. The woman said the Signora must have gotten up from her siesta and wandered away. It was the only time she was unattended."

Carlatti turned his back on the three of them and went to Immacolata, whose bruises had turned an ugly purple, the skin around them seeming to have shrunk away. He wanted to kill with his own hands whoever was responsible for this dishonor. Instead he stayed at her bedside, leaving only once to telephone the Commission.

By morning the young maid had made a full confession. By the following evening she had paid for her crime. Pasqualina was never pretty, but there had been a certain youthful wholesomeness to her fleshy features. Hereafter no one would look at her again without revulsion, and without remembering Immacolata Carlatti. The memories, one for each hour the old woman had lain alone there on the hill, one for each year of the old woman's life, were carved into her body. Pasqualina had tried to run away, but she had gotten only as far as the next town. There was, after all, no place to hide from the Commission. . . .

For ten days Carlatti kept his vigil, suffering Immacolata's agony as if it were his own. When she faltered, he became sick himself, wracked with bouts of nausea and migraine headaches. When she rallied, he felt stronger. By the tenth day her condition had stabilized enough for her to sit up, speak haltingly and take some broth. Elated by the improvement, Carlatti left Donna to nurse the old woman and returned to Milan.

With Carlatti in Sicily the furor over Dolcetta had quieted. Rumors that he was preparing to withdraw his bid had further lulled the Torre group into a sense of security. Once he was back, though, the bidding began again, even more frenetic than before.

Along with competition for Dolcetta, Carlatti began to move in and take over other companies, further stretching the limits of even his immense store of capital. It was as though Immacolata's grandson believed that his activity could stave off her death.

Four and five times a day he called to check on her condition, and his behavior tended to be prudent or reckless depending on the report he received. Parente advised caution. Even Bishop Desmond suggested a slower pace. No use, Carlatti was like a man possessed. All he seemed able to hear were the words Immacolata had said to him seventeen years before. "I can only remember and wait . . . for death or for glory. Which will come first? It is up to you, Stefano."

He did not take the charge lightly, and for a while it appeared he might even best death. Immacolata seemed to gain physically as her grandson expanded his empire, but the doctor had cautioned that short of a miracle there was little hope of recovery. His diagnosis was to prove correct. Once Immacolata's condition began to deteriorate, the decline was irreversible.

Carlatti couldn't accept it. The weaker she grew, the wilder he bid. His extravagance built upon itself, took hold of him. Not satisfied to take over the institutions of one continent, he began to bid for American companies as well. He wanted a global consortium to offer his grandmother, to save his grandmother, and he would pay any price to get it. In one thirty-six hour period when Immacolata's pulse dropped to forty he bought a chemical company in Germany, a shipping company in France, a resort development in Sweden and, most astounding of all, the troubled Jefferson American Bank in New York.

Only Dolcetta still eluded his grasp, and still he refused to back down. Parente, normally passive, begged him to withdraw while they still could, but words of caution only seemed to rankle, to make him more reckless. Alarmed by the news out of Milan, Bishop Desmond now tried to reason with him, but with no more success. The one-time good Samaritan who had answered the call of his Church would not be put off by its words of caution.

By the time Parente had reluctantly disclosed his fears to the Bishop and they had conferred on Carlatti's obsessive behavior, Carlatti had, unexpectedly, been dealt a trump card that made him feel invulnerable. Once he played it his triumph, so he thought, would be complete.

Chapter Eight

INDUSTRIAL MILAN had outgrown the original city and pushed out into the environs, marring the landscape of Lombardy with factories and warehouses. Ostensibly Lombardy Import-Export was just another scar on the countryside—a large, windowless box of a building due north of Milan. Inside the bare open room forklifts drove between the flats, lifting the crates of olive oil to be loaded into the fleet of waiting trucks and driven west to Genoa or east to Trieste.

Before certain crates were loaded, Pietro Lacrisso lifted a gallon can of olive oil in each hand and compared them, judging their weight. Satisfied, he dropped them back in the crate and gestured to the foreman waiting obediently to seal it. He moved on to the next, and the next, making random samplings. He did it all by touch, never using a scale. The exact measurement—the weighing to a fraction of a kilo, the filling and sealing—was normally the foreman's job, but Lacrisso was double-checking. In his business you could never be too careful. The most trusted lieutenant could become lazy, careless, or most unfortunate of all, greedy. Lacrisso signaled for another crate to be closed, stood on his tiptoes and slapped the foreman approvingly on the back. Pietro Lacrisso had all the qualities of the stereotypical fat man—the deep humorous voice, the belly-shaking laugh, the jovial disposition—everything except the paunch. In size and physique he was closer to a featherweight boxer—bandy-legged and compact— and his nose, which was so large it looked as if he'd borrowed it from someone else, bore the marks of other fists.

Lacrisso crossed now to the far side of the warehouse where his office was enclosed in a cube of one-way glass and flicked an electrical switch. It had taken some time for him to become convinced that he could not be seen when the floor of the warehouse was exposed to him so clearly, and for the first few weeks after the glass was installed he'd gone in and out several times a day marveling at the phenomenon. A wall panel slid open and he stepped into a narrow passage between the inner and outer walls of the warehouse, just wide enough for a steep metal stairway. The panel closed behind him automatically as he started up, his crepe-soled shoes muffling his footsteps.

He opened the door at the top of the stairs with an instrument that looked more like a Phillips-head screwdriver than a key and entered a gleaming laboratory. Secreted in the seven-foot space between the roof and the drop ceiling of the warehouse, the lab was sophisticated and modern. Electric coils and deep tubs were sunk into stainless-steel counters that ran the length of the room. Glass beakers and vials bubbled over blue heat. Here Lombardy Import-Export did its real job as the receiving and processing center for the converted drugs smuggled from southwest Asia through Bulgaria to the Commission. Lacrisso took delivery of morphine base that had been converted from raw opium in primitive bathtub-factories close to the poppy fields and processed it into pure heroin. His fleet of trucks carried the granular powder in the false bottoms of the olive oil cans to Genoa and Trieste, where it was shipped to distribution points throughout Western Europe and the United States.

Lacrisso proceeded to inspect the chemical lab even more closely than he had weighed the oil cans. The final stage in the conversion of heroin was the most critical. With billions of dollars to be gained, any mistake in the process of heating and filtering, drying and crushing was costly. And the Commission did not absorb losses with grace. Before leaving, he filled a small plastic bag with powder and dropped it in his pocket. Lacrisso, a generous employer, liked to bring a little present back to the city for his trusted lieutenant. Although he never touched the stuff himself, he encouraged Dante to do so. Loyalty had its price, and Dante had, after all, handled the matter of Lucco Torre's debt adroitly.

Driving back to Milan, Lacrisso fondled the necklace in his mind, lingering over each flower. He loved beautiful objects more than beautiful women, more even than beautiful men. Their charm inevitably paled, or worse, turned out to be an illusion. But an *objet d'art* was eternal. He'd never possessed anything as perfect as the Torre necklace. At night he wrapped it around himself and swelled with a passion greater than any he'd known before. In the best possible world it would be his forever, but in this world it was a commodity to be used like everything and everyone else—and suddenly its value had increased enormously.

Lacrisso was smiling as he entered the city. Like every other astute businessman in Milan, he had been following the battle for Dolcetta. Unlike the others, he held an edge. Stefano Carlatti would pay dearly for such an edge, and Lacrisso was happy to be of service . . . anything to help a friend of the Commission.

THE VOICE of Elena's secretary sounded through the intercom. "The guard just called from downstairs. Stefano Carlatti is on his way up to see you."

Elena's laugh rang with victory. It would give her exquisite pleasure to hear Carlatti beg. "Show him in as soon as he gets here. I wouldn't want to keep the gentleman waiting." She opened the compact she kept in her center drawer and outlined her lips, touched a black pencil to the corners of her eyes, smoothed the hair at the nape of her neck, pleased with much more than the way she looked.

Magnanimous as a queen accepting homage from a vassal, Elena invited Carlatti to take the chair beside her desk. "I am curious, *Signore*. Why do you want Dolcetta so much that you would risk everything to acquire it?"

Carlatti moistened his lips with the fine point of his tongue. "Let's say that I have a sweet tooth, and Dolcetta makes such exquisite caramels—my favorites."

Elena was neither charmed nor disarmed. "I presume you came here to discuss Dolcetta."

"Only incidentally." Carlatti smiled warmly. "First, something has come into my possession that I thought might interest you."

Elena started to protest in annoyance, but Carlatti stopped her with a hand. "It is a very beautiful, very old necklace of beaten gold and sapphire flowers. . . ." He took a sheet of origami paper from his jacket pocket and folded it into a flower. "Like this. I believe you would recognize it. I am not an expert on jewelry but I do know something about art. I would guess it dates back to the Renaissance."

Elena shook her head. "I am afraid you're mistaken. A necklace similar to the one you describe does belong to me. It has been in my family for generations and it is priceless. In fact" she smiled— "I wore it the evening before last in Geneva at the IMF meeting."

"I saw you there." He stood up to leave, composed and almost courtly. "Gold leaf and colored stones—an artful imitation. Nonetheless, I suggest you take it to your jeweler for verification. Or better yet, you might ask your son Lucco about it—"

"I shall do neither. Intimidation may have worked for you in the past, but this time you have chosen the wrong person to threaten"— she considered him as if he were less than an indentured servant— "you will never win Dolcetta, Signor Carlatti. Indeed, your visit today has guaranteed your loss."

Carlatti half-turned, his hand already on the doorknob. "I will visit you again tomorrow at this same time . . . and I will not remember what you have just said."

Elena waited until she was certain Carlatti was gone, then, her face ashen, called her car. There was no need to involve anyone else. Carlatti, she knew, was too shrewd to try to bluff her. First she would get the necklace, then her son. . . .

She found Lucco sleeping in the room she had once shared with his father and that he now insisted on making his own. She stood over him and watched him breathe as she had once stood over his crib wondering at the miracle that had pushed free of her body. Lucco opened his eyes slowly and smiled up at her, rubbing his eyes to make sure he wasn't dreaming. It was the first time his mother had ever been there when he woke up. Elena dangled the necklace over his face so that the colored blue glass scraped his nose.

His smile evaporated. Guilt strained every feature. Elena felt much the way she had when she had found Peter and Malcolm During in her bed. She slashed the necklace savagely across her son's cheek.

Lucco covered his face. "I didn't want to disappoint you, mamma." Blood trickled between his fingers and down the back of his hand.

Elena turned away. "No, you only wanted to steal from me. That's why you asked me to trust you."

"No!" But she didn't wait for an explanation. She knew too much already.

Lucco turned over on his stomach, staining the pillow with his blood and tears.

When Elena's anger cooled some, her resolve took over. He had paid dearly to deceive her, submitting to a man who repulsed him, a man who was master of duplicity . . . art, papers, jewelry—even his erection was a fake. He would put cocaine on his penis to prolong his erection so that Lucco was forced to pay, and pay again, and Lucco had endured each violation because he knew that Elena would never accept anything less than the best, and the man was the best at what he did.

When Lucco saw the forged necklace, perfect to the smallest petal, he knew he would have paid any price for it. The flaw, after all, was not in the forgery, but in himself.

* * *

PERCHED ON the edge of a high-backed chair opposite Elena Torre, Carlatti waited for her to beg. He was prepared to be magnanimous, even comforting. An alliance with the Torres was more than he had even hoped for when he had made the first preemptive bid for Dolcetta. Even powerless, Elena was beautiful, desirable. He looked forward to drying her tears.

But Elena was not cooperating as he'd hoped . . . her tone was still filled with the arrogance of power. "What exactly do you want from me?"

"I believe you have never sold Finaria."

Elena nodded imperceptibly.

"My offer of so many years ago still stands."

"And my necklace." Her voice reeked with disdain.

"Naturally you will also publicly withdraw your opposition to my takeover of Dolcetta. Give whatever reason you like."

She was all business. "As long as our conversation goes no further than this room."

"Of course." Carlatti offered his hand, Elena took it, maintaining her poise even in defeat. She had succeeded in keeping the Torre name free of scandal. And her humiliation had at least been private.

WHEN CARLATTI left, Elena began making the necessary phone calls, and the next morning the Torres' withdrawal from the Dolcetta bidding was a front-page story in *Il Corriere della Sera*. Elena was quoted as saying, "Stefano Carlatti merits admiration for building a financial group of scope. After careful consideration I have concluded that the effort to prevent his takeover of Dolcetta may have been ill-advised."

Carlatti telephoned personally to convey his thanks, but Elena cut him off. She had done what she had to. She would do no more. "There is no need to maintain the hypocrisy between us," she said. "Have the necklace delivered to my office immediately."

Acceptance was no closer than it had ever been. He attempted to counter with a soft laugh. "I don't have it with me just now. Perhaps when we meet again, another time . . . don't worry, Elena Torre, your necklace is in safekeeping. On my honor as a gentleman."

A GENTLEMAN's honor proved conditional, and Elena never received her necklace. Carlatti needed it as a continuing symbol of his hold over her. She did, however, receive thirty million dollars for Finaria—a good infusion for her bank, and helpful in affording the cost of her son's new bachelor apartment . . . he was no longer admitted to his mother's home except by appointment.

Without the support of Banco di Milano, Carlatti's opponents in the Dolcetta matter faltered, and when Carlatti renewed his frenzied bidding they withdrew completely. He had won, although knowing heads said it would have profited him more to lose.

Exhilarated by his victory, Carlatti phoned Donna in Sicily, only to learn that Immacolata had sunk into a coma. Minutes before he had sealed the bid she had given up on him and shut herself off from the world. Carlatti flew immediately to Messina to be at what everyone assumed was her deathbed, but his grandmother was still a tenacious woman. For six months, while he rode between despair and blind hope, she lingered, unconscious. He would allow no one else to care for her. He was watchdog, guardian angel and nurse. In deference to her he maintained his impeccable appearance, always clean-shaven, his shoes polished, the crease in his trousers razor-sharp.

Meanwhile, in Milan his empire teetered without him there to manipulate the flow of money. During his orgy of acquisitions he'd somehow juggled millions of dollars, keeping them spiralling around the continent and beyond. Through Dapro, his Swiss holding company, he had skimmed off the cream and borrowed to cover his new investments. One by one, as the components of his empire came under scrutiny, they were revealed to be empty shells. Notes were coming due. Stockholders were growing anxious, restless, and the longer Carlatti remained in Sicily the more dangerous, and suspicious, the situation grew. In the volatile financial market rumors fed on each other, ballooned. Talk of defaults, foreclosures and bankruptcy was driving already wary investors to panic, and in the scramble to save their own skins they began to dump their shares on the market. Once one Carlatti company began to sink, the loss of confidence in the others became contagious.

Bruno Parente went to Messina three times to beg Carlatti to return to Milan before it was too late. But Carlatti was obsessed with Immacolata, with the conviction that his salvation depended on her survival. He was alarmingly self-deceived. "Just another day or two," he would tell his old colleague, "then she will be better . . . there was such a change, just from yesterday, come with me, you can see for yourself. . . ."

Donna would shake her head at Parente but didn't openly disagree. Her husband's delusion was as consuming as his dreams had been, and in both she had been less a partner than an onlooker.

Urged by Parente, Bishop Desmond also made the futile trip to Sicily, personally gave Immacolata his blessing and returned to Rome, more frightened, he told a confidant, than if he had descended into hell. In fact, he felt he had done just that. If Carlatti failed, there was no question the Vatican Bank stood to lose billions of dollars. And he would be responsible. The Holy Father had given him the responsibility . . . adding to his alarm, the national Bank of Italy, the country's financial watchdog, began to take a close look at Carlatti's holdings. Graft and corruption might be endemic to Italian society, but that venerable institution had an unassailable reputation for integrity. Once the Bank of Italy's curiosity became public, the last vestige of investor confidence would be lost, and Carlatti's empire would begin to tumble like the proverbial house of cards.

Ironically Dolcetta, Carlatti's most satisfying "triumph," was the first to fold. When three more followed in as many weeks the Bank of Italy moved to offset a total collapse, which in turn could bring disaster to the whole Italian market. It was at this point that the investigator Marco Boni was called in to look into the full and tangled skein of Stefano Carlatti's affairs.

Chapter Nine

Boni's investigation was five months old when the coroner of Messina proclaimed Immacolata Carlatti dead. Donna's fervent prayers for her death had been joined by those of Bruno Parente and, God help him, Joseph Desmond.

Donna had never resented Immacolata. She had married Stefano knowing that their partnership would be a limited one. Still, death, she was sure, would be a blessed relief for the woman, for them all. For her husband it would, she devoutly hoped, be a release. Instead Carlatti was inconsolable. In the depths of his grief he felt his grandmother's death was a desertion, and at the same time railed against his Milanese enemies, blaming their "arrogant conspiracy" to block his takeover of Dolcetta for Immacolata's death.

To the relief of many, within months of the funeral he had moved to New York, his mantle of Vatican advisor had passed to Bruno Parente, and he had become a self-proclaimed exile, concentrating his still considerable energies on extracting the resources of the Jefferson American Bank, which he had purchased in the midst of his buying blizzard. If his headaches and nausea were stronger than ever, so was his resolve. On the body of Immacolata he vowed once again to resurrect the name of Carlatti, and exact payment from those who had killed her and driven him out of his own country.

CARLATTI'S GRIEF was a mandate to conquer new worlds. He would vindicate himself before his enemies. And the Jefferson American Bank would be his flagship. Accordingly, once in the States he moved quickly to acquire the necessary trappings: an office on Park Avenue, a twelve-room suite—complete with a panoramic view of Central Park—in the Pierre Hotel on Fifth Avenue, and a table reserved in the hotel café where he held court each day—ever the perfect host, courteous, amusing, thoughtful and persistent.

His quietly persuasive powers, his old-world manners, contrasted sharply with the driving style of the American businessmen he wooed and helped create the impression that this low-key Italian could be had. Many of them, set up to believe, were taken in by his propositions, even though once analyzed they tended to seem too good to be true. Which, of course, they were. Stefano Carlatti was using the same tactics that had worked on so many Europeans who prided themselves on their business acumen. He was a master of the game. In his Nietzschean philosophy greed was the guiding principle of life, the strongest motive. Not surprisingly he recognized it in others more clearly than in himself. He would offer a special accommodation as a show of good faith to a new friend, an opportunity to invest in his Jefferson National Bank for a song. Once the new associate took the bait, he would be led subtly into other ventures, each more entangling than the next, until he was caught in a silken web of fraud and deceit. Carlatti would then be in a position to loot the assets of his new associate–turned–victim, who was in too deep to seek legal redress.

While Marco Boni attempted to dig through the morass of Carlatti's Italian companies, at times comparing himself to an archaeologist sifting the rubble of an ancient civilization, Carlatti managed to reign in New York like visiting nobility—the grand financier from the old world educating the neophytes in the fine points of international finance and geopolitical economics. Remarkable but true, and it didn't seem to matter that he had left behind him the makings of a national disaster unequaled since World War II. That was long ago and far away, nasty rumors put out by jealous types that couldn't cut it, his new friends said. He accepted invitations to speak at the most prestigious forums—the Wharton School of Business, Harvard University Business School, the Georgetown School of International Affairs; the list was as impressive as his performance. He winningly deflected any potentially embarrassing questions from the floor with veiled references to the unnamed enemies intent on crushing him and impassioned denunciations of the Communists who were trying to seize his country and replace capitalism with their despotic brand of corruption. He was hailed as a champion of the free enterprise system and praised for rescuing the troubled Jefferson American Bank by bringing in millions of dollars in foreign currency and increasing deposits significantly in the first months of operation.

Few, if any, suspected what form Carlatti's rescue operation was actually taking. The new deposit-accounts did not come from good-faith investors but from the Commission's dirty laundry, as gingerly handled as long johns left on too long. At Family gatherings in New York and New Jersey he and Donna were honored guests treated with respect by the older members, but the young ones, the women as well as the men, were a different breed—arrogant, impatient braggadocios. The Commission was changing. The business of drugs had proved lucrative but also corrupting to the old order, breaking down the code of honor that had governed their affairs for so many years. As much as $45 billion was up for grabs, and no one was willing to listen to his elders or wait his turn anymore. The men Carlatti had first met with in Palermo were dead, retired or jailed, and their Families were at war over who would control the flow of heroin. The new lords changed faster than the seasons, the old rules were ignored, there were no standards . . . once the Commission's absolute authority was broken, everything and everyone was corruptible.

The only dialect they understood was power, and Carlatti understood that he was safe only as long as he possessed it. But there his self-insight stopped, endangering his new state of grace. He had become obsessed with regaining his empire and redeeming his name, and the esteem that he so quickly received in the States fed his needs, and his delusions. His financial sleight-of-hand was at first dazzling . . . but up to eighty percent of foreign-currency investments in Jefferson American consisted of shares in shell companies he still controlled through Dapro, his Swiss holding company. While claiming astounding paper gains, Carlatti was simultaneously emptying the bank's coffers and diverting the real money back to Dapro in an attempt to bolster those already bankrupt holdings, creating a sinister helix.

When their dividends dwindled, then sharply fell, stockholders at last began to question their charming new president. It was too late. Jefferson, like its European counterparts, was already an empty shell. Even then the authorities were slow to act. The Federal Reserve Board was poised to step in, but in a marathon meeting Carlatti convinced the FRB chairman that Jefferson's troubles were short-term. By the time the chairman realized that he had been taken in too, Jefferson was bankrupt.

THE BRASS plate inscribed with his name remained on the door, but Stefano Carlatti never returned to his Park Avenue office. And while depositors scrambled in panic for their money, he sat isolated in his hotel suite, still implacable, obdurate, folding origami papers.

BOOK TWO

Chapter Ten

The city waited outside. Fall colors were chiseled through the wall of windows that stretched high above Central Park. Against the blue of clarity and the white of innocence, the red of cardinals turned to rust, the gold of bullion turned to rust. Leaves flew before the wind that swept down from the reservoir, through the cramped zoo with its Victorian wrought-iron cages, molding the skirts of the women on Central Park South against their thighs like a second skin. Across the narrow channel of Fifth Avenue, flooded with yellow cabs, opposite the granite facade of the Hotel Pierre, seedy hansom carriages idled. The drivers in their battered top hats appeared as disconsolate as the horses pawing at the macadam, vaporous breaths curling like smoke signals.

Inside the Pierre Marco Boni waited, wondering where the women were going in their new fall boots, with their confident stride and swinging shoulder bags. To Henri Bendel's to shop in the chi-chi boutiques? To lacquered offices to threaten the male powerhold? To *nouvelle cuisine* lunches to swap titillating gossip? Another visit, another season, he would enjoy uncovering the answer. Now he turned back from the enticing vista to face his distinguished host. "You're looking much better than the last time I saw you . . . at your grand-mother's funeral. I assume she was a saint. Every Italian's mother and grandmother is."

Carlatti understood he was being baited. "Did you come all this way to offer your condolences after two and a half years?"

Boni concentrated once again on the package of origami papers that lay open on the Louis XV desk across the room. "You know why I'm here."

Carlatti's long slender fingers chose a blue sheet and began to fold it, each move precise, each crease exact. Two boats, one violet and one green, were already set to sail on a paper sea. Boni watched as the third took shape. He hadn't traveled three thousand miles for a lesson in the art of Japanese paper-folding any more than he'd come to express his sympathies. But Carlatti would not be rushed. His banking empire had collapsed on two continents. Five hundred million dollars of assets had been seized, and the spectre of a lifetime in prison shadowed his future. Still, seated at the ornate desk, just far enough away to forbid intimacy, he was as elegant as if he were attending a Milan salon.

"You should try it." Carlatti slid a black sheet across the desk. "The Japanese are wise as well as clever. Their origami teaches many things besides how to make colorful ornaments. Patience, for one. A valuable lesson for impetuous Italians like us."

Boni shifted a bit. He'd wait as long as he had to. His Louis XV chair was designed to be seen but not sat on for any length of time. It was an end chair, armless and straight-backed with legs delicate as a well-turned ankle but considerably less reliable.

"You've already taught me a few things about patience. You built an empire out of some threads as fine as Italian silk, and as tangled as a Gordian knot. I've been unraveling them for three years. Patiently, Signor Carlatti. Very, very patiently."

Boni wouldn't admit he'd become obsessed with it. Nor did he reveal how close he was to the end and how afraid he'd become.

He hesitated, not sure of how much power Carlatti could still command.

"You can give me a lesson if I visit you again. You'll be in jail by then, of course, so you'll have plenty of time on your hands."

Carlatti threw back his head and laughed.

"You are one of a kind, my friend—a lawyer with a sense of humor. But you are also short-sighted. Too bad. Otherwise we could resolve our differences like gentlemen." Carlatti folded the hull back and placed the blue sailboat beside the others.

"The Niña, the Pinta and the Santa Maria, I suppose."

"If you like." Carlatti smiled like an indulgent father."

"And you, of course, are Christopher Columbus, still believing there are new worlds for you to conquer."

"I always go forward, my friend. It is the only direction I know."

"With apologies to Galileo, Carlatti, but this time you're going to sail off the edge of the world if you try to go forward." He looked around the elegant drawing room, just one small part of the sumptuous ninth floor suite that Carlatti maintained as his permanent residence. "You must agree that this place, though not home, has certain advantages over, say, Asinara—the space, for one thing, the light, the view of those businesslike asses marching by. Come on back with me. Cooperate with the investigation and who knows . . . you still have friends who might appreciate any assistance you give us."

"I am a most cooperative man. But retreat, even retrenchment, is the vocabulary of defeat."

"If you don't come back with me you'll be a sitting duck for the Americans. They're closing in almost as fast as we are and we'll be obliged to cooperate." Boni stood up awkwardly, like someone who has been forced into an uncomfortable position for too long. "I talk to you, Carlatti, as a fellow countryman."

Carlatti chose another square of paper, a lemon yellow sheet, and began to fold again. "The Americans and I understand each other." His voice was soft. "After all, everything I know about money I learned from their occupying forces in Messina. The GIs also taught me to play poker. It's your move now, Boni." Carlatti placed the yellow shape beside the three ships. Instead of another boat, he had made a papal crown.

THE CERULEAN blue of the sky was fading to pearl gray. Carlatti still sat at the desk where Boni had left him. The stack of origami sheets had thinned. A whole fleet of paper ships sailed around the papal crown. He'd owned banks in four countries with billions of dollars in deposits. He had bought and sold companies with a snap of his fingers. He'd had offices in Milan, Rome and New York, a luxury apartment and a villa in the hills of Umbria. And now he was reduced to this single hotel suite, his holdings had gone down on two continents and this Boni was chipping away a little more each day at what was left.

Carlatti pressed his middle fingers against the bridge of his nose, smoothing the crease between his eyes to ease the migraine that was gathering force like storm clouds. No standards anywhere. No permanence. The Commission had changed. Even the Church. The old Pope had died a few months after Immacolata and his successor was an enigma, not even an Italian—and Parente . . . Parente was dispensing advice to the Vatican Bank like a physician dispensing aspirins. Parente . . . good lord. . . .

"*Nonna, ti prego,*" he said under his breath. But his grandmother was dead and he was alone. He still missed her as intensely as the first day he'd left Sicily to obey her trust. And he was still determined not to disappoint her. Power, as always, was the key. . . . "He shall be the greatest who can be the loneliest, the most hidden, the most devastating, the human being beyond good and evil, the master of his virtues, he that is overrich in will." Nietzsche, a genius, once again pointed the way. He wouldn't wait for the lawyer to make the next move. . . .

Boni had been right about one thing. He still had friends in his debt—the only kind worth having. He took a pen and began to total them against his enemies on the origami paper, like assets and debits on a balance sheet. When he was finished he folded the page. His fingers moved faster, unconcerned now with the object forming in his hands, intent only on the plan taking shape in his mind. Every man—even a Marco Boni—had a price. It was just that the currency wasn't always the same. If gold couldn't bend a man, then pride or power or love or lust or fear would.

He was feeling better. He would take care of Boni, and the rest would follow. Meanwhile he would need a few lira to show that the tap was still running, a few discreet words well-placed, a little pressure judiciously applied. After all, no formal charges had been brought against him as yet. He would insure that none were . . . public memory was short, soon the name of Carlatti would once again be spoken of with respect, and fear. . . .

Still a Sicilian to his manicured fingertips, at another time he would have turned to the Commission for the help he needed, but it was clear that the old order had changed and there was no honor among the new thieves. He needed a personal *condottiere* to see that his message was delivered.

Despite the tense, emotionally exhausting day, he felt exhilarated. Taking a key out of the desk drawer, he went over to the bookcase at the far end of the room. It was empty except for one book, *The Twilight of the Idols*, and a wooden box he kept filled with candies. He opened it and began to pop the caramels into his mouth, salivating with their sticky sweetness. He grasped another handful, and then another. Beneath his depleted stash a jewel gleamed. Carlatti pushed the remaining caramels aside and fingered the buried treasure—Elena Torre's necklace of Renaissance gold beaten into flowers and overlaid with sapphires and diamonds, the most uncontestable IOU he had ever held, thanks to Elena's need to protect her precious family name.

Chapter Eleven

GEORGE BANNIGAN loped along Macdougal Street whistling "Autumn in New York." The soiled streets of Greenwich Village passed beneath his feet, but he was seeing only the great jazzmen and bohemians who had haunted them a generation before. In those days the Village had been full of jazz. Bop was emerging, a new music full of Bird calls and Dizzy spells, and there was the Jazz Revival with Dixieland in full swing at the Village Vanguard on Seventh Avenue and at Nick's a few doors away where Max Kaminsky played, and at Condon's where Wild Bill Davison sounded loud and clear and out of the side of his mouth with George Brunis on trombone, cadaverous Pee Wee Russell on clarinet and Jess Stacy or Joe Sullivan on piano. The music at Condon's was hot, and that was cool.

Bannigan improvised a few bars. Maybe he'd catch some good sounds tonight, he thought, as he turned toward the Vanguard. A gust of wind caught him as he opened the door, propelling him forward on a collision course with a group of Midwesterners who were just leaving. He tried to flatten himself against the wall to let them pass and felt his heel come down on someone's foot.

"Excuse me, I hope I haven't crippled you for life."

Marco Boni gingerly moved his squashed toes, took a couple of tentative steps. "I think maybe this is not such a good spot to wait."

Bannigan peered at him through the smoke that seemed to cloud every jazz club he'd ever been to and tried to decide what accent the man had. "Are you waiting for a girl?"

"No, no," Boni said, as if the very idea were preposterous. He had no time to waste on girls, even liberated American ones.

Bannigan took the measure of the other man. "I'm waiting for someone too. Your name wouldn't by any chance be Boni, would it?" He'd been expecting someone small and swarthy.

"George Bannigan?" Boni held out his hand. He had expected someone older.

They shook hands, already wary of each other. Physically they were opposites. Bannigan was quite tall, blond and even-featured with a face so bland it could have been created to keep secrets. Almost everything interested him, from Reggie Jackson's RBI statistics to Stefano Carlatti's crumbling empire. Right now, especially Carlatti's remarkable career. Although he looked innocently boyish, in fact he was a seasoned professional with more busts to his record than any other Drug Enforcement Agency operator in the field.

Bannigan had gotten tied up with the DEA by accident. He'd started out in premed at the University of Santa Clara with every intention of becoming a dentist like his father. A month before graduation his roommate had bought some marijuana laced with arsenic. The roommate had been in a sanitorium ever since with an incomparable view of the Pacific, gazing out—like stout Cortez with wild surmise silent upon a peak in Darien—a permanent basket case. Which was when Bannigan's career goal had changed. Even now, though, walking down the street or waiting for his order in a restaurant, he'd find himself looking at people's teeth and wondering what it would be like to put his hands in fifteen or twenty different mentholated, garlicked, nicotined mouths every day. Dr. Bannigan had been disappointed and surprised by his son's decision. Being the eldest child, George had been inculcated from his earliest years with a desire to please his parents . . . at least initially.

Marco Boni, a lawyer with a nose, was less easily deterred. He might be diverted, as in the case of Elena Torre, but it was in the line of duty. Or so he told himself. Nonetheless, he had set his sights on Carlatti thirty-six months earlier, and he wasn't backing off.

Bannigan led the way to a table close to the bandstand and ordered hamburgers and draft beer for the both of them. A combo he didn't recognize was playing jazz with a Latin beat. Disappointing. He liked the sound pure.

"Do you like jazz?" He drummed his fingers on the tabletop, curious to find out what the Italians had on Stefano Carlatti.

"It is undoubtedly very fine, but I am uneducated in it." His Italian's English, rather incongruously, came out with a clipped British accent. "For me there is only one music—opera."

"*Die Meistersinger?*" Bannigan asked straight-faced, peering over his glasses. They had the kind of opaque frame no one else had worn in fifteen years.

Boni crossed and recrossed his legs, uncomfortable in the stiff designer jeans—obligatory for the Village, he'd been told—that he had bought just hours before at Saks Fifth Avenue after he had left Carlatti. "Wagner is German, which is very good for the Germans, but he was not Verdi or Puccini or even Donizetti."

"Listen to the mute sax." Bannigan leaned into the sound. "With a little exposure you might discover there's really more than one music. I play the sax myself . . . but not like that." His smile was apologetic.

"For me the greatest instrument of all is the human voice—Caruso, Gigli and now Pavarotti . . . and the bassos, Chaliapin, Scotti. . . ." Boni sighed as if he were remembering lovers.

He had lied to Carlatti at the Pierre . . . he only knew that the Americans were investigating the collapse of his New York bank; he had no clear idea what specifics, if any, they had on Carlatti.

He'd hoped to find that out tonight, but this George Bannigan seemed fixated on the music. His fingers drummed incessantly. Boni knew he would have to give up something first, although he didn't necessarily trust Bannigan to reciprocate. "I should have educated myself on your American jazz," he murmured, cutting into his hamburger.

Bannigan blew the head off his beer and gulped the brew. "You mean, when in Rome, and so forth?" He smiled. Bannigan was honing in on Carlatti's activities from the American end on the hunch and vague talk that the mob had used Carlatti's Jefferson American Bank to launder its drug dollars.

Each man had been led to believe that the other had valuable information that would help his investigation. Neither trusted the other, and so, for now, they were at a stand-off.

Chapter Twelve

Bruno Parente stood at the open terrace doors listening to the voices drift up from the private beach below—the high, slightly whining drone of his wife Anna, the exuberant cadence of their two teen-age daughters, the deep boom of their houseguest, Bishop Joseph Desmond, just back from a morning of water-skiing.

Parente preferred the rough-hewn country house in his native Cervino, the Alpine valley just south of the Swiss border, to this deluxe oceanside residence in Lyford Cay, but his family loved it, and the Bahamas did offer certain advantages that a banker could not enjoy in Italy.

Parente closed the French windows, shutting out the laughter below, and turned back with distaste to the *condottiere* from Carlatti. By choosing to send such an emissary, Carlatti had insulted him again. Or, more accurately, was still doing it. He might have succeeded to Carlatti's old position as advisor to the Vatican Bank, but here he was being treated, as in the old days, as though he were a subordinate, an accessory of power. Gian Gattino was grotesque—slimy and small with a voice that fairly slithered with menace. A caricature, but all too real. He was a lowlife, the kind Parente had spent a career trying to rise above. Parente knew him by reputation. Gattino had served in the Resistance during the war but somewhere along the line he'd sold out, had become a collaborator without conscience, an amoral *agent provocateur* whose specialty was the smear campaign. Now he performed for the highest bidder. Parente didn't want Bishop Desmond to see him in such unsavory company.

"Who let you in here?" he demanded. A private police force was retained to keep unauthorized visitors out of the exclusive compound.

Gattino leaned back in the pigskin sling chair and crossed his knee as if he had every intention of prolonging his visit. "Perhaps you didn't hear me too well. So many distractions." He gestured toward the terrace. "Or you weren't concentrating. Don Stefano is anxious to clear his name and regain the companies that have been wrongfully taken. But it is an expensive business. He is being persecuted like a Christian martyr in imperial Rome. He needs someone to intercede for him. . . ."

Parente tallied every insult Carlatti had made him suffer, then added this visit by Gattino and allowed himself a smile. "You are a convincing advocate." Carlatti couldn't have phrased it more eloquently himself.

"Good. So what answer should I bring back to Don Stefano?" Gattino pressed his case with unctuous politeness. "He would prefer a full envelope to empty words. $500,000 as a token of your old and close friendship . . . to start with."

"You can bring back my warmest regards—and nothing more."

Loyal service was in Parente's bones. In the brutal winter of 1942, when the Germans had needed more cannon fodder on the Russian front, he'd quit the University of Milan in his supreme naïveté and volunteered. He'd felt invincible as his division rode the train east to join the Eighth Army on the Don south of Stalingrad that fall. First the rain had come, next the *rasputiza*, the thick black mud that sucked at the horses' hooves with every step and covered the men with a sodden coat, then the winter with its relentless snows.

In the long retreat through the blood-red snow Parente had held together what was left of his men.

The Russian campaign had been a devastating yet glorious experience for Parente. Those few who had survived were bound by blood more closely than brothers. He still would die for his comrades-at-arms. But he would not lift a finger for Stefano Carlatti, his one-time friend and mentor, the man who had coached him in his own devious financial skills. Carlatti had always treated him more like a water boy than a partner, or even a disciple. Parente was now content, determined, to reap what Carlatti had sown and lost.

Gattino's fleshy lips stretched back revealing a gold crown. The esteemed president of Banco Bartolomeo would regret this day. The Sicilian code of honor was without mercy when a favor was not repaid, and unquestionably Parente owed Stefano Carlatti one. "This once, I will give you time to reconsider your answer," he told Parente.

"That won't be necessary, Gattino. You're on a fool's errand." When nothing could be gained, nothing need be given . . . Parente felt confident that his old friend was finished and could be ignored without risk. After all, he had long ago been through the valley of death and had survived. What did he have to fear from a fallen Stefano Carlatti?

Chapter Thirteen

Acouple of inches give or take on either side and the twin-engine Fokker would graze the jagged fangs of the Hindu Kush. George Bannigan looked out at the Khyber Pass, a gaping mouth surrounded by rocky teeth. Edged between them as tightly as plaque were the reasons he had traveled halfway around the globe to the treacherous mountain belt that girded the border between Pakistan and Afghanistan: pockets of color as potentially lethal as they were beautiful. Bannigan leaned forward to study the fields of poppies below, the flowers of pink, white and red blurring in a sunset of color.

He had been well briefed at DEA headquarters in Washington. The Khyber Pass was a dry treeless slash cut across the Sufed Koh from Afghanistan to the Valley of Peshawar in Pakistan—twenty miles of road, 3,370-feet high. Geographically it was a meager sliver of the global pie, but geopolitically its potential was devastating. For more than two millenia it had been a passage to invasion. Its rocky outcrops were soaked with the blood of generations. Darius, Alexander and Ghengis Khan had driven their armies through the Pass. It was still a lethal corridor, only now instead of marauders charging through, the dangerous traffic had been reversed. The tribesmen were exporting their own brand of devastation. Reputedly, they were the best guerrilla fighters in Asia, even more fearsome than the Montagnards of Vietnam—and understandably so. They had spent centuries defending themselves against invading hordes. The law of the gun still prevailed. On the Pakistan side the forts, most of them relics of the British Empire, were controlled by the government but the tribesmen remained a rule unto themselves. The government didn't dare impose its will on them. On the Afghanistan side the tribesmen were fighting tooth and bloody nail against the newest invaders from the Soviet Union.

Except for the poppy fields it was mean-looking country, and one had to be clever or cruel to survive in it. Bannigan wondered if he was enough of either. As the Fokker shuddered and sucked in a draught of wind between peaks, Bannigan shuddered with it. Of all the glorious spots on earth he had to end up here, pretending to sell guns to men who would slit his throat if they ever suspected his true purpose. His only comfort was the silver saxophone in its battered black case beside the cache of weapons stashed under his seat.

Maybe he'd done it all wrong and his old man had been right . . . he could have been a dentist with a lucrative practice in Santa Clara, a jacuzzi, a 36-foot Pearson, a Porsche, one-and-a-half kids and a sun-tanned wife with blonde hair and a yoga-conditioned body that could perform like an elastic band. Instead he had gotten angry . . . and now he was scared. Well, his boss had said he'd be a fool if he wasn't scared shitless every step of the way, but that was small consolation when it was his own ass on the line.

It had seemed more than a week ago that he'd been sitting in Leonard Hindle's office at DEA headquarters in Washington, a hill of pure white smack on the desk between them. Twenty-four kilos of the stuff had been seized at JFK International Airport in New York. It was the biggest haul since the French Connection, and Bannigan had been called off the Carlatti case and summoned to D.C. for a briefing.

When he got there Leonard Hindle had been sitting back in his swivel chair, a burned-out cigar stump planted between his front teeth, contemplating the heroin. Hindle was bald as Yul Brynner, a big man in every way—oversized, overweight and over-generous if he liked you. Every sound he made, whether a laugh, a snort or a spoken word, was a boom, yet to Bannigan's knowledge he had never yelled at anyone; his anger was felt rather than heard. A paper coffee cup with a picture of the Acropolis in blue sat on the edge of his desk.

"We know the stuff is grown along the border between Pakistan and Afghanistan," Hindle had said. "As far as we can figure, the ones really pushing the stuff are the Bulgarians, and you know they don't dare wipe their ass unless Moscow provides the paper. The Mafia is working like kissing cousins in New York and Sicily, buying the stuff from the Bulgarians and peddling it over here and all over western Europe."

"Moscow and the mob cozying up to one another?" Bannigan said. The Mafia had always bragged it was at least anticommunist.

"Strange bedfellows, but not all that surprising. Remember the Hitler-Stalin pact? Moscow goes by what it thinks serves its world plan at the moment, the Mafia by what lines its pockets. It's a vicious connection, and we really haven't been able to get inside it. There's more smack coming in here from southwest Asia than from the Golden Triangle and our Latino neighbors combined—*nine times as much.*"

"Fine, but what has all this got to do with me. I'm the guy on Stefano Carlatti's tail, remember?"

Hindle crossed his arms over his chest. He always wore short-sleeved shirts, and the length of his arms showed baby-white through the black hairs that were dense enough to brush. "I remember. So you tell me, George. Could Carlatti be in on this? He's Sicilian, isn't he?"

Bannigan hedged some. He still didn't have any proof that Carlatti's money was drug related, and Hindle didn't like mistakes. "I'm no financial whiz but I've got a hunch that Carlatti's probably the biggest laundry man this side of the Great Wall of China. At least it would explain where all the money came from."

Hindle grinned as if the Pirates had stolen the World Series and he'd just won the office pool—he was from Pittsburgh originally and was still a Pirates fan. "You bet your sweet ass it could. We're not talking about millions here, we're talking billions. Carlatti may not be the biggest cheese but that doesn't mean he's not connected."

Bannigan waited, his face bland, wondering what his boss was really driving at. The first week on the job he'd learned there was no point in trying to hurry Leonard Hindle.

Hindle removed his cigar just long enough to swallow the last of his coffee, then settled back again. "I want you to volunteer to trace this stuff."

"You mean I'm off the Carlatti case?" Bannigan didn't try to hide his exasperation. He'd spent the last six months trying to find the way back from Carlatti to his Mafia clients. Though he hadn't gotten anything definitive yet, he was sure that if he kept on digging it would pay off. He hated to be pulled off an investigation in the middle. A real disappointment. Whenever he'd misbehaved as a child his mother had said, "I'm not angry with you, but I am disappointed." He'd always wished she'd get angry and let him have it just once instead of making him bear the burden of her disappointment. Hindle was the same way. Under his rule the DEA was a paternalistic society, and Hindle, the paterfamilias, counted on his boys not to let him down.

"I'm not sure," Hindle said, as if he'd been waiting for the question. "Maybe I'm taking you off Carlatti and maybe I'm just asking you to start at the other end and work your way back. Could be you'll end up at square one again with Carlatti. Let's not prejudge it."

Bannigan traced his initials in the powder, the way he used to do in the sand at the beach. Hindle chewed on the end of his cigar as if it were a cud. "I'll leave it up to you, George. If you really think this is off the mark, you can always catch the next shuttle back to New York and go on nip-nipping at Carlatti's tail."

"Sure, and I could also work someplace else. Since when did this outfit get to be a democracy?"

"I mean it, George. I won't order you to take on this one. I could but I won't. It's like a no man's land. I need someone to go over there and find out who's behind it, how the stuff's getting out, and to whom it's going. If you go and you're not scared shitless every step of the way you're a horse's ass and I don't want you working for me. You'll also be a sitting duck. There's no way I can support you logistically or otherwise. Once I fly you in there you're on your own. We don't even know you if anybody asks."

"I hear there's a war going on over there. The Russians versus the Afghans."

Hindle leaned over the desk. "Yes, and I'm going to war against that southwest Asian smack. But I've got to know who's pushing and how it's getting through. I need logistics. All I've got to go on is the seat of my pants." He laughed. "You'd think that would be ample in my case but it's not."

George leaned back, as if to put more distance between them. Hindle never got mad, yet even his good humor was somehow intimidating. "So where do you want me to volunteer to start?"

Hindle smiled. "Where the poppies grow." He pressed a button on his desk and swiveled around. Instantly the wall behind his desk revealed a topographical map of southwest Asia. He reached back and pressed another button on the console. A dime-sized orb of light hovered over the relief. "Right here," he said, moving the light as he talked. It flickered like Tinkerbell along the rugged border between Afghanistan and Pakistan. "The Hindu Kush is no more than a splinter of land, eighty miles at its widest point, but that's where it begins."

"How do I get by over there? I can't exactly pass for a native."

"True, you look about as much like a Pathan tribesman as Robert Redford, though of course you're better looking than he is."

"So what am I supposed to pretend to be? The Great White Hunter?"

"That's Africa. You're getting your continents mixed up."

"An aging hippie in mid-life crisis?"

"Not bad. Maybe next time." The circle of light moved up the map. "You'll go in as a mercenary and gun runner with a Canadian passport. This area is called the Northwest Frontier Province, and right here in the middle of it is the city of Darnu. It's famous as a center for all sorts of firearms. You'll have a contact who can introduce you there—a native. He'll be your guide and interpreter until you get through the Khyber Pass. We'll give you everything to help you be convincing. That's the best we can do."

"You mean once I sell the guns, then I get to sell myself?"

"Guns and butter. Or rather, snake oil." Hindle's laugh boomed.

Chapter Fourteen

MILAN LOOKED festive. Everything—lampposts, storefronts, even the facade of Banco Bartolomeo—was festooned with yellow and blue posters. Bruno Parente gazed out the window of his limousine and wondered what grandiose promotion was being pushed now. He was glad to be home. The clamor and congestion of the city were a welcome change after the torpor of Lyford Cay. Still, he was pleased with the success of his vacation trip. Bishop Desmond had agreed to sit on the board of his new Bahamian bank, a clear indication that the carte blanche Carlatti had once enjoyed as financial adviser to the Holy See would soon be extended to him.

Parente stepped out of the car with an uncharacteristically jaunty air, and was instantly dwarfed by a phalanx of outsized bodyguards. At the front door he stopped and motioned them back so that he could read the poster. The big letters stood out thick, black and defiant, spelling his name for all the world to see. Parente's face turned to chalk as he read. It wasn't a circus poster or a promotion of any kind. It was a broadside denouncing the president of Banco Bartolomeo. "Bruno Parente has illegally and criminally misappropriated millions of dollars for his own financial gain in his partnerships with Stefano Carlatti. He has filtered the funds into private Swiss numbered accounts for his wife and himself—"

Parente didn't read any more. Only one person could have concocted such charges. He reached up and tore at the paper until every word was shredded.

"Go over every inch of the city and tear these down . . . these vicious lies—and don't let anyone stop you. I want every scrap of every paper in my office before noon." He didn't look at his guards as he ground out the muffled order.

By the time he reached his office his wife was already on the phone. No one had dared look at him as he passed, not even his secretary. "Have you seen the city . . . those disgusting posters?" Anna was sobbing.

"Everyone in Milan probably has." Parente felt like crying too. He had worked so hard to get to this office, starting out behind a teller's window after the war, taking Carlatti's way of patronizing him. Now everything was in danger of blowing up in his face because he had misjudged the reach of Stefano Carlatti.

"What are we going to do? It's so humiliating. How can we ever show our face again. The children can't even go to school. . . ."

Parente wanted to comfort his wife; appearances meant everything to Anna. But he couldn't find any words that wouldn't be a transparent lie. "Take the children and go to Cervino until this thing blows over."

"Will you come with us?"

"I wish I could hide there," he admitted. Just thinking about the place was comforting. "I'll come as soon as I finish with this business."

"What will you do? It's so humiliating."

Parente knew what he had to do but he couldn't tell Anna. "Whatever I have to," he said.

He remembered Gian Gattino's smile and realized how self-deceived he had been to think Carlatti was actually finished. The man would hold on with his damned polished fingernails to the bitter end. No one could ever break free of him. Descending into hell he would drag down as many as he could with him. Like the devil's own, he would have his lackeys, damn him.

Tomorrow or the day after Gattino would be back to collect the $500,000. Parente had to be sure it couldn't be traced back to him. The accusations on the broadside were damning enough. The bank investigator poring over Carlatti's affairs had already been sniffing at his door as well. Now the man would be back, even more curious than before. Parente was by nature a cautious man, but association with Carlatti had made him imitate the master . . . he too had over-reached.

By noon his sleek modern office, which Anna had decorated in disregard for the Renaissance architecture of the building, was piled with plastic garbage bags stuffed with yellow-and-blue posters, and Parente was thinking of his next move.

First he would personally watch until every scrap of paper was reduced to ashes. Then he would make a pilgrimage to Rome. Bishop Desmond was an understanding man. The Church prided itself on helping the needy, and it too had secrets to be kept.

On her way to the office that morning Elena Torre tapped on the shatter-proof glass that separated her from her chauffeur and ordered him to stop so that she could personally strip the broadside off a lamppost. Now alone in her office, she studied it curiously. Although the crudeness of the poster surprised her, there was no question in her mind who was behind it. It bore the clear, ominous signature of Stefano Carlatti. No one else, she calculated, could have the facts to back up such allegations.

Elena had never liked Bruno Parente. He was a small man in spirit as well as stature, not to mention one of her shrewdest rivals in the arcane world of Milanese banking. But that hadn't prevented her from investing in some of his ventures. As of that day she would cut all ties with his Banco Bartolomeo. An investigator had questioned her in the past about her association with Carlatti. She didn't want a second visit.

God knows she'd gone through a great deal to keep the Torre name and the Banco di Milano beyond reproach, including Carlatti's private humiliation of her. She would never, no matter the cost, allow the name to be tainted, even by association or innuendo.

Elena folded the poster and locked it in the safe at the far corner of her office. No one else knew the combination. Parente's public humiliation was a terrifying lesson. Even in exile Carlatti was too dangerous to ignore. Leaning against the window, she gazed out at the city she still considered her own. The golden Madonnina, suspended between heaven and earth on a spire of the Duomo, seemed to stare back at her. The morning light on the gold was blinding.

Mothers and sons, Elena thought. She knew the time had come for Stefano Carlatti to call in *all* his IOUs. Including hers.

Chapter Fifteen

THE PATHAN'S face was narrow and composed of acute angles, the most prominent of which was the beak of his nose, a classic shape as old as a Himalayan crag that could have been plucked from the head of a predatory bird. Mohammed sid Bawar had been waiting at the airport in Peshawar when the Fokker skidded down the too-short runway, and in the thirty-six hours that Bannigan had been in Pakistan he had been a second shadow. His onyx eyes watched more closely than those of a newborn's mother. He carried himself with the contained dignity of an elder statesman. Bannigan was impressed. The man, an enigma, could have been thirty as easily as sixty.

"What is there here in Peshawar that I should see or do?" Bannigan asked.

"Nothing, everything." Mohammed shrugged. "You have been briefed?"

Bannigan nodded, faintly disconcerted by the tribesman being familiar with such an alien thing as a *briefing*.

"Then you know that Peshawar is probably the oldest living city anywhere in the world. For twenty centuries it has existed on this very plain. Once it was a great kingdom, a jewel as rare as the Kohinoor diamond for which it is famous, encircled by orchards and fields of wheat. Now it is more humble but not without interest. We will stay here another day or two, then we will go on to Darnu and the business that has brought you here. My way is the best, though not the fastest, *malik-sahib.* You must feel a place through the soles of your feet to understand it. If you don't it can be very dangerous."

Bannigan, uncomfortable to be addressed with a title as if he were some jewel-encrusted ruler, deferred to Mohammed and allowed himself to be led through the streets.

Peshawar was one city with two distinct parts. The British section, relic of the empire on which the sun had set, was a gracious, composed garden of broad avenues and flowering bushes. The native section was a clamorous back alley, leading to another and another, each dense with traffic—water buffalo drawing open carts, bicyclists, three-wheeled taxis and the perennial bargain hunters, staple of every bazaar. The air was close and choked with smells—ginger and coriander and human sweat, gas fumes and animal dung. Bannigan held his breath and side-stepped a water buffalo being whipped forward by a small boy brandishing a lash of knotted grass. Just above his head hung a toothy grin, disembodied as the smile of the Cheshire Cat, signaling that he had reached the street of denture-makers. Indeed Bannigan felt as curious as Alice on the trail of the White Rabbit—only the stuff he was chasing, though just as white, was considerably less benign. He hurried on, weaving and bobbing through the crowds, afraid that if he let Mohammed out of his sight for a moment he wouldn't be able to recognize him in the sea of faces, all dark, wary-eyed and shadowed angles. The sense of unreality persisted with each step, like stepping into a 1930s Hollywood back lot. He half expected to see Ramon Navarro sashay onto the scene crooning the "Vagabond Song" . . . but that was India, land of snake charmers and sacred cows. Here there were rock-hard men peddling lethal flowers.

At an open stall piled high with grass prayer mats, pitchforks shaped from bent sticks and cots of woven grass rope and wood, he caught up with the guide. Mohammed pointed to a cot. Even though he carried a bedroll in his pack Bannigan nodded and watched as Mohammed haggled over price and purchase.

"You will need this when we go into the mountains," Mohammed said when an agreement had been reached. He didn't give Bannigan the cot. "It's called a *charpoy*," he said, carrying it under his arm.

Bannigan admired the skilled if primitive craftsmanship more effusively than it warranted. He had the uncomfortable feeling that everything Mohammed did or said had some other, larger significance that he somehow must be missing. He felt as if he were constantly being put to some test that he didn't understand.

The feeling intensified the next day. Mohammed drove him in a vintage Chevy sedan, maneuvering the narrow roads as if he were Mario Andretti at the Indy 500. They nipped past taxis, skinning the knees of the passengers who overflowed onto fenders, hood and roof. Careened around trucks elaborately painted with cartoons of jet planes, mosques and giant telephones. Zipped by women in voluminous skirts, their feet bare, their heads burdened with the bundles of fodder they effortlessly balanced. Bannigan turned back to watch them through the rear window, but the billows of dust the Chevy raised enveloped them.

By the time they reached Darnu the sun had dropped behind the mountains, softening the glare of the day. "The shop I will bring you to is the biggest in the town," Mohammed said. "When you sell your weapons there, everyone in the territory will know what your business is."

"Is that good?" Bannigan felt like a canary in the claws of a cat for safe-keeping. But Hindle had put him there, and Bannigan trusted his boss more than his own father.

On the trip from Peshawar, Mohammed's driving was so hazardous that Bannigan had been afraid any distraction could prove fatal and had tried not to show his misgivings. They got out of the car and opened the hump-backed trunk. Bannigan unzipped the two army-green cases and checked the contents. When he was satisfied he closed them again.

"How far do we have to go?" The cases were made of feather-light parachute cloth but their contents were considerably heavier.

"One street to the left and then one more ahead."

"Okay. Let's make tracks." He hoisted one case on each shoulder and nodded to the guide. He was, he decided, as ready as he would ever be.

The shop they entered was a room no bigger than a walk-in closet. One straight-backed chair stood against the wall. A girl knelt on the floor beside it, a hand-hewn rifle butt between her legs, polishing its stock with a cloth. Mohammed spoke a few brusque words to her, gesturing over his shoulder at his companion. All Bannigan understood were *"malik-sahib"* and "American," but that was enough. He expected the girl to bow. Instead she looked directly up at him. There was no arrogance in her face, but there was no deference or shyness either. Her hair was long enough to brush the floor behind her if she leaned back, long and shiny black as her eyes, which were still fixed on him.

Bannigan smiled at her. "My name is George Bannigan, what's yours?"

"Zenah Rahmir."

"Do you speak English?"

She shook her head and smiled back. Her teeth were small and white in front but on the sides several had rotted away or fallen out. He eased the cases off his shoulders and hunkered down in front of her, still smiling. "Can I call you Zenah?"

She nodded and made a gurgling sound somewhere deep in her throat, not so much a laugh as an expression of intense pleasure, a primitive sound. Mohammed interrupted, addressing the girl even more brusquely than before. Her face closed and she shouted without turning away from Bannigan. Immediately a man appeared at the door behind her. He was as old or as young as Mohammed, with the same narrow, unyielding face. He looked from Bannigan, still hunkered down in front of the girl, to the guide. Mohammed spoke quickly. His voice was apologetic, even fawning. Finally the other man nodded and turned back. Picking up the cases, Bannigan smiled at the girl and followed Mohammed, stooping to fit through the low doorway.

The room they entered was a wall-to-wall arsenal. From floor to ceiling were racks of weapons—everything from crude homemade rifles to Russian Kalashnikovs and M1 carbines—and shelf after shelf thick with handguns, bazookas, bayonets and knives, some with blades fine enough to puncture a pupil, others thick enough to stab through a body.

Bannigan laid his cases on the floor and opened them. Hindle had been as good as his word. The merchant peered in and bowed. *"Malik-sahib."* Bannigan wasn't sure whether the gesture was in deference to him or to his baggage. But clearly Rahmir was impressed.

"He wants to know if he can examine the guns," Mohammed interpreted.

Bannigan pulled the bags open wide and moved aside to allow him room to check out the loot. The merchant knelt down and clapped his hands—Bannigan thought in pleasure—until Zenah appeared a few minutes later with tea, almonds and raisin cakes. She didn't look at Bannigan when she served him. When he thanked her she didn't respond and disappeared as quickly as she'd come.

Rahmir handled each weapon, sighting and testing it, then laying it down in a pile. He paused to light an oil lamp in the windowless room, then went back to the instruments of his trade, occasionally emitting a few words of admiration that Mohammed dutifully translated. Bannigan asked for more tea to bring Zenah back. She wasn't beautiful but she was more interesting than a stack of unloaded guns, and there had been something about the open way she had looked at him.

Mohammed didn't translate the request, but Bannigan wondered if an interpreter was really necessary. Pakistan had been a British colony not so many years before, and he thought he saw the merchant's hand tighten around the Uzi submachine gun he was handling, although it could have been his imagination. Rahmir continued with his examination of each weapon, then the haggling ceremony began to determine a price for the contraband. Bannigan kept quiet and left the negotiations to Mohammed.

By the time business was concluded night had encircled the shop. Bannigan zipped one case inside the other, empty except for an M1 carbine and a 9mm Beretta, which he kept for himself. Mohammed explained that Bannigan was on his way to Afghanistan to offer his services—for a price of course—to the tribesmen fighting the Russians, but that he planned to move slowly through the countryside to get accustomed to the difficult terrain. Rahmir nodded in agreement. A man who lived by the gun had to be prudent if he expected to survive. Mohammed mentioned the Green Berets in Vietnam, the trouble in Salvador. Bannigan wondered if anyone in this remote arsenal had ever heard of either place but it didn't matter. His identity with Rahmir was established, now he could start selling the butter.

Rahmir showed them to the door. Bannigan would have liked to thank Zenah for the tea but the small outer room was empty as they passed through, and stepped into a black night without streetlights or stars.

"Do not think of Zenah Rahmir or any other woman you see, *malik-sahib,*" Mohammed's voice said in the darkness. "In this country a husband will kill any man who stops to look at his wife working in the fields, and a father with his only daughter has even less sympathy."

Bannigan glanced back over his shoulder. "Maybe I made a mistake selling Rahmir all those guns then." He could swear he saw a shadow move around the corner of the shop and a gaping smile shine through the darkness. Too much fuel for his overactive imagination, he told himself.

Chapter Sixteen

Bannigan picked a red flower and held the open cup to his nose. Back home in California his father had grown orange poppies in his garden, in front of the hollyhocks that bordered the brick path leading to the vine-covered arbor where he'd surrendered his virginity one summer night when he was seventeen. He was the only boy to graduate from St. Stephen's Prep uninitiated, but he hadn't wanted the first time to be with just anyone. Connie Mackay had seemed special all that summer, so special it hadn't mattered that it wasn't the first time for her too. After she went away to college, though, vacations never seemed long enough to make up for the time lost in between.

Up here flowers were less romantic. The poppies were red and pink and white, *Papaver somniferum* and there was nothing clandestine about the way the opium was extracted. For three days he'd been watching the farmers harvest their crop. When the petals fell off, they went through the fields and split the pod that grew at the base of each flower, releasing a rich, milky secretion. The pods could grow as big as an egg, depending on the size of the flower. The next day, when the latex had turned black and gummy like licorice, they came back, scraped the raw opium off with a crude iron scoop, and lanced the pod again. The farmers worked carefully and patiently, repeating the process four or five times for each flower, and hoarding every drop of the gum—raw opium worth more to them than whole fields of wheat or mustard.

Bannigan walked back slowly, skirting the field to the cave where he and Mohammed had encamped. It was far enough removed from the village to insure their privacy yet close enough for them to become familiar figures in the area. Now that he had seen the farmers gather the raw opium, Bannigan was curious to find out how it was processed, but Mohammed said it would be dangerous to appear too curious.

Mohammed had fought beside the British and something of their innate meticulousness had rubbed off. Clearly he was a survivor, but Bannigan was impatient. In the week that they had been camped in the mountains he had at least impressed the natives with his saxophone. If they hadn't seen him, at least they knew of him by now. He could move freely among them, and he took advantage of that freedom to slip away from Mohammed's watchful eye and search for the places—bathtub-factories they were called in Washington—where the opium underwent the initial step in its transformation to heroin.

BANNIGAN CRAWLED out of the cave, his black saxophone case gripped under his arm, and gulped the cold air. The night was clear and still. He climbed around the cave and down to a broad ledge behind it. A handful of people had already gathered, apparently anticipating another evening concert. Their faces were closed but their presence was proof that his music had somehow reached them, even if he hadn't. The first night he'd come here after dinner to play he'd felt like Pan. He was barely through the scales, though, when he noticed the first head peering around a rocky outcrop. Then another and another had appeared until he was surrounded. He'd just kept on playing, trying to decide whether the music had drawn them or whether they had been lying there to ambush him.

Bannigan bowed to his audience and took out the saxophone. A few more people gathered as he tuned up. He recognized some of the faces from the previous three nights. Tapping his right foot he blew the first notes of " 'A' Train"; the lyrics running through his head: "Hurry, hurry, hurry. Take the 'A' train. You'll find it the quickest way to get to Harlem."

Bannigan looked up. Above the group, partially concealed behind a ridge, he thought he saw a smile he recognized. He hadn't seen Zenah Rahmir since the day in Darnu. Anyway it was too late for her to be so far from home. When he finished the Duke Ellington number he looked up again, straining through the dimness. There was no one there, and there would be no one back at the cave when he returned. Every night when he got back from his concert the place was empty. Bannigan guessed that Mohammed snuck back to his family for a few hours, although he never asked and the guide never volunteered the information. In the morning when he got up, Mohammed would be making the coffee. . . . Bannigan played two more numbers, then packed up and waved goodnight. He wanted to turn in early and catch a couple of hours sleep.

Back in the cave he stretched out on the *charpoy* Mohammed had bought at the bazaar in Peshawar and folded his hands behind his head. He'd doze until just before dawn when the sky began to lighten, then he'd go back to the hut he'd found. He appreciated Mohammed's caution, but at this rate he'd have to set up permanent residence in the Khyber Pass.

BANNIGAN WISHED he were eight inches shorter and ten shades darker as he darted toward the door of the mud hut. From the outside it looked as bleak as any house in the village, only its isolated location set it apart. Easing his shoulder into the door, he forced it open and entered a room so low that he had to hunch over to keep from bumping his head on the ceiling. It smelled of ammonia, and of something else. Two vats the size of bathtubs were filled with water and the ammonia mixture. Behind them on a rack was a large screen for filtering, the final step in converting the opium to morphine base. The operation was rudimentary, primitive, but it got the job done and there were probably dozens more huts just like this one, crude factories turning out enormous quantities of drugs that somewhere along the line would be converted again, dried and crushed into heroin and finally end up being shot into the veins of junkies in Harlem, Miami, Chicago. . . . All he had to do was nose around long enough and he'd fall over them, just as he had this one.

He had seen enough. He crouched in the doorway, glad to leave the stench of ammonia, and looked around. There was no one in sight. No movement, no sound, not even the rustle of leaves in this treeless country. He pulled the door closed and refastened the make-shift wooden lock. Behind him a figure moved but the sun was not strong enough yet to cast a shadow, and by the time he finished fixing the lock it was gone.

Chapter Seventeen

T HE NIGHT was luminous, as cold as pure ice and just as clear. The rocky table was empty. Bannigan took out his sax and wet his lips so they wouldn't stick to the metal mouthpiece. No one had shown up for his evening concert but he began to play anyway, starting with "Tangerine," then switched to "In My Solitude," which seemed more fitting.

He looked up at the spot where he thought he'd seen Zenah the night before. There was nothing but cold stones and shadows. He wanted to stop playing but was afraid to. The circle of shadows tightened around him. He moved back so that he was leaning against the rock wall that formed the back of the cave. Mohammed would be gone already, he thought. The last notes of "Solitude" dissolved in the air. Bannigan pointed his sax up to the heavens and began to play "When the Saints Go Marching In." Leonard Hindle always said, "If you lose your sense of humor in this business you're as good as dead." Bannigan filled his cheeks and blew for all he was worth. He had no weapon except a knife that he carried in his boot, more for reassurance than defense. The guns were back in the cave, and the shadows were now marching in, pinning him against the wall. This was really being caught between a rock and a hard place. The shadows took shape the closer they came, wiry bodies with narrow shuttered faces. None of them came empty-handed, and they didn't wait for him to finish the number. "Oh, Lord. . . ." He missed the next note. The saxophone flew out of his hands as they threw themselves at him. So much for a sense of humor, he thought, bracing himself against the rock. They lunged at him with rifles, knives and pitchforks. Any one of them could easily have shot him at pointblank range, but they came at him, brandishing their weapons like clubs.

Bannigan reached for the knife in his boot and crouched down. If he could edge his way around to the mouth of the cave he might stand a remote chance. He cut an arc with his knife, side-stepping as he did, and split the nose of a man rushing at him. From the opposite side, a rifle butt caught him just above the ear. His glasses flew off. The attackers dissolved into shadows again. He lashed out with the bloodied knife as they rushed in on him, crushing him.

Bannigan's last thought was that Leonard Hindle would wait six months before presuming him dead.

SILVER, AN evening color, the color of moonlight and of Diana, moon goddess, chaste and fair. Bannigan's saxophone shone on the deserted ledge like an offering to her. Zenah Rahmir picked it up, wiped it clean on a patch of her skirt that wasn't soaked with blood and returned it to its case, which had gotten wedged in a crevice during the fight. She carried it back to the cave and laid it beside Bannigan's battered body.

She'd come to hear his concert as she had the previous night and had stayed for the fight, hidden from view out of fear someone might report her presence to her father. When the attackers retreated she had crept down to him. Only his clothing and size were recognizable. She looked for his glasses but there was nothing left of them except a bridge.

Zenah lifted his head onto her lap and called out his name. His blood seeped through to her skin. "George Bannigan," she said again and again. She reached for his hand and held it tight. It had felt soft yet strong when he shook hands with her in her father's shop. She'd never touched a man's hand before except her father's. He would kill her with those same hands if he could see her now. But he was in Karachi, and she had been careful not to let anyone see her. The villagers had come to Darnu talking about the music man, tall as a tree with hair like wheat. She knew it could only be one man—the man who had touched her. One of them had come to the shop that morning and spoken with her father about him just before he'd left. She'd listened intently. Her father was a just man. The American deserved punishment, but death. . . .

Still holding his hand, Zenah got up and began to drag him around the ledge toward the mouth of the cave. She was afraid the man who had brought George Bannigan to the shop would be there, but she was more afraid of the birds that were beginning to circle high overhead anticipating breakfast. They would begin with his eyes, the choicest parts first, then peck through his clothes until there was nothing left except scraps of flesh clinging to skeletal bones.

Inside the cave there was water, and she washed him as best she could. When his friend returned he would take care of the body, she told herself. Still, she was reluctant to leave it. He wasn't supposed to be killed, just frightened into going on to Afghanistan. She'd heard her father give the order. She didn't blame him. The American had been too curious. He'd broken into her father's factory. But the villagers had been overzealous.

Murmuring the prayers of the dead to Allah, she washed away the blood that encrusted his eyelids. She wondered what he would look like if she undressed him. She knew the body should be anointed before burial, but she had no oils. . . .

Chapter Eighteen

A REVERENTIAL hush pervaded the Istituto per le Opere di Religione. The IOR, the Vatican Bank, was quieter than a Roman church. The cassocked tellers counted out lira as if they were giving the number of *Ave Marias* to say for penance. Bruno Parente suppressed the urge to tiptoe as he walked to Bishop Joseph Desmond's office.

On his first visit a dozen years before he actually had begun to tiptoe until Carlatti's laugh had embarrassed him. "The money-changers here are no more sanctified than in your own bank—no less venal, no more virtuous," Carlatti had said.

Parente remembered how moved he had been, in spite of Carlatti's irreverence. It was his first time inside Vatican City, except to visit the basilica and have a general audience with the Pope. He had just been named president of Banco Bartolomeo, and Carlatti was presenting him to Bishop Desmond. He had heard of the American who had been made president of the Vatican Bank, but even so, hadn't been prepared for either Bishop Desmond's intimidating size or informal manners.

This time Desmond was tanned and glowing with welcome, and Parente was afraid.

"I had a great time in the Bahamas. I'm going to have to practice my water-skiing, though, before my next visit. I don't want a couple of teenagers showing me up." The Bishop laughed and clapped a large hand on Parente's shoulder. "I didn't expect to see you in Rome so soon." Parente was a changed man from the one he'd left just a short time before in the Bahamas. A gray patina coated his face . . . from fear, fatigue or both, Desmond thought.

"The trip is unscheduled. I haven't come for myself but to ask a favor for a mutual friend—Stefano Carlatti. He needs help—for his defense, he says. I think we know what that means."

"I thought the whole government was, as they say, in our friend's pocket by now." He didn't understand why the embarrassing business kept dragging on. Between them, Carlatti and Parente must have crossed enough palms to suppress the investigation and allow them to get back to business as usual.

"It helps to refresh memories." Parente's voice was dry enough to crack. He wondered if word of his humiliation had reached Rome yet.

Bishop Desmond closed the door and sat down behind his desk. "What's the price tag for jogging memories these days?"

Parente looked across the desk. The Bishop had everything he envied—the infectious grin that inspired confidence, the easy manner that defused any confrontation, and, of course, the purple cassock. "Five hundred thousand American dollars."

Desmond whistled. "That's quite a job. Even when he trips Carlatti does it in grand style."

Unlike Parente, the Bishop thought. He had no style, a simple, homespun man, not content to be himself. He seemed tight as a steel wire except when he was at home with his family, where he was warm and pleasant. He even cooked the dinners himself and the kids served them. They were good kids, Desmond reflected. He liked Anna, too, in spite of her pretentions. He should never have accepted a seat on Parente's bank in the Bahamas. Sentimentality had made him foolish. He had grown up in a big family, he'd missed the rough and tumble, the easy give and take, the affectionate joking, until the Parentes had made him feel like a part of their family. "What have you told the investigators? They must be at your heels."

"That's why I have come to you. The assistance Carlatti needs must not be traced back to me."

Desmond leaned back and linked his fingers behind his head. He was inclined to go for broke—even to pour sacred oil on troubled waters for Carlatti if need be . . . and he was not motivated by Christian charity. Millions of dollars of the Church's revenues were on the line . . . if any more of Carlatti's empire collapsed its fall would rival that of the Holy Roman Empire, and *he* would be the first one crushed. The innuendos and whispered accusations had already begun. Gossip spread like fire in the Vatican, and there were more than a few waiting to see him stumble—some who would willingly put out a foot to speed his fall. Except for three years in a Pittsburgh parish Desmond had worked in the Vatican ever since he'd finished the seminary, but he was still an outsider by happenstance of birth and he always would be . . . like Carlatti. It was, he suspected, one of the things that had drawn them together.

The Bishop looked across the desk at Parente and wondered what he had welched on for Carlatti to have taken such a stunning revenge.

"Will you help?" Parente was begging, an unpleasant sight.

"Anything for a friend." The Bishop's laugh was a hollow sound. He was just as frightened, but at least he hadn't been humiliated. Not yet. "On one condition." He leaned back and linked his hands behind his back, knowing that he could ask anything now. "We have a new Pope on the fourth floor who has never heard of Stefano Carlatti, unless he has read the name in the newspaper. But there is a cause very dear to his heart."

"Of course. Any favor for our new Holy Father." At the mention of the Pope, Parente was instantly reverential. Desmond wouldn't have been surprised if he had crossed himself. Ordinarily the Bishop would have been touched by such genuine reverence, but just now he had other considerations. After all, his performance as president of the Vatican Bank was under assessment by the new pontiff. "The Holy Father is the Pope of all the people, but none more so than his own countrymen."

"I understand." Parente's head bobbed.

"Have you met him?"

"I haven't had the honor yet."

"I will arrange it. He wants very much to help his people stand up to their Communist oppressors and establish a workers' union. He would like to support their efforts with something more substantial than prayers, efficacious though we both know they are. The power of prayer is not to be taken lightly—no more so than the power of money. Two potent weapons to put in their hands—prayer and Peter's Pence . . . if a way can be found."

Parente's head continued to bob. "I am sure there is a way to help the Holy Father."

Bishop Desmond smiled engagingly. "Tell Carlatti our prayers are with him." The new Pope was an outsider too, after all, which made them in a fashion natural allies, and the Polish Solidarity movement was dear to his heart. Watching Parente's back as he exited, the Bishop decided that God did indeed work in mysterious ways.

GRAY FOG blurred the profile of the Eternal City as Bruno Parente started north. He'd come to Rome and had been granted salvation— at a price, certainly, but one that he was more than willing to pay. He leaned back and closed his eyes, shutting out the murky yellow line of the Tiber, feeling relieved. The Bishop was his friend, and now the new Pope would favor him too. . . .

The limousine circled Vatican City and picked up the *autostrada* off Via Flaminia. Parente would have preferred to take the scenic old road that cut through the towns and villages, but the highway was so much quicker and he was anxious to reach Cervino while

Anna was still awake. They would have an iced vodka together and savor his new concordat. Carlatti would be appeased. Too bad he would never know the terms, though. More than any man, he would appreciate a cause dear to a prelate's heart.

CARLATTI SUCKED on a caramel. The temptation to have another was irresistible—and another until the box was empty and the priceless necklace at the bottom exposed, as he would expose Elena Torre—and her precious son—if she refused his request.

He licked the sticky tip of a finger. The idea was as flawless as the woman, and Marco Boni would be blind, blissfully blind, holding nothing back. The thought of pleasing Boni gave him pause, but so much could be gained. Every man was a dreamer when it came to his own performance, and Boni would be foolish enough to think that Elena Torre could truly want him.

Carlatti was enjoying his solitary game, choosing his own actors and actresses, orchestrating their every move, like the puppeteers he'd loved to watch in the marketplaces at home. He went back to the wooden box. It was Florentine, a deep rose color edged with gold and crammed with candies. Donna scolded him for eating too many carmels as if he were a child. She said that his teeth would rot—an enviable fear, he thought, so inconsequential for a man who stood to lose so much more if Elena Torre refused her help.

He opened the box, yielding as he was certain Elena would . . . Elena. He half-whispered the name to himself, although he never called her familiarly to her face. Even now, when he called in his I.O.U., he would address her formally as befitted her position and rank. He was always the gentleman that Immacolata had raised him to be, never allowing him to go barefoot in the streets of Messina even in summer or lapse into the dialect of his native island.

He dipped into the caramels again. He had told Boni it was his turn next, never revealing that he held the winning pair.

Chapter Nineteen

Marco Boni walked in awe, a response as alien to the audience around him as gaucheness. In July, 1776, while the Americans were signing their Declaration of Independence, the Empress Maria Theresa, Duchess of Milan, approved the plans for a new opera house to be built on the site of the medieval Church of Santa Maria della Scala. A matter of priorities. Ever since, La Scala has been the social, political and intellectual *agora* of Milan and the royal house of opera where the most magnificent singers, composers and conductors come to be judged and applauded. Boni had sat in the balconies as often as he could afford a ticket and kept every program neatly arranged in chronological stacks in a corner of his bedroom.

Tonight, though, he was entering another realm. The huge chandelier, with a lamp for each day of the year, illuminated the majestic proportions of the theater, the silver chains worn by each usher, the gold relief carvings on the curve of the boxes that were replicas of the originals destroyed when an RAF bomb gutted the house on the Feast of the Assumption in 1943. It was the opening night of a new production of *The Barber of Seville*. *Tout Milan*, everyone who was anyone in the city, was there, and everyone, himself included, was wondering why he was escorting Elena Maria Torre, president of the Banco di Milano.

She held his arm lightly, not appearing to lead him through a sea of jewels to her private box. The original boxes had been ostentatious displays of pedigree, with the coat of arms of the noble families that owned them on the outside and tapestried walls, frescoed ceilings and lacquered furniture inside. Now they were uniform in their red, white and gold splendor. Boni felt as if every eye and opera glass was focused on him and Elena Torre. Her arm tightened on his and he looked down at her.

"*Calma.*" She smiled as if she had heard his heart racing.

Elena resembled a Botticelli fantasy—coiled golden hair, flawless golden skin, tapering hands that Boni half-expected to flutter protectively to cover her breasts or genitals. Boni was a man continuously surprised by the unique beauty of the female body, no two the same— a comforting thought when all else seemed to be failing; the breasts alone were so different in size and shape, each woman's distinct— like snowflakes—and so much more interesting.

Elena sat down on the crimson seat now as if it were a throne and opened the program. "I hope you like *The Barber of Seville*, Signor Boni," she said without looking up.

He tried not to stare. She was the most fascinating woman he'd ever known, certainly the most powerful and very likely the most capricious. "Very much. Do you know that when it was first performed—I think it was in Rome in 1816 or '17—the catcalls and booing were so tremendous no one could hear the singers. Rossini himself was hissed at the end of the performance. He'd been leading the orchestra at the piano. The second night was the opposite—everyone loved it. It's my favorite *opera buffa.*"

"Good. I like operas that make me laugh, don't you? *Opera seria* is so *tragique.*" She rolled her eyes heavenward. Her gown was midnight blue and draped Grecian style across one shoulder. The other was bare—a glorious contrast, he decided. Sapphire flowers pierced her ears and around her throat was a necklace of sapphires and diamonds that looked as precious as a ciborium.

"Your necklace is very beautiful." Boni ran his finger along the edge of it. Her skin had warmed the cold stones.

"Thank you. Like the Torres it has its own history." He thought she flushed slightly but it could have been his imagination. A woman like Elena Torre didn't blush so easily.

"It looks very rare"—his finger still lingered at her throat—"as if it should be in a museum."

She moved away from his touch. He was good-looking enough in a rugged sort of way, stocky and broad shouldered with high coloring and dark eyes that looked at her like melting chocolates. And she thought she remembered him as a rugged, athletic lover. She couldn't be sure now. The sensation of his touch still pricked her throat. She had worn Lucco's necklace as a reminder, like a hair shirt while she served her penance, but maybe it had been a mistake. Boni was admiring it as if it were her own. She fingered it herself. "The necklace has been in my family since the Renaissance—and it always will be."

Boni smiled. He knew she was giving a marvelous performance, as good as any they'd see on the stage, and he wondered why he was so honored.

Boni did love women—but for a few hours only . . . he always went home to his wife before dawn. In his ideal world he would make love to every woman, once anyway, and one sympathetic woman would always be waiting for him. He hoped Bianca didn't know that his eye wandered, his body lusted. He would never broach the subject, though, and prayed that his wife was different from the women who came to him, that her secrets were different from his. He didn't even like her to go to the beach where other men could look at her and imagine how it would be. She was his. He possessed her in a way, he was sure, no man could ever possess the remarkable woman at his side.

Boni knew Elena Torre as a resourceful banker and a provocative woman. Although they'd met twice before, he was surprised when her secretary had called with an invitation to the opera—and flattered that she hadn't forgotten him. After all, Elena Maria Torre held a singular position in Milan society. Her reputation as a shrewd financier was unimpeachable; her lineage impeccable. The Torres were the oldest banking family in the city, admired universally for their cleverness but never at the expense of their integrity. They could trace their ancestors back to the Sforzas, but the family was in danger. There was only Elena left, and her son Lucco.

Boni had just begun his investigation of Stefano Carlatti the first time he went to visit Elena at the Banco di Milano, which resembled a baroque palace more than a clearing house for international currency. It was as imposing an edifice as the Temple of Jerusalem, except in one detail—the moneylenders were welcomed in its columned halls. Elena had received him in her private office, which looked out on the spires of the Duomo. The room, like its occupant, was elegant and reserved. As he'd looked at her that first time, Boni had thought she was even more haughty than beautiful, and maybe too careful.

"I am investigating the failures of Stefano Carlatti's Italian companies to liquidate any remaining assets," he had explained by way of an introduction. "But his business methods have been so devious they are proving difficult to resolve."

"What else did you expect? Signor Carlatti is a Sicilian, you should remember." Her voice was contemptuous. He was on tenuous grounds, groping for a way to cut through the jungle Carlatti had created, and she had sensed it. "Please bear with me, my investigation is just beginning and I was hoping that you could help me."

"Stefano Carlatti and I are the merest acquaintances." She began to go through the stack of correspondence in front of her, as if she'd already lost interest in the subject. "Of course I know him. I know everyone in Milan, but we have never been what you would call associates."

"But you were more than acquaintances, I believe."

"I think you should explain yourself, Signor Investigator."

"I am referring to certain business dealings you had with Carlatti—"

"What is it you want? The Torres have been bankers in this city for two hundred years and our conduct has always been above reproach."

"I am not suggesting otherwise. As you have just said, you are a prominent figure in our city, a leading banker and businesswoman, and as such I am appealing to you. Anything you can tell me about Carlatti's affairs will be held in confidence. You have my word of honor—"

"Have you any honor? I have found that it's a quality few men have, or feel they can afford."

At this point Boni hadn't cared what Elena Torre thought of him. His purpose was to find out what business she had with Carlatti. "I would like to know," he had said, choosing each word, "about the sale of the finance company Finaria to Stefano Carlatti. I believe that between you and your son Lucco, the Torres held a controlling interest."

"That is correct."

"You sold to Carlatti for what many considered much more than you could have gotten from another buyer. Why was he willing to pay so much?"

"Immediate gain is only one consideration. The sale of Finaria was in the best interest of all the parties concerned."

"Maybe I should talk to your son . . . for corroboration."

"I wouldn't do that, Signor Boni. Lucco takes no interest in business. In time he will—he is a Torre—but for now you would be wasting your valuable time. The transaction that interests you took place several months ago. He won't know what you're talking about, I assure you. Although the stock was in his name I controlled it, as I control every part of the Torre family holdings." She had stood up as she spoke and moved to open the door for him. "I wish I could help you, but I really know so little . . . any business I had with Stefano Carlatti is in the past. It is difficult to remember clearly. . . ."

At that first meeting Elena had been very formal, very correct, holding everything back. At the second, aboard her private plane, she'd been impassioned, holding nothing back—or so it had seemed to Boni. And now she had called and invited him to this glorious event. The house lights dimmed, but the lamps in the boxes remained burning, heightening the wonder of the theater. A century before, an audience disenchanted with the performance it had just attended rioted in the piazza outside. Tonight a hush of anticipation fell over the house. The conductor swept out from the wings, tails flying, baton already flourished. The lights in the boxes faded. The curtain rose. Boni held his breath. The first morning light was illuminating a square in Seville where Count Almaviva waited, surrounded by musicians. He was gazing wistfully up at the second-floor balcony where his lovely Rosina slept behind shuttered windows. He began to serenade her, calling her to wake up and make his heart swell with happiness.

The audience didn't wait for him to finish. A murmur of approval hummed like background music as he sang, *"Ecco ridente in cielo . . .* the glow of dawn is banishing the gloom of night."

Marco Boni never heard it. He was far from Milan, far from Seville, in Palermo, Sicily, listening to a different music, seeing a different vision. He was remembering his second time with Elena Torre three years before yet vivid enough to excite him still. She'd made him feel as if he'd climbed Mount Olympus, awakened Etna, brought down La Scala. . . .

Figaro was strutting onto the stage, boasting that he was the most important man in town . . . *"Largo al factotum della citta."* The barber of Seville, the big cheese, a man with a talent for rendering services—at a price. When Count Almaviva promised to pay him well if he arranged a rendezvous with Rosina, Figaro jumped at the opportunity. He was singing, *"All idea di quel metallo . . .* the thought of gold inspires me, making my mind erupt like a volcano," and Boni was remembering the second time, wondering again if Stefano Carlatti had been there before him.

Both clapped without enthusiasm. Memories and uncertainty had removed him from the shower of carnations that rained onto the stage. The lights were too bright. The audience too loud.

"Where would you like to go now?" His finger grazed Elena's bare shoulder as he slipped the sable stole over her arms.

"Home, if you don't mind. Will you come with me?" She turned to him as disarming as a child, and looked up for his answer.

"We can talk there," he agreed with a firmness he didn't feel, "and then you can tell me why you invited me here tonight."

Pride made him hope that memories of their second meeting had prompted the invitation, but he was wary. A discreet tryst would seem more her style than this calculatedly public show of interest. His picture on the front page of the paper wouldn't have attracted more attention.

So many people had come by to gawk at him during intermission that he'd felt like a display in a freak show. Elena had seemed amused by his discomfort and disdainful of her friends. "Look at the aristocratic Milanese," she'd said. "Like hunting dogs, always sniffing up a new scent, a new man."

Elena Maria Torre, as powerful as she was desirable . . . he would never underestimate her, and never stop wanting her. He slipped his hand through her arm and she covered his fingers with her own, like a possession.

Chapter Twenty

T HE SITTING room was the smallest room in Elena's sprawling co-op, and the warmest. The walls were deep yellow and crowded with photographs. Instead of the formal portraits that hung in the other rooms, there were pictures of her at five in a smocked dress standing between her parents, others of her in the summer with her father at Lake Como, and several of a little boy, undoubtedly her son. Boni looked for a picture of Carlatti but couldn't find one. It was an intimate room, he thought, possessed of a comfortable, lived-in feeling. The sofa and side chairs were upholstered in yellow-and blue-striped silk with contrasting fringe at the bottom. The drapes were yellow satin and drawn so that not even the night could intrude. A bowl of yellow and white freesia filled the room with perfume. A table was opened in front of the windows with a cold supper of crayfish, stuffed breast of veal and endive salad. They hadn't touched it yet. It was almost too perfect to disturb. Every detail of the setting was exquisite—the hand-embroidered linen cloth, the silver candlesticks, the Ginori china.

The crystal chimed as Elena touched her glass to his. "I want to help you, Marco. I'm afraid I wasn't as cooperative as I might have been the first time we met." Elena folded her leg under her and curled up on the sofa beside him.

"The second time was a definite improvement."

"I was selfish."

"Then I hope you never change."

It was drizzling outside. They had run from the door of La Scala to the waiting limousine. Intimidated by the bodyguard in the front seat, Boni had discussed the opera as they rode the few blocks to Elena's apartment. He had expected a liveried butler to greet them. Instead she unlocked the door herself.

The crystal chimed as she now touched her glass to his. "It is true, Marco Boni, I do want to help you, but you have to take me into your confidence. There is little that goes on in this city that I don't know. I didn't take your investigation seriously before. You were so vague the first time, and the second time rather annoying. But the Parente business has changed my mind." Boni thought her grip tightened around the stem of the flute, though it could have been his imagination.

Since his trip to New York he had come even closer to dissecting Carlatti's empire. The public denunciation of Bruno Parente had given new impetus to his investigation, and he was anxious to find out what she could tell him. He wet his lips with the champagne, aware that her naked shoulder was brushing against the sleeve of his jacket. "Have you ever heard of Dapro?"

Elena took the glass out of his hand. "Take off your jacket . . . it is so rough."

He got up to remove it. "We were talking about Dapro."

"Dapro." She stood up with him. "The name sounds familiar, German or Swiss, I think. Trust me, Marco, and I will help you. Just let me change first, then we'll have some supper and talk about Stefano Carlatti. That should please you." She turned her back on him. "Could you unzip me, please. I told the maid not to wait up." Elena glanced over her shoulder at him. "What would you like me to wear?"

"Your skin."

Victory came so easily. She laughed and the midnight blue slipped off her shoulder. The dress slithered to the floor as she turned slowly to him, naked except for her necklace. "Come," she murmured, reaching for his hand.

Boni took her in his arms, his investigation definitely stalled. He reached up to unclasp her necklace.

"No." She stopped his hand with a kiss. "I want to wear it when I make love to you." She was humming *"Ecco ridente in cielo"* as she took him, her prize and victim, into her bed.

It was dawn when Boni tiptoed into his own bedroom, carrying his shoes in his hand so as not to wake up Bianca. She lay on her side, curled in a ball. At the first sound of his footsteps she closed her eyes, pretending sleep. She was glad at least to have him back, she wouldn't force him to lie about where he'd been or whom he'd been with. The tears dried on her cheeks while he undressed. She felt his weight on the bed first, then the tug of blankets being pulled from her. She moved under the sheet so that her body touched his. She could tell from his breathing that he was tired but she had been waiting for him all night. She edged back closer, insinuating her rump against his stomach. Her nightgown had ridden up as she moved so that it was bunched around her waist.

Marco lay still. He didn't much like coming from another woman's bed to her. It made him feel too guilty. But not, he thought, guilty enough. Bianca moaned in her pretend-sleep and pressed tighter. She moved against him as if she were dreaming of making love, and felt his response uncurling. The silent coupling, like two strangers, excited him. He slid his hand around her belly and felt her. She was waiting for him.

For the next few moments Bianca forgot the calls that had begun when Marco came back from New York. The voice was always a man's, muffled, and the message was always the same: "Tell your husband we're watching you and your children. He'll know who's calling."

There were tears on her pillow when he withdrew. She pulled her nightgown down and turned over.

Marco smiled. "Were you waiting for me?"

"No, I was sleeping."

He smiled again and closed his eyes, grateful that she had relieved the burden of guilt.

Bianca nestled in the crook of his arm. She would let him sleep, then when he was rested she would show him the anonymous letter that had come in the morning mail. No matter his philandering, Marco was single-minded about his family. If he believed his family was in danger. . . . Bianca crossed herself and prayed until it was time to get the older children up for school.

CARLATTI FOLDED a paper coffin and looked around the sumptuously-appointed Hotel Pierre suite. Leased elegance, paid for by the month. There was no permanence anywhere, even among friends. Parente had thought he could be ignored with impunity, but then he had always been a limited man—wily enough but naïve, floundering in murky waters too deep for him.

Carlatti glanced up at the condottiere, who fidgeted on the Persian rug, impatient for praise and for the bonus he had earned. "How did you find my forgetful friend?"

Gattino grinned, an unpleasant sight. "He has recognized the error of his ways."

"Fine work, Gattino," Carlatti said. He was $500,000 richer and Parente hadn't even begun to bleed yet. From his headquarters overlooking Fifth Avenue, he felt like a commander marshalling his troops. He folded a second coffin and considered his tactics. So much had changed, and so little. Immacolata was dead three years now, and still unavenged. His enemies in Italy were still welding the nails to crucify him, and now the Americans were copying them. An unoriginal people—automobiles, Disneyland, football, everything they created lacked subtlety. But for the first time, the sweetness of revenge was close enough to taste.

Except for Gattino's restless shuffling, the suite was silent. The noises of the street were too far below to be heard through the double-paned windows. Only the tops of the trees, bare gray sticks across the street in the park, and the opaque sky intruded. Carlatti chose paper for a third coffin.

Parente had just started to pay—Gattino could see to that. And Marco Boni . . . a pincer attack appealed to his combative nature. Boni would be squeezed from two sides, flattered by Elena, frightened by Gattino. It was just a matter of time before he fell silent. Carlatti finished the last coffin and closed his eyes. Parente and Boni were business, but Elena Torre was pure pleasure. His tissue-thin eyelids fluttered in ecstasy. The sweetest revenge of all was making her perform at will, like his kept whore.

Chapter Twenty-one

ALTHOUGH SHE was ready to swear before Allah that her eyes had never left Bannigan for a second, Zenah must have slept. It was the only explanation, because the bloody bedroll was empty. Bannigan had lurched off the mat and was crawling toward her on his hands and knees. His eyes looked like soiled glass, his mouth was half-open in a grimace, the closest he could come to a smile. Congealed blood coated his teeth, the skin around his mouth was purple and swollen. He pointed to his lips, pleading for water.

Zenah shrank back until she was flattened against the wall of the cave and tried to scream. No sound came out. Before she could try again he lunged for her and pulled her down. His face contorted in pain, making him appear even more frightening, and he clamped his hand across her mouth.

"Don't be afraid, Zenah. You know me, my name's George Bannigan." Even though she wouldn't understand him he hoped the soothing sound of his voice might calm her down. "I brought your father weapons and you brought me tea in his shop, you came to hear me play the other night, I think. I've lost track of time. I saw you hiding from the others. You must have helped me." He went on talking although his mouth was so swollen that his words were slurred. "I know I couldn't have gotten back here by myself—you probably saved my life. I want to thank you." The sound of his voice seemed to quiet her. He didn't blame her for being afraid of him. If he looked anything as awful as he felt, he'd scare off Dracula.

Tentatively, Bannigan lifted his hand an inch. When she didn't try to scream again he released her. The water was still out of reach. He began to run his hands over his body, no bones appeared broken although all two-hundred-six of them felt as if they'd been pulverized.

Zenah watched him closely as he examined himself. He tried to smile again, touched his lips.

"Water?" The word was spoken in a clipped British accent.

He nodded, flabbergasted. She got the water and held a cup up to his lips.

"I learned English at school. We all did, although some remember more than others. When my father was a young man, Pakistan belonged to Great Britain."

"Why didn't you tell me in Darnu . . . at your father's shop?"

"Sometimes it is better not to know. My father would have been displeased."

"How does your father feel about you being here alone with me?"

Zenah shook her head. "Sometimes it is better not to know," she said again.

"Seems to be the popular philosophy up here—those three tired old monkeys." He acted out the words. "See no evil, hear no evil, speak no evil. Only I didn't catch on in time."

Zenah watched him curiously. "My father is in Karachi until tomorrow night."

Bannigan wasn't sure if she was defending her father or explaining herself. He studied her face, an ancient puzzle. In the Hindu Kush, society was structured as canon law, stern as the Torah—a paradigm of conformity.

Without his glasses Zenah's black hair melded into the depth of the cave, her features appeared rounder, more yielding. He wondered why she'd risked so much for someone who could never be anything except a stranger.

"I thought you were dead. That's why I was so frightened," she was saying. She had saved his life and she was apologizing.

"Maybe I was supposed to be."

"No. My father believed you merited punishment and wanted to convince you to leave."

Rahmir. It fit. The local arms merchant was also the drug lord, probably a government advisor in the Northwest Frontier Province as well. His English too must be impeccable. "I can think of subtler ways to make a point," Bannigan said. If curiosity had been his only transgression he might have escaped with a light beating. But he'd also compromised Zenah by asking her name and so he was mobbed. Would they come back to finish him off?

Bannigan knew he had to start moving around if he was going to get out of there alive. He managed to get up on one knee, and no further. He felt as if a meat cleaver was dividing his cranium. Zenah held him under the arm to steady him. Leaning on her, he pulled himself up and took a first, tentative step. Zenah hovered by his side. He wondered how far she would go to help him . . . and how far he would go to take advantage.

Bannigan didn't like using her, but scruples were a luxury now. He touched her cheek. When she didn't pull away he caressed her again, smoothing her cheek, threading his fingers through her hair and brushing it back from her face. Her hair felt coarse and oily. "I think I should get away from here before your father gets back."

She nodded, and remembered how George Bannigan had looked. Now his face was distorted, overgrown with stubble. She also hoped he wouldn't stop.

"I don't think I can make it out on my own. If Mohammed comes back soon. . . ."

"He won't. He has probably reported your death already."

Bannigan went on stroking her face as if he'd forgotten what he was touching. He was wondering if Hindle would send some other poor sucker hotfooting it into this no man's land. "Could you go to him?" He knew the answer. If she did she would be dishonored. "I'm sorry." He closed his eyes. "I'll try it alone. How bad can it be."

Zenah now drew away from his touch. She had inherited her mother's sex and her father's shrewd intelligence. But in her tribal, patriarchal world, she would never be allowed to use the latter because of the former. "There are other ways beside Mohammed."

Zenah was sure no one would come near this place for several days. The Pathans were superstitious and would not want to disturb the birds or the dead. Still, she crept out cautiously, carrying the empty canteens, aware of every shadow. The birds circled high in the sky now, not yet willing to give up a feast. A stream ran close by the cave. After she'd refilled the canteens she placed them at the entrance and tossed a stone in. She didn't wait to see if Bannigan could reach them. He had to begin to help himself again.

It was dusk when Zenah returned with an Israeli-made Uzi concealed under her skirts. Bannigan had cleaned himself as best he could with the water she'd left, dressed the worst of his cuts with antiseptic from his first-aid kit and put on clean clothes. It had been agony and had taken him all day. Judging from Zenah's expression, his efforts had been an improvement.

"Now I can recognize you again, by the way you look as well as by your touch." Her frankness was without guile, almost masculine.

"That's because I have my glasses on. I always carry a second pair, I'm lost without them. Not blind so much as stupid." He knew it was psychological, but the glasses clarified much more than fuzzy outlines. Some people, he knew, said they couldn't hear without their glasses. Bannigan found it difficult to think without his.

Zenah produced a small package of almond cakes wrapped in white paper and tied with string from the pocket of her skirt. "You must hurry. My cousin has already started. His mule train will pass close by here. There will be room in it for you."

"Why will he take me?"

"Because I have asked him to—he works for my father. And because I have promised him this." She drew the Uzi from the voluminous folds of her skirt. "For this he will keep silent."

Bannigan fingered the almond cakes. He knew she wanted to go with him, but she was too proud to ask for herself. And he couldn't bring himself to offer, no matter how much he owed her. "I think I'll save these to eat on the way." He rewrapped them awkwardly and zipped them into his knapsack. The combination of oily pastry and thick honey was more than he could stomach.

She watched him without offering to help as he tried to hoist the pack on his back. He felt like a cripple. Sweat stood out on his face. At the fourth try he succeeded. The straps cut into his ribs where the rifle butts had been.

"Will you be all right, Zenah?" He stood in front of her, feeling awkward and guilty.

She nodded. "There is no one to miss me except my father and he has not returned yet."

"I'll miss you, too . . . and remember you." Bannigan cupped her face in his hands and lifted it up to his lips. He felt like a damn hypocrite. Or a fool. Or both.

THE THUD of the jackboots forced Bannigan to hunker lower under the straw mat. Through the slats of the wagon he could see them scuffed and splattered with snow. The boots pounded against the cold. The snow furled around the greatcoats. Bannigan shivered more from fear that the Soviet troopers would stop the mule train than from the frigid temperature. But the soldier waved his Kalashnikov, signaling for them to pass. His orders were to stop and search every conveyance. A waste of time. He'd never found anything worth more than a couple of rubles and his tour of duty was almost over. In thirty-six hours, before the mule train got as far as Kabul, he'd be on his way home to Stalingrad.

The wagon jerked forward, and Bannigan bit his fist to stifle the gasp of pain. The trip through the Khyber Pass, stuffed between sacks and smothered under straw, had been as rough as a second beating. He'd escaped from Pakistan and entered the war-zone of Afghanistan where, something told him, a battered unkempt American gun runner hiding in a ramshackle wagon would be accorded something less than a hero's welcome if discovered. The Russians were burrowed in the surrounding foothills. Their field guns and tank turrets jutted through the snow—a disturbing sight. But the mule train appeared too inconsequential for them to bother with.

The overland trail was bone-breaking and long, stretching across three continents. Once they crossed Afghanistan they went through Iran to Diyarbekir in eastern Turkey. Bannigan had to stay hidden the whole time. He'd been cramped for so long he felt like a coiled spring that would never be able to unwind again. By the time they reached Turkey he was almost unrecognizable. All that was left of the clean-cut bland-faced American who had arrived in Peshawar six weeks before were the glasses, and even those were replacements. Although the swelling in his face had gone down, his skin was encrusted with layers of filth and congealed blood. His hair was shaggy and matted, and a full curly beard shadowed the lower half of his face. The only food he'd had were the almond cakes Zenah had brought him and some dried beef that was left in his knapsack.

As the wagon bumped along the rutted roads the driver maintained a low, nerve-wracking wail for the better part of each day. To Bannigan it sounded like every other Moslem song, atonal and forlorn. The driver's turban was wrapped in snow, and flakes glistened on his beard. Bannigan had no idea what Zenah had told the man, and he decided it would be better not to try to find out. Even when they stopped the driver didn't acknowledge Bannigan's presence. Being ignored so totally for so long, as if one were a corpse, was disconcerting. Still, it was a sight better than being abandoned a thousand miles from nowhere, and he was still on the heroin trail.

Coming through the Khyber Pass, to distract himself from the pain, Bannigan had investigated the cargo. Beneath the sacks of onions were cakes of morphine, wrapped as carefully as Zenah's almond cakes. A coincidence—or Zenah had done even more for him than he'd realized. She had said the driver worked for her father, but Bannigan hadn't quite put two and two together until now.

Chapter Twenty-two

No one at the DEA could remember the last time Leonard Hindle had worn his jacket in the office. The brown worsted strained across his shoulders as if the slightest additional tension would cause it to rip down the back. Hindle hunched over his desk, hugging the Acropolis in both hands. His lips moved, reciting the tribute he would give at the memorial for George Bannigan. The service was scheduled to start in ten minutes. Hindle wasn't ready for it. Never would be.

Hindle would have liked to be able to forget how he'd pushed Bannigan into the job, and what the pricetag for his cover had been. Gun-running was an expensive business. It was also going to be tough to justify the cost of all those high-powered weapons he'd shipped out to Pakistan, without even a body to show for it.

"An unfortunate incident." The report from the field had been too correct. The requisite information was provided, but no answers. Hindle felt like flying out there himself and finding out what the hell had gone on. At least he might be able to bring back Bannigan's body. He gulped the coffee dregs and crushed the container in his fist. The last drops spurted out, staining his speech. It didn't matter. He stuffed the pages in his pocket and pulled himself up. There would be no public acknowledgment of the loss, just this private service for the staff. Dr. and Mrs. Bannigan had declined his invitation to attend. They would have their own memorial in California with their remaining children.

THE THIRD floor conference room looked the way Hindle felt—dismal. The chairs had been pushed back against the walls as if the floor was scheduled to be washed any moment. The lights were dim. The piped-in music was a romanticized "Body and Soul," probably orchestrated by Lawrence Welk. Bannigan wouldn't have liked it. Hindle stood at the podium with a massive arrangement of white gladiolas and carnations—the two flowers he hated most in the world. The room was full of faces that wouldn't recognize Bannigan if he walked through the door. He had never worked in the D.C. office and he'd never made friends too easily anyway.

Hindle fixed on the only other person in the room who cared for George Bannigan besides himself. "Will you turn that goddamn noise off, Hattie, so we can hear ourselves pray."

Instantly he regretted the irreverence. Hattie's only fault was that she had tried too hard to make it nice for George. She hurried out, holding a handkerchief under her eyes like a safety net. Hattie Carmody had been at the DEA for thirty years, twenty of them as secretary to the director, a deceptive title. Hindle relied on her for more than funeral arrangements. Although her taste ran to angora sweaters and ceramic figurines of bears in toe shoes and pastel tutus, her knowledge of the agency was encyclopedic and her judgment of people astute.

"Body and Soul" was suspended in mid-note, leaving a void. Hindle cleared his throat. "I prepared a few words about George Bannigan but since none of you knew the guy I'm not going to deliver them. If it's all the same to you we'll recite the Lord's Prayer together and say Amen."

Hattie tiptoed back in the room just in time to hear him. He wished she hadn't. She would think George deserved something more personal, and she was right. "Hattie Carmody will lead the prayer." Her voice rose above the others with each word and at the end she went on alone. "Into your hands we commend George Bannigan, a noble spirit who shall be missed." Hindle murmured, "Amen."

Afterward the others started to move toward the door. The phone on the conference table jangled, a raucous intrusion. Hattie hurried to answer it, efficient even in grief. The operator was holding a collect call from Ankara on Hindle's private line. Hindle came off the podium in a rush. He never refused a call on that line. Only a handful of his best field operators and his mother had the number.

"Jesus H. Christ. We just finished burying you." He sat down heavily on the edge of the table. "I don't believe in the resurrection, you sonofabitch, though Hattie here evidently does.

"You're in Turkey? You are a turkey . . . so am I." Hindle eyed the hated flowers. "Now I'm stuck with a three-foot funeral piece and no body to pin it to. I've a good mind to drag you home and pin it on your ass."

Hattie was humming as she pushed the chairs back around the table. Although she could have left it for the maintenance crew, she preferred to return the room to the exact condition that she had found it. "Actually it's not a wreath." He laughed. "It's an arrangement—a Hattie Carmody special. Maybe I should make her wear it. Can you talk?" He was shouting. "I want a full report. I'll alert the embassies in Istanbul and Athens to expect something from you for the diplomatic pouch in the next few days. Get to whichever one you can—and Bannigan, be careful. I'm not going through another damn funeral service for you. I think that music you're always playing has affected your brain. You may think you're cool, but you're not a cat. You've already used up one life and that's all you're entitled to. You're on borrowed time now."

"I'm sorry, sir, your call has been disconnected." The overseas operator came on the line. Hindle gently laid the receiver in the cradle.

"You do good work, Hattie," he said, still holding on to the phone. "Thank God it isn't always necessary."

"Are you bringing him back?"

"I don't think he'd come. He's riding shotgun on an international transport bound for Bulgaria."

"What did he say?" She came up beside Hindle and touched his arm.

"Just that he's sore but as safe as can be expected, whatever the hell that means."

Chapter Twenty-three

Bianca Boni waited until her two youngest were asleep, then took the magazine her sister had brought her that morning out from under the pile of ironing where she'd hidden it and went into the bathroom. She sat down on the toilet seat. Although it was the new issue of *Gente*, the magazine was already dog-eared and fell open quite naturally to the only page that interested her.

Bianca had known for a long time that Marco was unfaithful, but he had never before humiliated her publicly. Everyone she knew had looked, pointed, gossiped about the picture—her family, her friends, the parents of her children's schoolmates, even the teachers and the parish priest. Marco must be in love to be so thoughtless. Bianca had cared when her husband had been unfaithful but it had never hurt so much because she was sure of his love. With five children in nine years, there had been many months when her body was distorted with a child. She didn't blame him then. By comparison, other women must have been irresistible.

Bianca studied the glossy photograph. Even alone, she didn't cry. The woman was pretty, but no prettier than she would be dressed in beautiful clothes with perfect makeup. A comfortless thought, because Marco was holding the woman's arm with the expression of someone who had been transported to paradise. If he had stripped and beaten her in the piazza in front of the Duomo, Bianca's mortification wouldn't have been more complete. It had disrupted their lives, devoured Marco's time and energies, and terrified her. She hated it, and she hated Stefano Carlatti and the time-consuming investigation. Now she hated Elena Torre. The caption beneath the photograph identified her as the president of Banco di Milano. Why did she want to be bothered with Marco? He was a hard-working lawyer and a dedicated family man, when the temptation was not too great.

Bianca didn't want to know that her husband loved Elena Torre, that he went into the bathroom while she was brushing her teeth and teased her neck and shoulders with kisses until she was ready to be taken right there at the sink; that he warmed her cold hands at night between his legs. She got up and looked at herself in the mirror. She had a clear-eyed, unobtrusive beauty. Dark lashes shaded dark somber eyes, dark glossy hair worn long like a girl, although her body had lost the supple line of youth. The baby was still nursing and so it retained an added roundness. Her breasts were so full that when the baby slept too long they exploded with milk.

At least Marco came home every night, although she was usually asleep by then, exhausted from chasing after five children single-handedly. Her sister had told her to make him pay for the disgrace but she was afraid to risk what she had. If she accused him they would never be the same together. But could they now, when he had looked at another woman that way, and in public?

The baby started to cry before Bianca had decided what to do. She hid the magazine beneath the ironing again and went to feed him. The older children would be getting home from school any moment. They would be hungry too. Then there was the supper to start. She never knew if Marco would be home these days or not.

The baby was still at his mother's breast when the other children burst in from school. Bianca looked at their faces flushed from running, their enormous eyes, their cheeks streaked with dirt, and felt their terror. She hugged them fiercely against her. There should have been three of them. . . . "Where is Francesca?" Her first-born, her oldest, a miracle unequaled in life, always taking so seriously her responsibility to shepherd her younger brothers home each day.

The boys gasped out a story fractured by sobs. Bianca clutched them tighter, afraid to leave them at home alone, afraid to take them all with her to find Francesca. She could call for help, but each moment lost . . . her mind refused to function, she worked on instinct alone.

GIAN GATTINO had watched the children coming out of school from a Fiat station wagon parked across the street. They seemed to tumble out in their enthusiasm, backpacks strapped on, knee socks falling, hats forgotten or pulled down too far. He looked at each one, waiting for a specific face—intense, serious, with a head of black curls like her father. Now she came down the steps with a younger brother grasped firmly in each hand.

Gattino knew each of the Boni children by sight. He had watched them go in and out of their apartment many times. He waited, in no hurry, as the other children dispersed, then crossed the street and began to follow them, whistling, hands in his pockets. When they reached the next corner he called softly at first, then louder, "Francesca. Francesca." The child turned, wide expectant eyes, anticipating a friend.

"Who's that?" The boys tugged at her. They always wanted to run ahead but she held them more firmly than their mother, serious in her responsibility as big sister.

Francesca stared at Gattino, uncertain. She knew she should never speak to strangers, yet the man knew her name. She looked around. Across the street a woman was carrying a string bag of groceries, hurrying home to cook them for supper. Otherwise there was no one around. She looked back at the man. He was small and wore a turtleneck and three-quarter-length coat. In another step he would be able to reach out and touch them.

"You don't know me, Francesca, but it's all right," he said, "because I know you. Your father is Marco Boni and your mother is Bianca. You have two other little ones at home besides these two."

His easy assured voice held her, but there was something about him, the way he said her name, the way he smiled at them that frightened her. She turned away.

"Run," she whispered under her breath to her brothers and pushed them forward, knowing instinctively that it was too late for all of them to escape. Every other day they wanted to run ahead, and she insisted on holding them together, three abreast. "Run," she commanded again under her breath when they hesitated. They bolted then.

"Tell mamma," she whispered after them just as Gattino's arm snaked around her shoulders.

Francesca didn't move. She was watching her brothers until they turned the corner, hoping that it wasn't true—her fears.

"You're a pretty girl and very smart, I think." His arm tightened around her. "How old are you?"

Francesca heard herself answering clearly. "Eight years old. My birthday is in May."

"So is mine," Gattino said. It was in November. "You and your brothers go to school back there, don't you?"

She nodded.

"Come on, you can show it to me." Anyone seeing them walking back toward the school might have mistaken them for father and daughter; the man had his arm around the little girl and was speaking quietly to her.

"I bet you have lots of friends."

Francesca nodded.

"So do I." They were in front of the school again, and he led her back up the front steps to the door. "Do you know what else I can tell just by looking at you? I can tell that you are your father's special girl."

It was the first time Francesca smiled. Gattino bent over her and murmured, "Do you love him very much?"

"Yes," she nodded, still smiling.

"Good. If you love him very much, then you'll do something for me. Tell him to stop—he'll understand what I mean. And if he doesn't stop, I will come back with all my friends and with these." He drew a knife from his pocket and a length of rope tied in a noose. He took Francesca's finger, which was ice cold, and ran the blade along it, and rubbed the rope across her cheek. Gattino smiled, feeling her tremble. "When we are finished with him, we'll nail his body right there on the front door of your school. So you'll remember our little talk. . . ." He pricked her finger with the knife and smeared the bead of blood on his own. "Tell him to stop, Francesca—for you, his special girl."

Gattino pinched her cheek and turned away. It was part of the job and he was well paid for it—not his favorite part, but so be it.

Francesca didn't begin screaming until Gattino had driven away. When her mother came racing down the street, two babies in her arms, the two boys clinging to her skirts, Francesca was hunched on the steps of the school like an orphan. They had heard her hysterical sobs long before they saw her.

It took several hours for the child to stop crying long enough to tell her mother about the man. She told what he had said, but when she tried to tell about the knife and the rope she became hysterical again. They were too awful to say, and she was afraid no one would believe her. The tears had washed the blood from her finger. All that remained was a red pinprick to remind her that it hadn't been a nightmare. It was too much, even for a big girl as she was, to accept that.

WHEN MARCO got home from Elena he had to sleep in the children's room with the two babies. The three older ones were huddled together in his big bed with Bianca. She got up when she heard him come in and slipped out, being careful to close the door behind her. She didn't know how to tell him about Francesca. She didn't even know how to act with him anymore.

Marco looked at her—the sleepless eyes circled with black, the pale face, the nervous fingers playing with the string of her nightgown. "What's the matter, Bianca, *carina?*" He opened his arms to her, and she fell into them sobbing. He hugged her, loving her more than ever, perversely, because Elena in her fashion brought him such pleasure. He smoothed her hair, thick and black, and kissed it because it smelled of her body, her milk, her sleep.

When Bianca was calmer she led him into the kitchen and sat down heavily at the table to tell him about Francesca. Marco listened with his face half-buried in his hands, cursing Carlatti in his soul.

"Francesca never wants to go back to school. If she doesn't go, she thinks you'll be safe. Then she can't find your body hanging on the door."

He shook his head. "I wish it were that simple. I'll talk to her in the morning."

Bianca knew that wasn't enough. "The boys are just as frightened as Francesca."

"I'll bring the three of them to school myself. When they see me walk away safely they'll believe it was just cruel words to frighten us—"

"Are you sure that's all it is—first the calls, then the letters, and now this? Just cruel words to frighten us?"

Marco did not answer right away. He didn't want to lie any more than was necessary. At the same time he wanted to ease Bianca's fears. "Carlatti is a man—not so different from other men, with a sweet tooth, especially for caramels. I suppose that anyone with enough provocation can become a killer. If you were dishonored or my children hurt . . . I could see myself doing it. Still, desperate as he is, it's hard to believe Carlatti is a killer. I don't know. Anyway, just seeing me the same as I always am should make Francesca forget the worst of it."

Bianca looked up at him, her lashes slick with the tears that had begun again as he talked. "Are you the same? Is this case worth so much to you that you would destroy your family for it?"

"Do you want me to do less?" At the moment it didn't occur to him that she was talking about Elena Torre too.

"Yes, if it means we will have a life together again, and be a family again, and the children won't wake up in the night screaming, and I . . . I. . . ." She burst into tears, but she could see he wouldn't give it up—any of it.

Marco came around the table and pressed her head against his chest. "If you had seen Francesca today you wouldn't be so stubborn," she said.

He shook his head. Each attack on his family strengthened his determination not to stop until Carlatti had paid for every fraud, every theft, every act of terror. "It wouldn't be fair to Francesca or the other children if I gave up now. Terror can't be allowed to win. What lesson is that to teach our children?" He wiped the tears from her cheek as he held her. "I'll go to Rome and ask for more help— a bigger staff and protection for you and the children. I know how difficult it has been for you, *carina*, but it shouldn't be much longer. Can you stand by me a little longer, Bianca?"

"I married you forever, Marco, not just for nine good years. I want it to be forever, but sometimes I wonder if you feel the same. I don't want to lose you. . . ." There was no guile in her. She covered his shirt with tears and kisses. Before she couldn't cry, now she couldn't stop. She wanted to lie with him in the babies' room, but he was afraid the older children might wake up in the night and be frightened if she wasn't there. She didn't mention the photograph.

Chapter Twenty-four

BRUNO PARENTE wiped his face with the sleeve of his flannel shirt and leaned against the pile of logs he had cut, winded and happier than he'd been in weeks. A pair of young sheepdogs slept a few yards away. Curled in balls of fur soft as down they looked like pillows that had been forgotten in the dark grass. Parente loved every moment in Cervino, but the late afternoon was his favorite time. The sun was just beginning to drop and the mountains that encircled him seemed to blush the palest pink beneath its glow.

He breathed deeply, inhaling the smell of freshly mown grass, more fragrant than any perfume, then picked up the ax again and swung it over his shoulder. The strong, sweeping motion sliced through the bark into the pulp of the wood. He would split a few more logs, he thought, before starting back to the house to clean up and make supper—a rich soup of white kidney beans and broccoli. The soup base was already simmering. All that was left to do was add the small, tubular maccaronis, pick greens for a salad, cut the bread and open a bottle of wine, a barola, blood red and full-bodied.

Parente swung the ax again, working every muscle into the rhythm of the swing, until the tool seemed like an extension of his arm and everything else was forgotten, even the humiliation he had suffered at the hands of Stefano Carlatti. He thrived on the simplicity of country life—on the invigorating work on his farm, the simple, robust meals he liked to cook for himself. He felt secure and content on his beloved country estate. The dour banker, close-lipped and suspicious, was a stranger. He sang as he worked, *"Sul Monte Bianco e sul Cervino,"* an Alpine choral song about the courageous mountain men who died in World War I defending these summits with their own blood. Sometimes Parente wondered why he had ever left the mountains he loved. The wealth meant relatively little to him. He had simple tastes and few interests outside his family and this place. But position was important to Anna, and he had grown accustomed to power.

The log split in two perfect halves. Parente put down the ax and added the fresh wood to the pile he'd already cut. In the distance he saw a vague movement and thought it must be his children coming home. They had gone riding with their cousins, although he hadn't expected them back so soon. In the war he'd ridden for miles through the relentless snow with the Russian tanks at his heels until his horse collapsed beneath him, a chestnut mare with three white feet and a white diamond-shaped blaze. He'd shot her with his service revolver and sliced up her carcass for dinner. He hadn't ridden much since.

Squinting into the distance, he saw that it was a single figure, probably a neighbor on his way back from hunting. He could be a giant of a man but silhouetted against the mountains he looked like a dwarf. The pink had deepened on the distant peaks. He whistled to the dogs and picked up the ax again, intending to start back to the house. A warning bark stopped him. The dogs had scrambled up and stood like statues, ears cocked. All at once they began to bark again and tore across the field. Parente took his jacket and followed them, still carrying the ax. In the fading light he recognized the voice before he made out the face.

"Call off your hounds, Parente, before they bite the hand you feed." Gian Gattino's mocking laugh desecrated the blessed mountain air;

his presence defiled Parente's sanctuary. He would have liked to set the dogs loose but . . . well, there was Anna to think of, and the children. Men like Gattino and Carlatti, maybe even Desmond, thought only of themselves. He had never been a free man. Parente gave the command to heel, and the dogs bounded to his side still growling deep in their throats.

"What are you doing here?"

Gattino didn't come any closer. "Just passing by. It's so peaceful here, though." He turned in a full circle, waving his arms, encompassing the mountains and the pastures. "I may decide to stay. You certainly have the room."

Parente was silent. For Gattino to come here to Cervino to invade his home was unforgivable . . . an even worse insult than the others he'd been made to suffer.

"I should tell you," Gattino spoke as if they were old friends, "Carlatti sends his regards. He appreciates your gift—a generous gesture, I believe those were his exact words—but just an appetizer. He is ready to receive the next course, so to speak."

"No. I did my part . . . half a million dollars, and I had to go hat in hand for that."

"Just the appetizer," Gattino repeated. "Then there is the soup, the fish, the entree, the salad, and of course, the fruit and the dessert. If you were a cordial man, Parente, you would invite me into your home where we could sit down and discuss these things like gentlemen instead of standing in an open field like barn animals."

"The field is too good for you, Gattino. You should go back to the swamp where you came from."

Gattino tried to move closer, but the dogs stopped him with teeth bared. "I thought you understood, Parente. Evidently you're a slow learner. A pity for you." In the distance they heard Anna calling. "Carlatti believes the investigator Boni would be interested in you too, if presented with certain inducements. Of course he would never say a word to compromise a friend, even to help himself. But someone so ungrateful, so forgetful. . . ."

There was fresh snow on the mountain slopes for skiing, and the lakes between the ridges were thick with ice for skating. For the first time Parente felt the cold and shivered. Anna was calling to him again, her voice sharpened by worry. He didn't want her to see Gattino. It would upset her too much, shatter the security she felt here.

"How much more does Carlatti want?"

Parente put on his jacket, turning up the collar against the draught that chilled his neck. Although he'd been quite good as a boy, he hadn't done winter sports—skied or skated—in years. His children, of course, did, and Bishop Desmond. Yes, the Bishop was a great athlete. Parente had planned to invite him to the mountains for a week later in the season. Under the circumstances, the invitation would be extended sooner than planned.

PARENTE ONLY knew one safe road, and it led back to Rome. He took it with a certain grim confidence, knowing that the Pope's beloved Solidarity was stronger for his efforts. He had served His Holiness well—and would again, if the need arose.

The sting of winter had turned the city gray. The street peddlars had abandoned Piazza Navona, and the azaleas were gone from the Spanish steps. Rain splattered the cobblestones and washed the saints and serpents, the *putti* and pagan gods. In winter when the weather chilled the earthen colors, Rome was a city of stone and statuary.

Against such a backdrop Bishop Desmond resembled an advertisement for a winter vacation. He greeted Parente with enthusiasm, talking affectionately about Anna and the two girls, the perfect snow for downhill skiing, and the indefatigable energies of Stefano Carlatti. If the snow was good, he promised he would spend a week in Cervino.

It wasn't the promise that Parente had hoped to secure, still he remained hopeful—even confident.

"Give me a couple of days to see what I can do." The Bishop put a smothering arm around his shoulders. "Don't worry, we'll come up with something, short of pawning the Pietà I hope, to keep our friend Carlatti happy. It's the least we can do." That we had better do?

Parente spent most of the next two days in his room at the Excelsior Hotel on the telephone, checking with his vice-president at Banco Bartolomeo or consoling Anna who had remained in the mountains in anticipation of even deeper mortification. It was a front room, too noisy for adequate rest. The windows looked out on Via Veneto, an all-night street fabled for *la dolce vita*. He noticed the women below, as he noticed the rest of the topography, without a second thought. In nineteen years of marriage he had never been unfaithful to Anna.

When Parente, forty-eight hours later and much more tense, crossed the Tiber again he was advised that Bishop Desmond was unavailable. He had gone into retreat at an undisclosed monastery beyond the reach of telexes or urgent cables.

Parente told himself he should have anticipated Carlatti's appetite. The first swallow had made him voracious. A third demand would follow this one, then a fourth and a fifth, just as Gattino had promised. He remembered his father's face covered with leeches that grew fatter and fatter as he watched. He couldn't have been more than five when his father had gotten sick, and the doctor had prescribed the blood-sucking worms to draw out the infection.

He scratched his forehead nervously. In a way Carlatti was forcing him to submit to the same barbaric treatment. He was having trouble just keeping himself afloat. His investors' faith in his Banco Bartolomeo had been shaken by the scandal Carlatti had instigated, and Marco Boni's staff was pressing to look at the books.

Parente stayed in Rome for another week, praying that the Bishop would be inspired again. Finally backed into a corner with time running out, he approved an unsecured loan to his Bahamian subsidiary that was passed on to Gattino. It was easier to juggle eggs than paper, but Parente was desperate to deliver himself from the greater threat.

Chapter Twenty-five

I THINK I am falling in love with you."

Elena went on brushing her hair as if Marco had said he thought it might rain. She was sitting at her dressing table under the Morandi still-life. Giorgio Morandi had been an unassuming man—a clerk who lived with his sister all his life and painted the simplest things in the subtlest colors. Eggs, bottles, a dish—ordinary objects, elemental shapes that his pigment and brush made extraordinary. Elena considered him her own discovery. She had seen his work in Rome when she was a student and they were selling for nothing. Now there were retrospectives and high prices.

The only art Marco was interested in was the woman at her dressing table. Each stroke of the brush through her hair excited him. "I said, I think I'm falling in love with you." He watched her face through the mirror. One eyebrow arched slightly, otherwise she appeared unaffected.

"Is that so remarkable? You make it sound as if you'd achieved an impossible feat."

Boni sat propped up in the center of her bed, his knees pulled up and his chin hunched over them. She had never brought any of her lovers home while Lucco lived with her. In spite of their lovemaking, it felt strange . . . and too intimate . . . to have a man watch her in her bedroom. She had never shared it with anyone before. If she told him that, Marco probably wouldn't believe her, and even if he did he wouldn't understand.

"It's not incredible. It's terrible. I must be crazy. I have a wonderful wife and five children—"

Elena shrugged. "You make it sound as if we were eloping."

"Would you?" She was smooth and golden like an apricot, even under her arms. He'd never seen a woman who shaved her armpits before except in American movies. Her slip was apricot silk. He wanted to reach over and peel it off. One strap had slipped off her shoulder, and underneath it she was naked.

"Romeo and Juliet? That was in Verona, Marco. You're getting confused. This is Milano, and we are too old to play the parts."

"What do you feel for me?" He wanted to go behind her and take her in his arms again, but she was leaning into the mirror smoothing a cream into her skin, the first step in the exacting task of putting on her public face. Marco thought she was too beautiful for makeup, but she saw it as a protective shield.

Elena tilted her chin up and massaged the cream into her throat. "Why do men always have to be told how well they performed, how passionately they're desired, how irreplaceable they are?" She chose a pale mascara for her eyelashes. "What's the matter, Marco? Did your wife throw you out of bed last night?"

"Bianca has nothing to do with us." Since La Scala, Marco had seen Elena twice, sometimes three times a week and she'd never been cruel before. It was obviously a mistake admitting that he loved her.

"You're right, of course." She smiled but the effect was strained because her lips were drawn back in a tight line so that she could trace their contours with a siena-colored pencil. "I would probably like her very much. You should spend more time with her. I'm not good for you anyway. I distract you from your work." She began to fill in her lips with a sable-hair brush. Sometimes, caught up in his energetic lovemaking, she found herself forgetting Lucco and Stefano Carlatti, and why she was making love to him.

Marco unfolded himself. "Bianca wants me to stop. She's frightened for the children, and for me."

"We're all afraid of something." Elena stepped into black alligator sling-backs and stood up. Her voice was as sharp as her heels. "The other day a man terrorized my daughter on the way home from school. She's eight-years old."

Elena was pulling a dress over her head as she spoke. "What are you going to do?" The question was smothered in cashmere.

"Carlatti is a fraud, a thief and a cheat, but I don't think he's a killer."

She watched him put on his jacket and straighten his tie. "He is a Sicilian, Marco."

"So was Bellini."

"I'm going to Rome for a few days to try to get a bigger staff so I can clear up this mess before my children are too afraid to go out of the house. And when I come back I'm going to pay a call on your friend Bruno Parente. Shall I give him your regards?"

"By all means, though I'm sure he won't be as cooperative as I am."

"I hope not. He's a little short for my taste."

Elena laughed. "I didn't know you were particular."

"I wasn't until I met you. Now—"

"Call me after you've seen Parente. I'll be curious to hear what he has to say."

PALM TREES shaded the Bank of Italy. The rains had stopped and the dark fronds nodded in the breeze sweeping up the boot. Inside the bank the atmosphere was less positive. Ugo Mazeppa's thick fingers smoothed the edge of the desk, picking up the particles of dust that had formed there since the cleaning woman had dusted the previous evening. He shook his head at the findings. A dirty city, thick with the dust of centuries, and a dirty business, this Carlatti case. It was an unsavory task, arduous, thankless, and quite possibly dangerous. And Boni was performing it brilliantly—too brilliantly. His large head swayed in the opposite direction from the palms, east and west, as Boni described the threats to himself and his family. He wanted a bigger staff; the longer the case dragged on the more frightened his wife Bianca and the children became. . . .

Mazeppa wasn't surprised by the threats. He'd seen gentler men than Stefano Carlatti turn vicious when cornered. But his hands were tied. "If the pressure is too great, I can accept your resignation . . . an understandable decision on your part without stigma. But I can't promise you more help. We have no one to spare."

"I'm not asking for myself, but for my wife and children. Even if the threats are empty they need reassurance for their peace of mind, and my own—a quick resolution, or at least the hope of one."

"Personally I am sympathetic, Marco. But like everything else, we have limitations." His face was wide, the refined features almost lost in the generous expanse of flesh. Only the lower lip was full, as if the sculptor had forgotten to chisel it.

Carlatti's money had been heard. Influential voices in the Christian Democratic party had spoken out in parliament against his continuing persecution. To deploy additional resources now would just stir up more debate and bring the bank under fire. Mazeppa was too tired to challenge the Philistines head-on. During his twenty-year tenure he had earned an admirable reputation by being sensitive to the political climate, tempering integrity with pragmatism—a critical lesson Boni had yet to learn.

"I can't resign now. I know Carlatti. He's just waiting for his chance to insinuate his way back. We were lucky the first time. We stepped in before he made the whole country bankrupt. But the next time. . . ."

Mazeppa concentrated on the motes of dust. "Maybe he has learned his lesson."

"If you believe that, you have to presume a certain humility, and Carlatti's pride is as enormous as his greed."

"Is yours so much less, Marco? Think of your children first. Carlatti is our past, they are our future."

"Unfortunately he doesn't see it that way."

ALTHOUGH THERE was no ski slope or golf course in Assisi, Bishop Desmond suffered the deprivation without complaint. There was a fine 18-hole golf course in Rome, between Via Appia Nuova and Antica, where he liked to play a couple of times a week. But in Italy golf was not a game of power and politics as it was in the States. The Italians had never embraced the game with feeling. Probably because, at heart, it was a solitary sport that didn't appeal to their gregarious character. In golf you were really competing against your own best effort. Strength, control, precision—they were the prerequisites, and Desmond needed them now more than ever, for a much more serious game.

The Bishop seemed too large for the monk's cell that he had been assigned. It was a high, narrow room with a single high, narrow window, bare floors, a cot too short to accommodate his full length, a bedside stand, straight chair, and prayer with St. Francis's hymn of thanksgiving. Still, he was grateful for the sanctuary.

Sheltered behind medieval walls, surrounded by the meadows and foothills of Umbria, the town had changed little. In the adjacent basilica, Giotto's frescoes described the saint's life—the wealthy young man giving his father back everything that money had bought him, even the clothes on his back, becoming a beggar and adopting a new family—the birds and animals of the field.

Francis had been either very holy or very foolish. Desmond knew he wasn't the first and he hoped he wasn't the second. A foolish man, the Bishop thought, would have rescued Parente again. Instead he'd gone into retreat to distance himself and the bank from his Milanese advisers.

The first favor had not been as effective as he'd hoped. Although influential voices had been raised in Carlatti's support, the investigation went on as if it possessed a life of its own. Parente, he felt certain, would be drawn in next. And then, inexorably, the path would lead to the papal city-state, and to his own door.

A priestly retreat was normally a time of silence and seclusion set apart from earthly concerns—a period of soul-searching and meditation. The Bishop's meditations, though intense, were limited to his own salvation.

The Vatican was charged with danger. Decisions reached miles away had made the atmosphere within the Apostolic Palace tense. From his narrow window Bishop Desmond looked out beyond the medieval parapets to the Umbrian fields, the green expanse broken occasionally by a line of cypress trees. Gossip in the curial halls was that the Pope had warned a Kremlin emissary that he would fly home to be with his people if the Soviets launched an invasion. A twentieth-century crusade against the infidel with the Pope leading the charge. Desmond didn't doubt for a moment that he would. Although the cell was cramped, he was grateful for this safe haven. The tensions within the Vatican dictated prudence, and Desmond's position remained precarious. Although Parente's assistance had been appreciated, the Pope was preoccupied now, and the Bishop's critics within the curia were growing bolder. Any false move now might be beyond redemption.

Desmond bounced on the edge of the bed, testing it. There were no springs, and the mattress was so thin he wouldn't have been surprised to learn that one of St. Francis's brother monks had slept on it. Stretching out his long legs so that six inches of them hung over the foot, he closed his eyes and thought of skiing in Cervino and vacationing in Lyford Cay. He would miss the Parentes, especially the children. They'd had good times together.

Loyalty was an admirable virtue, the Bishop thought, but it wasn't something to be crucified for.

Chapter Twenty-six

BANNIGAN SAT on a load of unprocessed morphine base, heading for a country that might easily wipe him off the face of the earth without a trace. Hindle's jibes notwithstanding, he felt as if he really had come back from the dead. A primitive Turkish bath had restored his skin to a shade only slightly darker than his natural color. His weeks huddled in the mule wagon had given his body time to heal.

From the height of the TIR cab he looked out at the shepherds lolling on the scrubby hillsides of Greece, keeping a half-watch on their meager flocks. Olive leaves glinted silver in the sunlight. An eminently reassuring country, he thought; it looked exactly like the description in his fifth grade geography book.

They'd driven the width of Turkey, skirting the center of Istanbul, crossed the suspension bridge over the Bosporus and were cutting through the northeasternmost point of Greece that sticks up like a sore thumb between Turkey and Bulgaria. The TIR carrier—one of the hundreds of Transport International Routier trucks that criss-crossed Eurasia moving cargo across international boundaries, unimpeded by border checks—was a vast improvement over the mule train. So was the driver, an exuberant man with a handlebar mustache, oil-black hair and a flash of white teeth. Like every second Turk, his name was Abdul. Bannigan didn't have to stretch his imagination to picture Abdul in balloon trousers, flashing a scimitar between his teeth in place of a rose. But he wasn't complaining. His saxophone was in the back of the truck, buried with his knapsack beneath half a ton of morphine. The Beretta was folded into his sleeping roll with the extra ammunition. Only the M1 was gone. A gamble, but now Bannigan was confident it had been worth it.

When he'd realized they were coming to the end of the journey, he'd given it to the mule driver. They had just passed through the border point of Iran when they stopped for the night. He'd waited until the driver was asleep, then pulled the carbine from his pack and prodded the man into wakefulness. The night was obdurate and black, but the terror in the Pathan's face was clear as day. He had prayed aloud. Bannigan recognized the cadence.

"Help me and I will give you this." Bannigan had patted the stock. "An American M1—very good. If you don't help me I will kill you with it." He had pushed the barrel into the driver's chest. The words were crude enough to be understood in any language, but he acted them out anyway.

It had taken time and not a little ingenuity for Bannigan to make himself understood. Comprehension dawned slowly, and with it incredulity. Bannigan wanted to go on with the drugs. The Pathan looked at him as if he were crazy. "Very dangerous," he warned, but he wasn't one to look a gift horse in the mouth. His head had bumped against the rock-hard ground with each enthusiastic nod. His relief had been extravagant, and his cooperation commensurate.

Five days later Bannigan was riding shotgun in the cab of the TIR transport to learn the route from Diyarbekir, Turkey, to Sofia, Bulgaria, and teaching Abdul to sing "Tangerine." His name and passport number had been sent to Sofia for checking. When no police connection was found, he was, he figured, in business.

Because of the TIR logo they zipped across borders unchecked, even passing through the notorious customs control at the Bulgarian line without being stopped. Because of their special cargo, Abdul had sent the license number and approximate time of crossing ahead and they were waved through without question.

Once in Sofia, Abdul maneuvered through the traffic as surely as if it were his hometown. He'd made the trip too often to count, and the procedure never varied.

"What happens to our cargo from here?" They'd just dropped the keys off at Kintex, an innocuous modern building of concrete and glass that housed the Bulgarian import-export exchange, and were crossing Liberation Square.

"Kintex stores it," Abdul said.

"Forever?"

Abdul shrugged. "How would I know? I drive from Diyarbekir to Sofia, from Sofia to Diyarbekir, from Diyarbekir to Sofia. . . . But I have met other drivers staying here at the hotel with different routes, Sofia to Trieste, Trieste to Sofia. They admit they carry the same thing I do, if they have too much to drink. I never drink too much in Sofia. It is safer to do other things too much, then you're too busy to talk. I've been driving for six years, no trouble—and that is why."

"Good advice," Bannigan said. "I'll take it after you tell me what the Bulgarians get out of all this."

"Ten percent off the top in hard currency—that's what I hear, anyway. I'm only a driver, and you, my friend Tangerine, are too curious. It is better not to ask. I have driven all these years with no trouble. The reason—"

"I know, you don't talk."

He put his finger over his lips. "I may wonder, but I never ask."

"Who pays the Bulgarians?"

"The *buyuk baba,* the big grandfather, Abuzer Ugurlu. We work for him and he works for the Bulgarians. A happy family." Abdul slapped him on the back, making Bannigan unpleasantly aware of his strength. "Why are you so curious?"

He shrugged. "I just like to know who I'm working for, that's all."

THE HOTEL Vitosha-New Otani made Vegas look like an oasis of good taste. The thirty-floor white tower was built by the Japanese without a hint of oriental subtlety, except for a landscaped garden and a reflecting lily pool. Otherwise it was strictly show-off Western, pandering to the vices at least officially prohibited in the communist world—prostitution, gambling, moral decay. An apparent anomaly in a communist capital, until one considered its purpose. . . . To lure the international tourist trade the Bulgarians had built a pleasure dome that would put Kubla Khan's to shame, a place equipped with bowling alleys, saunas, bars, a gigantic swimming pool, overpriced boutiques, casinos, pretentious restaurants, and a raunchy nightclub show.

Bannigan and Abdul were installed in adjoining rooms on the seventeenth floor, the area usually reserved for the relays of TIR drivers. It was a long way from a Pakistan cave or the flat-bed of a mule train wagon, and when he stretched out on the king-size bed, Bannigan wasn't worrying about who was picking up the tab.

Judging from the grinding and grunting noises coming from next door, Abdul was taking advantage of his rest and relaxation furlough from wife and children. Bannigan was more temperate. The first night he sat in the tub, replenishing the steaming water as it cooled until his skin had shriveled so much he was afraid it might dissolve. Then he slept for fourteen hours. By the second day he was a new man.

He bought a guidebook and took to roaming around the city, always ending up in the vicinity of Kintex. Its official business was regulating imports and exports, but its unofficial business was more interesting. Everything contraband or illegal was Kintex's stock-in-trade. Bannigan could never get close enough to investigate though, and time was running out. In another day or two he would be going back to Turkey with Abdul, unless he could find a way to follow the heroin trail the next step. The meeting of Eastern transporters and Western distributors was a critical point. If he could nail the European wholesalers, the pick-up points, the processing plants, they could put a real crimp in the heroin flow. Abdul had said the next stop was Trieste, Italy. A coincidence? Bannigan wondered, or else Hindle had been right. He was coming full circle. Bannigan hadn't thought about Stefano Carlatti in weeks. Now he began to wonder if maybe he'd been on the same case all along. He'd started at the opposite end and was slowly working his way back—to the ultimate paymaster.

LEONARD HINDLE waited five days to receive Bannigan's report from Istanbul before contacting the American Embassy in Sofia. The information he received did little to improve his sleep. A man answering the description of George Bannigan had been observed being escorted from Liberation Square by three men, believed to be security police, after playing the saxophone there without a license and begging for coins. An official inquiry would be arranged through the Canadians upon request.

After he got the report Hindle went back to counting sheep at night—and cursing the infinity of numbers.

Chapter Twenty-seven

I~N~ L~IBERATION~ Square Czarist and Bolshevik Russia coexist in apparent harmony. Seated at an outdoor cafe, a visitor can take in with a sweep of the eye an undistinguished, equestrian figure of a czar cast in bronze, the Tsoum department store, the domed face of the Alexandr Nevsky Memorial Church and the bland facade of Kintex.

The view from Bannigan's vantage point was almost as good. He'd staked out a spot for himself directly in front of the mounted bronze czar, and had begun to play his sax like an itinerant street musician in Manhattan. A bilingual sign, propped up in the bottom of his instrument case, said "Passage to Trieste."

It was impossible to blend in with the foliage in Sofia. Everyone was watched. If the police happened to overlook you and you evaded the electronic bugs in your room, Kintex security would be sure to have you under surveillance. Bannigan would have stood out in any event because he was so fair. Now his long hair and full beard made him more obvious—like a sheep in a wolf pack.

Since he was already conspicuous, he had decided he might as well make a spectacle of himself. It would, he figured, be harder to be suspicious of someone who deliberately drew attention to himself. If one insisted he was crazy, people tended not to believe it; deny the charges and one was certifiable. Well, it was a long shot but it was the only one he had.

As he played, Bannigan watched the big cars pulling up in front of Kintex. Even in the bowels of the communist world drug traffickers stood out like Harlem pimps with their flashy style. At first he was conspicuously ignored. Then a few tourists stopped to listen, and a few more, forming a semicircle around him. The instrument case began to fill with coins. Abdul watched him from the cafe across the street, where he was having lunch with a whore. Bannigan recognized her from the hotel bar. He waved and kept on playing.

A policeman came over and stood at the edge of the group. A few minutes later two men crossed the square from the Kintex side. Bannigan had no illusions who they were. He switched to "The Internationale." The crowd laughed, enjoying itself and the concert, but as the men elbowed closer it began to disperse. No one in Sofia wanted trouble.

"American?" The policeman's tone was not sympathetic.

"Canadian. My passport is over there with Kintex." Bannigan stopped blowing to wave the sax across the square.

The policeman looked at the others for an explanation. One of them spoke rapidly, translating what Bannigan had said. Then the policeman turned his attention back to Bannigan. "You are a TIR driver."

"You've got it. I drove here from Turkey with Abdul. See him sitting with that whore?" He pointed to the cafe. The table was empty. The man looked suspicious but Bannigan didn't give him a chance to say anything. "I've been all over the place—Iran, Pakistan, Afghanistan . . . saw your Russian friends fighting over there . . . Turkey, Greece." He hoped he sounded as much like a fool as he felt. "Now I want to get a look at Italy. Not that I don't like your country. Sofia's the greatest. It's got everything . . . and it's all free. That's my idea of a socialist people's republic—"

"You are supposed to drive back to Diyarbekir where you came from," the man interrupted. "You have a transport."

"I know, I know, but Abdul can go it alone. He's an old hand at that. You see, I have a taste for spaghetti with tomato sauce, just like I used to get back home at Johnny's Italian Restaurant in Manitoba. Lots of garlic and meatballs that stay with you for a week, if you know what I mean."

The Bulgarians were staring at him as if he were a UFO. The English speaker started to translate, then thought better of it. "You will come with us."

"Great." Bannigan pocketed the change and picked up his case. "Maybe you can help me. I've heard some of your trucks go to Trieste. The drivers talk—like old women." He laughed, although no one joined in. "Where are you taking me?"

No one answered. He had to pinch himself to remember he was playing for real. It could have been a reel from a movie he'd seen a hundred times—caricatures of Russian bad guys, only these were Bulgarians, a fine point that made no difference. Bannigan had a bad habit of splitting hairs.

The inside of Kintex held no charm. The windowless cube of a room they crowded him into had cinderblock walls a shade darker than pasteurized American cheese, linoleum floors and accoustical tile ceilings. The furnishings were pre-modular plastic: stain-resistant, heat-resistant, water-resistant, laminated-wood, chip frames covered in nubby synthetic tweed. He settled down in the only chair without waiting to be asked, crossed his knee around the saxophone case.

The three men left him and were instantly replaced by a fourth, who eyed him curiously.

Bannigan tried a fool's smile. "Nice day. Fine weather you have here."

"You are on a visit to Sofia? A beautiful city, no?"

Bannigan nodded.

"The Hotel Vitosha is incredible, better than anything in Canada, or even America?" The accent was so thick Bannigan had to guess at every other word.

"It certainly is incredible," he agreed.

"You are a musician?" The guard pointed at the case. He had a thick peasant body and broad florid face—a young man, probably no older than Bannigan, although his hair had already begun to thin.

"Sometimes. I do a little of everything . . . whatever I can to see a new place, make new friends. Like you. Right now I'm a truck driver."

"I have never been outside Bulgaria." The guard sighed. "Once I almost went to Yugoslavia on holiday but I decided too far." His voice never rose above a stage whisper.

Bannigan nodded. "I would like to go to Italy, if I can find a way. I've never been there. Instead, I'm supposed to go back to Turkey."

"Ah." Understanding had apparently struck. "So many people are going to Italy . . . a very busy route." He nodded, full of wisdom, proud to show his private knowledge, to indicate that he was privy to important state secrets.

Bannigan waited, afraid to appear too curious. Abdul had warned him: curiosity was a crime in a communist nation.

The guard moved closer with the expression of one itching to share a confidence. "Do you play rock and roll?"

"That's kind of tough to do on this baby." Bannigan patted the case. "I play jazz mostly."

"I like rock. I hear it sometimes on Radio Free Europe . . . you understand?" He whispered "Radio Free Europe" like a monk breathing an expletive in chapel.

Bannigan nodded. He felt as if he were in the twilight zone. A Kintex guard tuning in to Radio Free Europe to get things jumping. He should put that in his report to Hindle, if he ever got to make it. "What rock groups do you know?"

The guard pressed a warning finger to his lips and pointed to the walls around them. Sofia, it seemed, needed the services of a special exterminator. The whole city was crawling with bugs.

"The Rolling Stones . . . 'I Don't Get No Satisfaction.' "

"You like Mick Jagger?"

"You know him?"

A Bulgarian groupie. Bannigan couldn't believe it. He shifted his saxophone case. Maybe, just maybe, the guy could help him? It was worth a try anyway. "Pretty well . . . he doesn't get to Canada that often."

"Mick Jagger is a friend?" The guard couldn't have been more impressed if Bannigan had walked on water.

"You know how musicians are—we all sort of stick together." He shrugged. "Want me to send you some of his records when I get back? If I ever do, that is." He looked around the closed, windowless room. "After Italy I thought I'd head home. Looks like your buddies don't want me to go, though."

"No, no, a routine check, nothing serious." His face dropped.

"What about the records?" All still sotto voce.

The Bulgarian was shaking his head. "No good. I have no . . ." He moved his finger in a circle.

"Stereo?"

"Very expensive, even for me with this good job. Go back to Turkey, play your music, forget about Italy."

Bannigan wondered what their conversation would sound like on the tape . . . a blur of sibilants between desert stretches—the fault of the equipment, or a cause for suspicion? He drummed on the rim of the case. "I could ask Mick to autograph a picture for you."

Bannigan was afraid the guy was going to kiss him. "Why don't you write your name down for me so I don't forget."

The guard shook his head and his finger, putting his whole body into the negation. "No, no. I tell you, and you remember. Boris Stasiak." He tapped his forehead. "Better to keep everything up here."

"Okay." Bannigan repeated the name carefully. "You'd better give me your address too so I can mail the picture to you. If you help me get to Trieste."

"Go home from Sofia," he whispered. "Much better."

Bannigan repeated the Bulgarian's name and address, a memory check to encourage his confidence. "I have to go to Italy first." His voice was getting hoarse from all this whispering.

The guard leaned close. Some things, it occurred to Bannigan, were immutable, uncorrected by ideologies or wars—like picking one's nose and smelling of garlic. Everyone in the world did them at one time or another. A thought for the day. His mother had always encouraged her children to choose a thought for each day, in much the same way that she gave them a choice of salad dressings—Italian, French, Russian or her own Green Goddess—preferably a gem of wisdom such as Cleanliness Is Next To Godliness. "Will you help?"

Bannigan caught himself in the middle of a word. The English-speaking man who had ushered him out of the square came in with Abdul.

"What are you doing here?" Bannigan jumped up, ready to be released. So far he'd been lucky but he had no idea how much scrutiny his passport would take. "I thought you'd forgotten I was still alive." He grinned at the two men.

"Good news." Abdul ignored his question and clapped a large paw on his shoulder. "We leave for Turkey in the morning. It will be good to get back . . . no? Sofia is wonderful—but in small doses." His big laugh filled the cubicle. "Too much exercise . . . bad for the heart."

The guard seemed to sag. Maybe the Bulgarian had known all along it was too good to be true, or maybe they'd each been putting the other on.

The security officer was returning Bannigan's passport. "You may go now. But in the future you will remember there is no music permitted in Liberation Square without a special license from the prefect of police. For you it is beautiful music. For others"—he raised a single eyebrow—"it is disturbing the peace. A point of view."

Bannigan saluted and picked up his saxophone. From the look of it he was exchanging one guard for another. Abdul put an arm around him possessively, and they went out into the square together. It was bright with stars. If he hadn't had Abdul around his neck, he might have hotfooted it directly to the American Embassy, just a short walk from the hotel.

Bulgaria. The name itself sounded coarse. Big peasant Slavs with heavy hands and features as leaden as their bread. Like Boris Stasiak's. Before dawn he'd be on the road to Turkey. Abdul's arm around his shoulders was as permanent as a cement collar.

"You were happy to see me I bet." He stuck his free thumb into his chest. "Abdul very reliable, many years driving. I swore you were a harmless bum. Not too bright." He favored Bannigan with the familiar flash of pearls. Abdul would never require the services of George Bannigan, D.D.S.

Back in Bannigan's room at the Vitosha, Abdul shut the door and leaned against it.

"Am I under house arrest?" Bannigan was defiant.

Abdul pointed to the walls, just as Boris had done. "I thought I was a slob, but look at you. Now I think I am neat as a housewife."

It was clear why Bannigan had been detained. Every drawer was turned over. The few possessions he owned had been combed through, pockets of his trousers turned out, the bedpack opened and slit so that the lining could be examined. Down was everywhere—tufts of it clung to the carpet and spread. Bannigan roamed around the room, inspecting the disaster. He didn't even bother to look for the Beretta.

"Are you missing anything?" Abdul's eyes followed his every step.

He shook his head, wondering why they'd let him go if they found the gun. "I didn't have a helluva lot to lose. Maybe a pair of dirty athletic socks, that's about it—and they could have walked out by themselves."

"No worry. Abdul will take care of everything."

That was exactly what Bannigan was worried about. Abdul would take care that he went straight back to Turkey. He had to play it by ear, but by dawn he felt tone deaf.

THE SUN was slanting off the czar's bronze shoulder when the drivers crossed the square to Kintex. Half a dozen trucks were already lined up in front. Abdul got his papers and tossed his gear into the last

176 · R. A. SCOTTI ·

cab, motioning to Bannigan to do the same. The carriers were packed, the motors warmed. Bannigan looked for Boris among the uniformed men who were checking cargoes and papers. He was nowhere in sight.

The truck pulled out and passed the white-elephant of a hotel. Bannigan was tempted to open the door and roll out the way they did in the movies. But then he'd still be in Bulgaria. "What are you carrying this time?"

"Rifles, submachine guns, explosives. If we hit a big bump—poof." Abdul threw both hands up in the air, neglecting the wheel, and laughed. "Also American and British cigarettes."

"Nice little business you've got for yourself."

"Not for myself. I'm just the driver. I deliver whatever is in the truck, and don't ask too many questions."

"Not like me."

"I warned you before." He didn't look at Bannigan. All his attention was concentrated on the road ahead. "I think you were missing something more than your socks last night. In my jacket."

Bannigan reached in the pocket and pulled out his Beretta. "Where did you get it?"

Abdul shrugged. "I have an Italian friend who says a little prayer to Saint Anthony and you find many things. Of course, I don't know Saint Anthony. But maybe you do."

Sofia shrank behind them. Bannigan didn't bother to look back. Up ahead a truck was pulled over on the shoulder with the hood up. He recognized the TIR logo. Abdul passed it and pulled over. "I always stop for another truck. Then if I'm in trouble they will stop for me."

"What's the trouble?" Abdul called. The driver's head was stuck in the engine as they approached.

"Maybe the radiator. Where are you headed?"

"Diyarbekir. You?"

"Trieste."

"Want some company?" Bannigan saw his chance and took it before Abdul could stop him. The driver's shoulders shrugged. Hurrying back to the truck, Bannigan grabbed what was left of his gear. When he got back the new driver was wiping his hands on his trousers. Abdul had gone into the bushes to relieve himself.

"Better ride with the cargo until we get over the border."

This one's English was better than Abdul's and spoken with an Italian accent. Bannigan didn't hesitate. After the mule train, anything would be luxurious. He slumped in the darkness on a bed of morphine and listened to the noises outside. The padlock snapped shut. Abdul came back, whistling "Tangerine." The tune grew fainter. Bannigan heard Abdul's truck pull away. Then the hood closed, the cab door slammed, the engine turned over and they were rolling down the highway, turning northwest toward Italy.

Chapter Twenty-eight

ALL BONI's efforts to examine the books of Banco Bartolomeo had been deflected with promises of cooperation that were never kept. But this time he was confident that Bruno Parente could not evade him any longer. His tireless digging was beginning to pay off. He had solid evidence now that pinpointed how the Carlatti-Parente partnership had operated. Boni settled down in Parente's office, feeling that he had the banker cornered.

"After months, years really, of piecing together scraps of information from telexes, stock transactions, account books and the like, I think I have finally begun to reconstruct the system that enabled Stefano Carlatti to dominate the Milan market." He leaned back in the chair, prepared to press for a court order if he had to.

"Fascinating." Parente made the word sound flat. "I would be interested to hear your theory . . . purely out of curiosity, of course."

Boni tapped a cigarette from the pack and lit it without asking permission. There was no ashtray in sight. It was hard to imagine this man, who seemed to wear his life like a straightjacket, charging across the Russian steppes, Boni thought. But the record was clear.

He had fought with courage, even heroism, under the cruelest conditions. Boni pushed the smoke through his nostrils. "I have found a pattern of fraudulent foreign-exchanges, concentrated bribery and the illegal exportation of millions of dollars, either alone or in collusion with his favorite partner, your own Banco Bartolomeo. Instead of being used for exports, the money taken abroad was either funnelled back for speculation here at home or secreted in fiduciary or trustee accounts for his own self-interest."

Boni flicked the ash from the cigarette into his hand. "All the activity seems to have been filtered through Dapro, a Swiss holding company that Carlatti still controls. I'd say Dapro is the key to the whole operation." He didn't add that access to Dapro would be a deathblow for Carlatti.

Parente listened without apparent emotion. "An interesting theory, and one that I'm sure you will pursue as far as it goes." He seemed to Boni to be a small gray spot on a vivid landscape. The decor of the office was a striking contrast to the man himself. An abstract slash of blue, the same shade as the upholstery on the chairs, filled one wall. The others were covered in moss-green ultrasuede. The same blue-and-green shades were melded in a diamond-patterned wall-to-wall carpet. The desk was as long as a bed and gleamed with polish. On a cornice affixed to the opposite wall was a Byzantine ikon of some indistinguishable saint. A room too controlled for personality, too precise for spontaneity. It was like a picture painstakingly filled in so that every color was kept strictly within the lines. In that single aspect, it reflected Bruno Parente.

"How far do you think it goes, Signor Parente?"

Parente opened a desk drawer and slid an ashtray over to Boni. "You're in a better position to answer that than I."

"I'm not so sure." Boni ground out his cigarette with ostentatious care. "I thought the books of Banco Bartolomeo might be enlightening."

Parente folded his hands in front of him as if he was preparing to pray. Boni hoped he would need to before they were through.

"I've told you before," Parente said, "I am prepared to cooperate in any way I can. However, I must remind you that my bank is not under investigation. True, I was associated with Stefano Carlatti on several ventures, like so many other bankers and businessmen I could name. But that doesn't give you the right to presume I am guilty by association."

"I presume nothing until I have the facts," Boni told him. "Then, of course, it's no longer a matter of presumption."

"Isn't it? One man's facts can be another's fiction—it's all appearances, Boni, and right now you're looking poorly." Parente smiled. "I am being hounded by a close, even intimate friend of the president of Banco di Milano? Not a pretty picture. You have chosen your friends foolishly. An investigator should be impartial above all."

Boni ignored the threat. Thanks to Carlatti, he was a veteran of intimidation. "Grant you it is a tangled skein. But so many threads, however twisted—fiduciaries, proxies, options—have led me here, to this door. You can cooperate, Signor Parente, or I can get a court order opening your bank's books to my staff. Then, of course, it becomes public record, lively grist for the gossip mill. I don't think you need any more embarrassment."

"Perhaps, although it might be wise to remember that the scales of justice are sometimes weighted. But we were talking about Dapro, I believe, and not about Banco Bartolomeo in which so many Milanese have placed their trust as well as their life savings." His eyes narrowed. "I advise you to look to other banks in more hospitable countries for your answers—Monex, for instance, in Switzerland." He got up and went around the desk until he was uncomfortably close to Boni. "It's just a suggestion. Who knows? Its vaults may contain some interesting surprises."

He opened the door for his guest. Outside, the office was like an armed camp. After Gattino's last invasion, Parente had armed himself with a phalanx of bodyguards. He had doubled security at his city and country homes as well as the bank, and traveled between them in a bullet-proof limousine at a cost twice his own annual salary.

He watched Boni pick his way through the line of guards. What was it Carlatti had said when he led him into temptation twenty years ago? "We will use each other. It is the safest way."

In that moment Parente got back his pound of flesh.

STEFANO CARLATTI hadn't been out of his hotel suite, even to go downstairs to the dining room, since Boni's visit to New York, sure that his enemies were everywhere waiting in ambush. Elena was performing well, keeping him one step ahead of the investigation all the way, but she hadn't dissuaded Boni. Nothing, it seemed, had. Boni kept inching forward with no indication that either his patience or his perseverance was wearing thin. It would only be a matter of time before he pressed for an extradition order, unless he was stopped. Threats were no longer enough. Carlatti needed reliable help.

He dismissed Parente out of hand. There was nothing to fear from him and little more to be gained, but he couldn't be eliminated. His banks would collapse with him and their secrets revealed to the world. Parente's own fears would destroy him in time. Another danger, threatening him obliquely, Carlatti thought. He was restless and impatient in his last redoubt.

Donna fretted over him when he allowed it, chiding him for eating too many sweets. His appetite had never been good. Now he had little taste for any food except the caramels that he had delivered twice a week in five-pound boxes and consumed at a prodigious rate. Little else gave him pleasure, although Donna's care, which he had always scorned, was oddly comforting—simple tastes and homely concerns.

She went out every day, regardless of the weather, and always came back chattering about what she had seen in the stores or where she had been for lunch. Once he would have cut her off. Now he found himself looking forward to the minutiae with a certain enjoyment. They were so simple, so very clear.

Donna would go on as long as his attention held, embroidering her recitation to fit her husband's mood. Most afternoons she never went near the stores or restaurants she talked about. There was nothing that she wanted, except peace of mind, so she had no reason to shop. And she couldn't understand going out and paying an exorbitant price for lunch when she could cook a much better meal for herself at a fraction of the cost.

Three days a week, though, she consulted with a psychiatrist about her husband's deteriorating condition. She didn't dare bring him to the Pierre for fear of antagonizing Stefano, but she listened to every word, even when she didn't understand it fully. The doctor called it "a classic case of acute paranoia, intensified by depression. He sees enemies everywhere. Old friends are against him. And the worse the paranoia grows, the more dangerous the isolation."

The other afternoons Donna spent in church. She sought healers, physical and spiritual. If she couldn't get help for Stefano one way, she would try another.

Chapter Twenty-nine

ISTANBUL, HONG Kong, Alexandria, Trieste—cities by their geography and history posed between two worlds. Trieste is located on the Adriatic Sea, in the curve of the continent, at the tip of the finger of land that Italy crooks into the Istrian Peninsula. A port, an apex between the communist East and the free West, a vacationer's Eden. The colors of Trieste are mixed and subtle. Instead of bright primaries there are turquoise, blue-green, beige tinged with pink against a background of white stucco. Tourists from East and West ride donkeys, swim in the gulf, romance on flowered balustrades.

Like Venice, Trieste is a jewel of the Adriatic, but one without glitter—a pearl. For Bannigan, it was a black pearl. He'd been squeezing by on a surplus of luck and the kindness of strangers. In Trieste he ran out of both.

The TIR transport had crossed Yugoslavia with impunity and entered Italy. The Italian customs officer in a dark blue uniform collected their papers and directed the transport to a loading dock. Bannigan helped the driver carry out one of the crates. The officer inspected it, then a second, a third, not satisfied until half a dozen boxes lay open. Each was filled with earthenware dishes, blue with crudely painted yellow-and-pink flowers. A service for four, the sugar bowl and creamer were separate, Bannigan thought. The customs officer pulled out plate after plate, wrapped in corrugated paper to keep them from breaking.

The customs officer stamped the crates fragile, and stamped their passports with their date of entry. He did not question why one of the crates had been opened, or why there were only three saucers for four cups.

DANTE LOFFREDO never actually picked up a crate, but his eyes touched each one of them as they were transferred from the TIR transport to the truck marked "Lombardy Import-Export." Bannigan wondered what cupboards in what countries the dishes would ultimately fill as he heaved crate after crate from the back of the TIR down to the man on the ground, who caught it, swiveled and chucked it up to the third man standing in the back of the panel truck. He had peeled down to his undershirt, blue and purchased in Rome, and streaked with sweat, caused not only by the physical labor but also by the fact that Dante was watching him almost as closely as the crates.

Stretching back to ease the strain of bending and lifting, Bannigan looked around, trying to orient himself. The customs officer had bought the story that he was hitching across Europe, playing his instrument for room and board when he was lucky, Dante appeared more skeptical, although he had gone along when Bannigan offered to help unload the truck to pick up a few dollars. Across the street from the warehouse shed where they were unloading stretched the port of Trieste. A huge oil tanker blocked the view of the fishing skiffs that were coming back to port with the morning haul. Farther down the coast the luxury yachts and schooners were docked.

Dante, Lacrisso's man, was shouting now, his voice as grating as his face. Although Bannigan did not understand the words, he got the message—"Get back to work." Wiping his forehead with his arm, he grabbed another crate and swung it down. He was trying hard to make sense of it. The shipment was supposed to be morphine base, one step removed from pure heroin. Instead it seemed to be nothing but plates and cups and saucers and bowls. It looked like Abdul had fed him a lot of crockery. Riding in the back of the truck, he'd pried open one of the crates and emptied it, checking the construction for a false side or bottom, then carefully repacked it and hammered the top back with his shoe. For good measure, he had kept a saucer. Wrapped in the corrugated paper, it was wedged in his duffel bag inside a knot of dirty laundry that the customs officer had not bothered to investigate.

There were a dozen more boxes in the back of the transport. Bannigan slid them forward one by one, giving the other men a breather, then began to ease them down. Fifteen minutes at the outside and they'd be done. As Bannigan climbed down, Dante pulled out a wad of lira notes and counted out five thousand, making it clear that he should take the money and split. Five hours of sweat for ten bucks and nothing more, not even a clue. Bannigan wasn't about to rush. He'd come a long way to reach a dead end.

Picking up his gear, he walked along the edge of the loading platform, putting a few yards between himself and the trucks, and stripped off the undershirt. He balled it up, unzipped the duffel and began wadding the shirt into the bundle of dirty clothes, trying to decide whether he should go on to Rome and ask the regular DEA officers there for help or follow the panel truck to Milan alone. He was tempted to write Lombardy Import-Export off, except for Dante. The man seemed unnaturally suspicious. Either Dante didn't trust strangers, or Bannigan had missed something.

Bannigan was whistling "Sing, Sing, Sing" and tilting toward Rome when he felt rather than heard someone come up behind him. He turned too fast. The laundry slipped. As he fumbled for it, the bundle began to open, exposing the brown edge of the corrugated wrapping.

"What's that?" Dante's voice was uncompromising, like the rest of him; he was either too broad for his height or too short for his width. Bannigan didn't need an interpreter to understand what he said.

Stuffing the clothes into the bag, he put one hand on the platform. Before he could vault up, Dante's fist jabbed out. Bannigan ducked but the brass knuckles caught him in the forehead and spun him around. Although his head was spinning, he pulled himself up on the platform. Dante was shouting for the other men. Bannigan didn't wait to find out what price he would exact for stealing a saucer. A karate kick caught Dante at the side of the head. He staggered back a couple of steps, more surprised than hurt, just as the others came rushing up.

Bannigan grabbed the bag and the saxophone case and ran. He heard them behind him but he didn't look back. Jumping onto the hood of the truck, he skittered up the cab and along the roof. Footsteps sounded on the pavement below. He saw a pair of shoulders and leaped, bringing down the man under him. Dante loomed over them from the roof of the truck, shouting curses and threats. The man beneath Bannigan lunged for his throat, but the fall had shaken him, slowing his reflexes. Bannigan rolled off him and sprinted up, pausing only long enough to scoop up his gear, then headed across the street for the docks.

It was December, too cool even in Trieste to run around half-naked. Tourists and fishermen stared as Bannigan streaked by, pointing the way that the thief had gone to the trio who chased after him. He was winded, but he forced himself not to slow down. The footsteps behind him seemed to grow louder, or he only imagined it. He was afraid to take the time to look around. The style of the boats changed, from working vessels to modest pleasure cruisers to white clouds balanced on the turquoise sea. The shoreline curved, momentarily blocking him from the view of his pursuers. He darted toward the water and with a flying leap sailed onto the deck of a forty-foot sloop as it slipped out into the gulf. The mainsail shook, then caught the wind as Bannigan sank down into the hold and found that he had exchanged his three pursuers for a pair of women whose interest in

him was equally single-minded. From where they lay, sprawled together, he appeared like a *deus ex machina* for their amusement.
Although they were only going as far as Venice they agreed that
they could use a cabin boy for a change.

It was a brief though eventful journey, and Bannigan was relieved
when it was over. From Venice he took the train to Rome.

He was just south of Bologna when the shipment from Sofia reached
the Lombardy Import-Export warehouse. Pietro Lacrisso's tastes were
much too refined for pastel crockery. He pulled off the wrapping,
discarding the dishes, and slit open the two layers of brown paper,
working carefully along each edge. He separated the layers, and examined the powder that had been flattened between the sheets of paper.

Chapter Thirty

G EORGE BANNIGAN had met the type too many times to count: tweed jackets, oxford-cloth button-down shirts, gray flannel or khaki slacks, loafers. Prep school and ivy league all the way from their easy charm to their casual insolence. Sturges Grahame was like all the others, and Bannigan hated him on sight. The landed aristocracy of America—white Anglo-Saxon Protestant, and arrogant.

"You say you're with the DEA?" Grahame shifted his gangly frame in the club chair and brushed back the shock of sandy hair from his forehead, scratching his scalp as he did. A flutter of dandruff drifted down on his collar.

Bannigan didn't bother to nod. There was no point in going over his credentials again. He must have told them to everybody in this CIA office in Rome, even the cleaning woman, a dozen times. He'd have much preferred to deal with his own people, but when he had found out that the two regular DEA officers were in Sicily checking out the Bulgarian connection from that end, he'd had no alternative but to go across a piazza or two and try for help from a so-called sister agency. Oh, brother.

Grahame waited for his acknowledgment, then went on anyway. "That much we know is legit. I had you checked out in Washington." He smiled engagingly. "That's what all the foot-dragging was about, as you probably guessed. You know how it is. We can't just have any joker coming in off the street with a cock-and-bull story and expect us to swallow it. As for the rest of it, Brannigan. . . ."

"Bannigan."

"Whatever. You must admit your story's pretty hard to buy. Especially here in Rome where every time you turn around some poor sucker is getting his kneecaps blown off—or his head. Sofia is full of Turks? So what else is new? You should see Berlin. It's getting so bad there that one out of every three Teutons is a Turk, if you know what I mean." He chuckled at his little joke. "It would take another Führer to clear them out. A frigging shame. So far, at least, they've kept to themselves. No dilution of Aryan blood." He knocked on the desk, which was made of cedar wood.

"Heil Hitler." Bannigan could feel his gorge rising.

"Touchy, touchy." Grahame wagged a finger in his face. The temptation to bite it was almost irresistible. Bannigan would have liked to lay back and level the guy, but that would be like nailing his own coffin. Anyway, he needed the pansy.

"I don't give a flying fuck how many turkeys are in Berlin—or capons either for that matter. I'm telling you—"

"I know exactly what you're telling me, and you may as well be telling it to the Marines." Sturges Grahame considered him from a position of social and intellectual pre-eminence. "Even as we sit here, right under our noses, a coven of Turkish mobsters is spiriting massive quantities of smack across Europe to the Bulgarians, who are passing it on to Italy in empty pink-and-blue coffee cups. All this was confided to you by some sort of security cop in Sofia who just happens to be a rock and roll aficionado. Next thing you're going to tell me he subscribes to *Rolling Stone*. It sounds like an Edward Lear limerick. There once was a cop from Bulgaria, who suffered from rock and roll hysteria . . . *You* finish it, Brannigan. . . ."

"Bannigan."

"You can't have too much to do if you're wasting my time with this nonsense."

Grahame was looking from the bearded, long-haired creature who had taken possession of his office to the filthy knapsack and battered music case tossed on the floor, and composing a report to Langley in his mind re the rogue elephant behavior patterns of other U.S. government agencies. "I have a word of advice for you, Brannigan . . ."

"*Bannigan.*"

"Of course." His smile was as genuine as a plugged nickel. "We don't need you boys from the DEA coming over here and teaching us our business. We're on top of the situation. We know all about Kintex. It specializes in smuggling contraband out of Sofia, cigarettes and the like, and bringing cigarettes in for the Mideast crazies. If anything else was coming in with the crockery besides cigarettes, we'd hear about it. We have our sources."

"If you know about it, we could work together and close it down."

"You make it sound like a corner candy store. Not so simple, Brannigan."

Bannigan swallowed the bile. "You could disrupt the route, though, and just maybe keep a lot of heroin off the streets of New York."

"We'll look into it, of course. Every report gets checked out, and if we find anything—"

"I know . . ." Bannigan got up. "Don't call me, I'll call you."

Grahame stood up and held out his hand as if they had just been introduced at the country club. "Nice meeting you, Brannigan. We must do it again some time."

Bannigan slung his pack on and turned his back on Grahame.

"Just a second."

Bannigan stopped at the door, but didn't turn around.

"Don't, as they say, make waves, Bannigan, or you'll find yourself back in Washington posthaste. You have my word on that. And one other thing. Don't get any ideas about playing Superman."

Bannigan found a room at a *pensione* at the top of the Spanish Steps, just across the street from the posh Hassler Hotel, and invested in a writing pad, pen and envelope. Then he did what he should have done before he went to see Mr. C.I.A. Sturges Grahame. He found a barbershop. As the white sheet swaddled him, he closed his eyes and did not open them again until he felt the flick of the whisk-brush across his shoulders. He laughed out loud at his own reflection, feeling as if he were meeting an old friend he hadn't seen in years. The effect was uncanny. After weeks of going unshaved, his skin was as smooth as a baby's. Except for a couple of fresh scars, he didn't look a day older than his high school yearbook picture. Years had been taken off his life with the beard.

Still laughing softly to himself, he went back to the *pensione* and began his report. "There once was a cop from Bulgaria, who suffered from rock and roll hysteria. He confessed to a Yank, a lot of Turkish hanky-pank, That was pooh-poohed by an American superior." It was well into the night when he finished writing in his neat, precise script. The next morning he took his report to the American Embassy in Piazza Barberini, to be carried by diplomatic courier to Washington.

Bannigan bought a guidebook and a stack of Italian magazines and waited for Hindle's response. It was his first visit to Rome, and he was a model tourist. He climbed to the top of St. Peter's dome; stroked the filthy cats in the Colosseum, half-expecting them to turn into lions; gorged on *gelato* in Piazza Navona, ogled the whores on Via Veneto, went to St. Peter's Square Sunday at noon to see the Pope, ate artichokes in the Jewish ghetto, rattled the sacred bones in the catacombs, watched the sun set from the Pincio. And waited. He thought he was in love for the first time—with the music of the fountains, the orange-tiled roofs, even the crazy drivers. In the evenings he studied his phrase book or flipped through the magazines. And waited. In *Gente* he found a photograph of Marco Boni coming out of La Scala opera house with a beautiful woman. Bannigan thought it would be worth looking up Boni just to meet her.

When Hindle's answer finally came, Bannigan had overdosed on altars and art and could roll five Italian phrases off his tongue with a perfect accent. The answer was curt: "Cut the crockery and get back to work."

Bannigan smashed the saucer he'd filched and examined each shard. It looked like Grahame and Hindle were right, but Bannigan had a tendency to keep on banging his head against a brick wall. Sometimes until he knocked himself out. He collected the broken pieces, wrapped them up again in the corrugated paper, packed his new duffel bag and threw three coins in the Trevi Fountain. Maybe, in addition to the woman, Boni could fill him in on Lombardy Import-Export. The sign on the back of Dante's truck had read: "Lombardy Import-Export, Milano." Boni's home turf.

LEONARD HINDLE had gotten to 1,357 sheep and was still counting. He did not blame Sturges Grahame for dismissing Bannigan out of hand. The CIA boys followed orders to the letter and by note, even if it came to blowing up Castro with a trick cigar. Hindle always found himself going back to that bit of lunacy when he contemplated his sister agency across town. The straight arrows from Langley had probably been trimming the Christmas tree and singing, "We three kings of Orient are . . ." when the best and brightest of them came up with the notion.

Hindle had read Bannigan's report a second time, then gone directly to the CIA director. He almost wished he hadn't, but he'd been in Washington too long to risk laying so much as a little toe on somebody else's turf. The agencies guarded their territory as compulsively as street gangs.

The director, a former navy man, had been cordial, admirable in his frankness. He had shrugged off Hindle's concern. "We appreciate your interest, of course, but you should know for the record that we're on top of it. Kintex is much more than meets the eye. Your Bannigan was one hundred percent right on that score—although Grahame could never admit it without my authority. We zeroed in on the Bulgarians a long time ago. They have a nasty little business going for themselves—or I should say for their Kremlin paymasters. Anything to destabilize the West. Every little bit helps, they know. Actually, we like it that way." He grinned. "Perverse though it sounds, their nasty little business works out quite well for us. We all use their smuggling route to get our people in and out of eastern Europe. You don't like it? Neither do I, but it works, and that's the *modus operandi*. It probably saved your Bannigan's hide. I did a little digging before you came over and turned up a report from one of our field hands—a Turkish native, goes by the name of Abdul. It seems that if it weren't for our Abdul, your Bannigan would be cooling his heels in a Bulgarian prison right now. He's a regular—a good man—we've been using him for years."

"I know Bannigan got himself in some trouble, although I don't have all the details yet," Hindle admitted.

"You owe us one, Len. I won't forget." The director held his shoulders at attention. A spit and polish man, short hair, scrubbed nails. Hindle felt like a slob. Latrine duty for him. He tried not to slouch. "Are you telling me that I've sent a poor sucker halfway around the world risking his ass for information you've been sitting on like a goddamn ostrich on an egg?"

The director snapped each nail, beginning with his pinky. "I'm giving you the facts. You interpret them any way you like. As it stands now, the route is used for smuggling drugs out, heroin mostly, that gets splattered all over Europe, the States too—and running guns back in for the Middle East crazies. An ugly picture, but that's our business—yours too."

"You make it sound like a piece of cake."

"As long as we know about something, we can keep it under control. It's what we don't know that's worrisome."

"And what you don't know is how the smack is getting from the Bulgarian Commies to the first families of the U.S. Mafia."

"We suspect that the Mob is involved in all major drug trafficking, but you're right, I can't cross every 't' and dot every 'i' for you."

"We're talking about sixteen hundred tons of southwest Asian opium, not alphabet soup."

"That's your particular headache, Hindle. I've got enough of my own."

HINDLE TRIED to get back to the damnable sheep, but when he started to count again, all the lambs he saw were being led to slaughter. He wasn't normally superstitious, but the memorial service for Bannigan had given him the heebie-jeebies. He had the discomfiting sensation of having staged a dress rehearsal, and Hattie's unusual behavior had set him further on edge. Normally she was close-mouthed and practical, both feet planted squarely on terra firma. But like many Irish she had a black, morbid streak. Ever since the memorial, she'd been going around the office muttering like Cassandra. Now, he realized, more than Bannigan's life was on the line. If George didn't come up with something concrete—who was receiving the shipments, how the heroin was being processed—the whole colossal exercise would go down in DEA annals as Hindle's Folly.

He shut his eyes, knowing it was a futile gesture. In the morning he would have Hattie book him on a flight to Italy. He was due for a vacation, and he might as well make it a working one. Somebody had to make Bannigan forget the damn crockery and start crossing "t's" and dotting "i's."

Chapter Thirty-one

BANNIGAN TOOK the express train to Milan. He had new clothes on his back, bought the day before at la Rinascente, one of the two biggest department stores in Rome, and Marco Boni's address in his pocket. The secretary he'd talked to at Banco d'Italia had been obliging—maybe too obliging, Bannigan thought. Then he caught his new/old reflection in the train window and shrugged it off. Anything for a pretty face, he decided.

The train compartment was empty except for one other passenger, a not-too-prosperous businessman from the look of him, a salesman possibly, sitting diagonally across from him. Bannigan was beginning to create an entire scenario of the sleeping stranger's life. Then he caught himself in time. In restaurants he often ate in silence so that he could concentrate on the conversation at the adjacent table. He listened to strangers in waiting rooms and movie lines. A voyeur of other lives. His curiosity was insatiable.

In Milan the blend of civilizations was harmonious—Romanesque domes, Gothic pinnacles and glass-enclosed skyscrapers, stunning in the simplicity of their clean sweeping lines, all within the medieval gate. But it was also too business-like.

195

Bannigan found a *pensione* a few blocks from the railroad station, where he unloaded his brand new duffel bag, also bought at la Rinascente, and his saxophone case. Then he went to a nearby *trattoria.* He was flush for the first time in two months—Hindle had wired a generous advance along with his less than generous reply—and Bannigan took advantage of his prosperity, consuming two orders of spaghetti, a loaf of bread, a slice of beef, a plate of spinach, and a double espresso. By the time he located Boni's apartment it was already evening. He rang the bell several times and was just about convinced that no one was home when a woman's voice called through the closed door, *"Chi c'e?"* "Who's there?"

"Un amico di Marco Boni," Bannigan said, complimenting himself on his linguistic talents. *"Americano."*

The last word was met by a barrage of hysterical words, not one of which sounded complimentary. They spilled out of her so fast they ran into each other, leaving Bannigan at a total loss.

"Non capisco, signora. Parla Inglese?" The phrase book had advised when in trouble to say these two simple sentences: "I don't understand. Do you speak English?" Inside the barricaded apartment he heard children arguing, the pitch of their voices unmistakable regardless of the language. A baby began to cry.

"Signora Boni?" he called again, wondering what it would take to convince the woman to let him in. He thought only New Yorkers were so reluctant to open their doors to strangers. Italy seemed so much more civilized. *"Piacere di fare la sua conoscenza."* "It is a pleasure to make your acquaintance." He went on running down the list of basic phrases in the stilted book-Italian he'd memorized on the train trip from Rome. At least he was getting a chance to practice his latest lesson.

The door opened a crack, just enough for one dark eye to look him up and down. It looked like a disembodied eye in a Picasso painting, he thought. Bannigan smiled for her benefit, knowing that his face was impossible to mistrust. He could commit almost any crime and get away with it, because no prosecutor in the world could find twelve honest men and women willing to believe that he was anything but a very nice boy who was always respectful to his father and never forgot a Mother's Day. In some ways true.

"George Bannigan, American police," he said.

"*Grazie a Dio,*" Bianca murmured, and opened the door another crack. Between her few words of English and his fractured Italian, they managed a halting communication. Bannigan walked away with Boni's office address and the distinct impression that the lawyer was in trouble. He was tempted to call it a night and look for Boni in the morning, but curiosity got the better of him. The picture his frightened wife made, surrounded by a cluster of children, all looking up at him with the same dark, mistrustful eyes, stayed in his mind like a painting.

Fog crept down from the lakes and caused the night to thicken. A faint drizzle clung in the air, the minute beads gathering in Bannigan's hair. Farther to the north, where the Parente family waited in seclusion for the Bishop's retreat to end, it was snowing. After a few false starts, Bannigan arrived at the office in time to see the windows blacken. A few minutes later Boni came out and stopped in the doorway, peering cautiously into the opaque night.

"Boni," Bannigan called, and started across the street.

Boni froze at the sound of his name and retreated inside the relative safety of the building. Bannigan moved under a street lamp and waited. He thought he saw the emotions skim across the Italian's face—apprehension, uncertainty, and then recognition.

Boni pushed open the door and shook hands. "George Bannigan. You're the last man in the world I expected to see tonight." Relief made him effusive. "I can only imagine one thing that would bring you to Milan and to my office on a miserable night like this . . . Stefano Carlatti."

"Yes and no. I need your help, and your wife's behavior tells me you maybe need mine."

Boni pumped his hand again. "Maybe this time we can talk about more than music. I was just going for some supper."

Ristorante Ticinese was comfortable and well-lit—two lines of tables with long white cloths set at right-angles to the muraled walls—a neighborhood restaurant with good prices and even better food. Although he'd devoured a huge dinner, Bannigan didn't need to be persuaded to have a second.

Boni studied him while they ordered, trying to figure out what was different. He looked exactly the same, except for his maroon sweater, which was definitely Italian—the stitching at the shoulders was unmistakable—and for two other things. He had a scar as dark as a raspberry going up from the end of his left eyebrow half an inch, so that it formed a vee above his eye.

"Where did you pick that up?"

"In the Hindu Kush in the middle of an outdoor concert. An over-enthusiastic fan was wielding a rifle butt. . . . I'll spare you the gory details." Bannigan touched the scar, his red badge of courage. It gave his face character; at least that's what he told himself.

Boni grimaced. "Imagine if he didn't like the concert . . . I had forgotten you were a musician as well."

"I'll play for you one day, if you promise to confine your response to clapping or catcalls."

"And the other?" Boni pointed to a bulge about as big as a melon ball in the middle of Bannigan's forehead.

"What can I tell you? I came face to face with a wall in Trieste—about twelve inches thick—by the name of Dante something. I don't know what he normally does for a living, but I'm pretty sure he doesn't compose cantos. That's about all I can tell you, except that he knows how to give a beating."

"It sounds as if you've been keeping busy," Boni murmured. "The Hindu Kush is a long way from a jazz club in Greenwich Village. Have you given up on Carlatti?"

"Yes and no . . . I don't know myself." Bannigan raised both hands, indicating his uncertainty. "Right now I'm interested in Lombardy Import-Export. Have you heard of it?"

"Everyone in Milan knows it, at least by reputation. It belongs to Pietro Lacrisso. His olive oil is very good—one-hundred percent *pura*. His other interests aren't—extortion, loansharking, prostitution, or so it's said, although he has never been charged with a crime or spent a night in jail. A clever man, very smart, very tough, with the most civilized tastes. A connoisseur of the fine and not so fine things of life. Have I told you enough?"

"Enough to start." Bannigan hesitated, then decided if he was going to get the Italian's help he'd better begin to trust him. "I know he's involved in smuggling heroin into Italy, but I'm not exactly sure how. He could be an independent or he could be a middleman for somebody bigger, like the Commission. Do you know if there's any connection between Lacrisso and Carlatti?"

"I'm trying to sort out Carlatti's businesses with legitimate fronts. I haven't even looked into the others, if there are any. But we did find one transaction between them . . . harmless enough, as I recall. If you have time tomorrow I'll ask one of my investigators to look it up for you. I think Carlatti bought a piece of jewelry from Lacrisso. It must have been very special because he paid for it with stocks— very many stocks, all of them . . . how do you say . . . blue chip? The stocks were transferred to Lacrisso's account in Banco Bartolomeo. The president of that bank happens to be an associate in many of Carlatti's ventures—a collaborator, I'm sure, although I haven't been able to prove it yet."

A circle isn't supposed to have any angles but the one Boni just drew had more than Bannigan could count. He was humming when they finally closed the restaurant, "Turning and turning in a never-ending line. . . ." The tables had been stripped as they talked and the chairs turned up on top of them.

"You still haven't told me what you want from me?" Boni paused in the doorway to light a cigarette, and flicked the wax match onto the pavement.

"And you haven't said why your wife apparently thinks you need an American policeman? Shall we toss a coin to see who talks first? You're heads, I'm tails." He took out a twenty lira coin and flipped it in the air.

Boni watched perplexed, only half-understanding his American idiom. Bannigan lost the coin in the fog and saw its descent too late. It rolled down the street and skipped off the sidewalk into the gutter. Like trying to pick up a fumble on your own goal line, he thought, chasing after it. Retrieving the coin, he slapped it down on the back of his hand.

"Heads." He turned around, ready to hear Marco Boni's full account. What he got was more graphic than any words. Two men were closing in on Boni. One yanked his arms behind his back. Boni spat his lighted cigarette at the other, who came in from the front and delivered a driving fist to the stomach. Boni's voice was a thud of pain. He doubled over. An uppercut to his chin sent his body jerking back up again.

Bannigan crouched in the gutter, grateful for the fog, took off his glasses, put them in a solid metal case, put the case in his pocket, reminding himself to ask Hattie Carmody to send a second pair. Then he scrambled back. The man was poised to punch Boni again. Bannigan brought him down with a flying tackle. The fist that had been propelling forward on a trajectory for Boni's lower abdomen met the sidewalk instead with shattering force. The man screamed out with the agony of four knuckles splintering.

Bannigan hesitated for a moment, caught between a desire to bring the man's head into the same close contact with the pavement as his hand, and the need to go to Boni. He chose Boni, who was flailing at his assailant with both arms. Boni was strong and agile but clearly unskilled, and the attacker was a man nearly twice his size.

Bannigan came up behind him with a karate kick that caught his assailant in the small of the back. The man whirled around and lunged for both of them before they had a chance to set themselves again.

Dante Loffredo stopped hugging his shattered hand long enough to struggle up to a kneeling position and pull a Walther out of his shoulder holster. Dante liked to moonlight. He didn't do it for the money so much—Pietro Lacrisso was a generous employer—as for the pleasure it gave him. Dante enjoyed the work. He liked to bring a man to his knees with his fists—and the richer, the more powerful the target, the keener his enjoyment. He should have been a boxer, only he didn't like taking punches. He preferred to have his opponent held or bound, which was why he always worked with at least one other, even though it meant cutting him in on the stipend. He would have brought two of them tonight if he'd known Marco Boni had company.

Dante was good at his work, the best enforcer in the business. That was why Gattino had chosen him to teach the nosey lawyer the lesson he had stubbornly refused to learn any other way. Positioning his right arm under the shattered hand to support it, he aimed carefully. He was supposed to get Boni, but he wanted the blond one even more. And it wasn't just because of his hand. Dante couldn't believe his dumb luck. At first he hadn't recognized the American without his glasses. But it was the same one he'd met up with in Trieste. The ache over his left temple was still there to remind him. There couldn't be two of them stalking around northern Italy as quick as this big cat.

Dante's companion had now collared both opponents, was about to bring their heads together like coconuts. Dante waited, Walther cocked, and laughed at the terror he could read in Boni's face. He would have enjoyed seeing the American's face even more, but his back was turned, a perfect target. Just as Dante's man started to hurl them together, Bannigan slashed out with a second karate chop, directed at his windpipe. The man promptly dropped them and clutched at his throat with both hands, gasping for air. His face engorged and turned an ugly purple, like a fresh bruise. He tilted forward, hovering for a moment in suspension. Bannigan was about to finish him off with a blow to the gonads when Boni launched himself at him, bringing him down. The man lost his balance and crashed on top of them, the three of them writhing together in a tangle of twisted limbs.

Bannigan's move had surprised Dante as much as his man. His finger had hesitated on the trigger, and in that instant, seeing the flash of the muzzle, Boni had leaped through the void. Now he and

Bannigan were huddled behind the other man's massive girth as if it were a sandbag.

"What do we do now?" Boni, more accustomed to the labyrinths of paper trails than the alleys of violence, had never fought before, but with his life on the line he was learning fast.

"Lose ourselves in a crowd if we can find one at this time in the night." Bannigan peered over the giant body. "Our friend's getting up. Do you think you can run?"

Boni grimaced. His left leg was pinned under the man. It might as well have been sunk in concrete. "Do I have a choice?"

"Not unless you call a forty-five caliber bullet an option. On the count of three, roll out. One, two . . ." He heaved the hulk of the strongman just enough for Boni to extract his leg. "Okay, let's go. You lead, I'll follow. Head for wherever there'll be the most people."

Dante's first shot grazed the human sandbag at the same instant that Boni and Bannigan abandoned it. The fog closed around them, preventing a second shot. Boni's leg ached but he forced himself to run on it. He heard Bannigan's tennis shoes flapping like duck's feet, a soft, flat sound behind him, as he turned down Via Giuseppe Verdi along the side of the opera house. The doors of La Scala had closed hours before. Running past, he crossed the piazza and staggered into the Galleria. The glorious arcade, with its expensive shops, restaurants and cafes, was the drawing room of the city. From the center dome of lead and glass, four arms stretched in cruciform beneath vaulted ceilings. Ordinarily the arms were full of shoppers, lovers, tourists and Milanese charged with the political, social and artistic issues of the day. But the late hour and the dismal weather had driven all but a handful of people home.

Inside the Galleria they slowed to a walk, Boni limping badly. Bannigan caught up to him and took his arm. "I'm sorry I got you mixed up in my unfinished business."

"Do you know him?"

"He's that twelve-inch wall I was telling you about. I can't figure how he tracked me here, though."

"I don't think he did. He was going for me. You were a bonus. He didn't even see you at first."

Bannigan glanced around. "Well, he does now." Dante was framed in the entrance of the arcade, his face in the sudden light glowing a sick white. "We'd better keep going."

Boni groaned. His face was almost as chalky as Dante's.

They passed beneath the central dome and started down the opposite arm. At the end of the Galleria Bannigan hesitated, knowing that once out of its relative safety they would again become targets. He looked out. A vast empty square spread in front of them, and across it lay the cathedral, its spires swallowed in the fog.

"We can hide in the Duomo," Boni murmured. "He won't follow us in there."

Bannigan didn't share the faith, but Boni was already half-running, half-skipping. Bannigan loped along beside him. Even the pigeons had deserted the square. They tried three doors, feeling more desperate with each attempt. Dante's form was obliterated by the night, but he was just behind them, his footsteps sounding louder every second. Finally they found an open door at the side.

The church closed them in a stranger's cool embrace. Even their whispers echoed in its vaulted emptiness. Surprised by its flamboyance, Bannigan let his eyes travel in every direction—the length of the nave with its five measured aisles, the height of the pillars that rose uninterrupted to the ribbed vault. Statues in canopied niches stood at their tops instead of capitals. Boni blessed himself and motioned Bannigan to follow as he approached the altar to give thanks for the sanctuary. Halfway there he froze. A sliver of light crossed the aisle. Dante had followed them into the deserted house of God. The door shut, extinguishing the light.

At the door Dante hovered motionless, waiting for a sound that would tell him where they were hiding. Boni and Bannigan flattened themselves against the wall, slunk along the aisle, working their way toward the Medici tomb in the south transept, where the elevator was located. It was Boni's territory. Bannigan followed.

Once inside the elevator Boni sank against the wall.

"Where's this taking us?" Bannigan whispered.

"To the roof. We may have to spend the night there, but at this point it's not hard to think of worse things."

"Is there another elevator?"

"The only other way to get up is to walk—almost two hundred stone steps."

"Dante's in no shape to do that." Or so Bannigan hoped.

When they got to the top Bannigan took off his jacket and made a roll of it to keep the elevator door from closing. They crouched together in the walkway between the flying buttresses, prepared to wait for morning.

In spite of the cutting wind and the dank chill, Bannigan began to nod. It seemed like months instead of hours that he'd been in Milan.

"On a clear day," Boni was saying, "from up here the whole city is laid out in front of you, and the Lombard Plain beyond all the way to the snow-capped peak of Monte Rosa in the Alps."

On a perfect day in sunlight it would be spectacular, Bannigan thought. "Maybe by morning the fog will lift," he murmured as his eyes closed.

"Are all Americans optimists?"

"No, only the—" A noise, vague at first, now unmistakable, stopped him. It had sounded like a rhythmic knocking, but as it grew louder it became clearer and closer. Boni tensed beside him.

"The man must be made of cast-iron." Bannigan cursed and wished his Beretta wasn't zipped into a duffel bag in the *pensione*.

They heard Dante's labored breathing before they saw him, stooped and dragging but no less deadly.

"I'll lead him," Bannigan whispered, pointing to the stone stairs connecting with a higher walkway. "When he comes after me give him a few minutes, then follow. Do something to distract him. I'll try to take him when he turns."

"Why don't we try to get back to the elevator?"

"Too late." Dante had pulled out Bannigan's jacket and the elevator door eased shut.

Bannigan sprinted toward the stairs, taking them two at a time. Still clutching his battered hand, Dante charged after him, panting heavily with every step. Boni couldn't see either of them but he could hear Dante's labored grunts. Holding onto the sculptured concrete to pull himself up, he tested his leg. The rest and the cold had stiffened it, but he limped after the other two, gripping the scalloping for support.

The cruelty of the wind intensified the higher they climbed. At the base of the central spire, Bannigan turned and waited. He had climbed as high as he could, short of shinnying up the pinnacle. He heard Dante's footsteps first, then his breath, short and heaving, not enough of it left to curse.

Abruptly Boni's voice pierced the curtain of wind and fog. "I'm behind you. Throw down your gun." Even though he'd been expecting it, hoping for it, Bannigan tensed, then jumped and just caught the edge of a flying buttress, dangling by one hand over the city. Vertigo came over him. Spires and finials and buttresses swirled over the height of the cathedral. Dante, only momentarily distracted by Boni's attempt at bravado, fired blindly. The shot, flat and muffled, ricocheted down toward Boni. Bannigan chinned himself up, swung and just managed to catch the side of Dante's head with his toe before he lost his balance and fell, bringing Dante down beneath him.

Bannigan lunged for the gun but Dante held on, squeezed off a shot. Bannigan rolled away just in time and clambered up the steps to the central spire. The bullet had been so close he'd heard it travel past his left ear. Dante was crawling up the steps on his hands and knees. The pain was intense, obliterating everything except his need to kill. Bannigan hugged the spire, protected only by the fog. At the top of the steps Dante fired again, shattering the concrete foot of a statue on a lower pinnacle, then somehow pulled himself up and crept forward, inching his way closer. The Walther was aimed at Bannigan's chest. There was no place to go except over the edge.

One hundred meters to splatter the squares inlaid with white marble in front of the Duomo.

The wind lashed him against the cold towering stone, but Bannigan was sweating. Hindle's warning came back to him too late. He had already used up one life in Pakistan and was living on borrowed time. Maybe they still had the arrangement of gladiola and carnations hanging around the DEA to pull out for a second service—

A sudden sharp sound of metal hitting stone, very close. Dante lurched around, and Bannigan dove for the gun, but Dante clutched it as if his fingers had been forged with the butt. Forcing Bannigan back against the rail of the walkway, Dante tried to bring the gun up to his throat but Bannigan managed to wedge a knee between them and push. Dante was thrown back against the opposite rail, with Bannigan coming after him. This time, instead of going for the gun, he grabbed at the broken hand and twisted it back behind Dante's head. An agonized scream. And as with gilded eyes the Madonnina gazed down from her lofty height atop the central spire, the body of Dante Loffredo somersaulted over the walkway and began its spiral descent gracelessly to the piazza below.

"Boni," Bannigan was calling. "Where are you?"

"Down here, on the roof." The answer sounded so close it was startling. "Looking for my keys."

"How in hell did you lose your keys?"

"I threw them to distract him. If I don't find them I won't be able to get into my house tonight, or into my office either."

Bannigan had to laugh in relief. Or rather at Boni's comic relief. "Saved by house keys? I should have them cast in bronze." He got down on his knees and began crawling over.

Boni sat back on his haunches and watched Bannigan's approach with admiration. He had just killed a man, after all. "Where did you learn to fight like that?"

"At the movies. The Saturday morning matinees in Santa Clara had special cowboy and Indian flicks for the kids at ten o'clock. . . . And the DEA filled in some gaps."

"You are very brave—"

"That's not courage, it's a reflex action. And that's the truth. You saved my life with your diversion."

"Butch Cassidy and the Sundance Kid." Boni smiled and held out his hand.

Bannigan smiled as he shook it. Actually he'd walked out in the middle of "Raindrops Keep Falling on My Head." The bicycle in the rain routine had been a little too cute for him to stomach. But he didn't tell Boni that. He touched his cheek where Dante's Walther had caught him, and winced.

Boni was still watching him curiously. "What made you look me up?"

"I saw your picture in *Gente.*"

Boni groaned. "I think everyone in the world has seen that, except my wife, thank God. She's too busy with the children to read foolish magazines."

"You didn't let me finish," Bannigan said. "I saw your picture, and I wanted to meet the woman you were with."

It was Boni's turn to smile. "You and every other man in Italy. For you, though, I will make an exception, on one condition. . . ."

"Hey, there were no conditions between Butch and Sundance."

Chapter Thirty-two

Bannigan recognized her immediately from the photograph, although the hard, glossy finish hadn't done justice to her. She looked softer, more sensual in the flesh—much more than just a beautiful woman. Boni had been as good as his word—even better, because Elena Torre was sitting alone. In spite of the season she was having a *granita di caffe*, at a cafe in the Galleria.

Elena looked up and smiled at him as if they had already been introduced. "Marco is so sorry, but he can't meet us here today. It seems he injured his leg—something very heavy fell on it, I think, and now it is giving him great pain. He tried to call you at your *pensione* but you must have been out sightseeing."

"I slept all day. I haven't seen anything of the city except at night in a thick fog, and then it was a glimpse of La Scala, the cathedral and this arcade. On the run, you might say." He transferred his gaze reluctantly from Elena's face to the glass dome overhead with the allegorical half-moon mosaics just below.

An article in the newspaper had identified the man found splattered on the marble piazza in front of the Duomo as Dante Loffredo, a longtime employer of Lombardy Import-Export. Although passing reference was given to his suspected underworld connections, his death was officially designated a suicide. No mention was made of a gorilla discovered around the corner from La Scala.

"Georgie or Giorgio? Which is it?"

"Just plain George." An uncertain half-smile formed on Bannigan's lips and he danced on the balls of his feet, shifting his weight like a boxer, tense and nervous. Elena burst out laughing and instantly regretted it, because Bannigan's face turned a bright pink. "Will you join me for something?"

Elena had thought men couldn't blush. She was sure Milanese men couldn't, once they'd outgrown short pants, but this Bannigan wasn't anything like them. He'd be eaten alive in their world, she thought.

"Why did you go into such dangerous work?"

"So I could come to Italy and meet you." What the hell, it was the best he could manage under the circumstances. He sat down beside her.

"But wouldn't you be more likely to be sent to Harlem or South America? I only know what I read in the newspapers about your American drug problem. Here it is bad too, but not so bad."

"I've worked in both places."

"You seem so . . . so. . . ."

"Boyish?" He smiled again. A shy smile. "It's helpful some times."

"A beard might help."

"Too itchy."

"Marco said you were here on business." Elena chose her words with delicacy, not wanting to reveal Marco's confidences or her intimate knowledge of their affairs.

"Getting to know your country and its people is my business." He tapped the blue guidebook that stuck out of the rear pocket of his chinos. "I was on my way to see the cathedral, but I could use a guide, especially a beautiful native guide—"

"Actually I was born in Tremezzo on Lake Como. My family has a villa there."

He took her arm. "That's close enough."

She looked up at him curiously, wondering if he was naturally presumptuous or too naïve to understand the position she held in this city. He *was* boyish—tall and blond and open-faced with an exactly proportioned body and even features, relieved from perfection by pale-rimmed glasses. A Renaissance master's ideal, she thought, yet he was all-American. He could never pass for anything else. And more, he was a surfer from California and a saxophone player, if her information was correct.

"I'll call my car."

He looked at her. "Let's walk instead. It's just across the square. Then you can tell me what else I should see."

"I don't dare. I'm not brave enough. I leave my secure apartment to get into my impregnable car to drive to my guarded office. Windows, doors, tires—everything around me is bullet-proof. We all live like that in Milan." She shrugged. "It doesn't eliminate the terror but it offers the illusion of safety, which is comforting."

"Marco Boni doesn't take care of himself that way . . ." Bannigan said, as much to himself as to her.

"No, but he is very foolish. See those two men over there, looking in the window at those fine leather shoes? They are my bodyguards. I never go anywhere without them."

"Never?"

It was her turn to blush, but of course she didn't.

"Will you come with me? I don't want anything here and it will be dark soon." He didn't know why he wanted her to say yes so much. She was Marco's girl, and he wasn't a thief. Just a killer, he mocked himself.

The square in front of the Duomo was clean—not a drop of blood to indicate that a body had lain on the sacred pavement. He made a point of walking on the spot where Dante had fallen. Elena Torre proved to be a better guide than any book. She seemed to know every inch of the city, and she showed him things he never would have discovered on his own.

They walked for miles without tiring, side by side but never touching. Somewhere in the distance, almost forgotten, the bodyguards and limousine trailed.

Finally the night stopped them. Bannigan thought nothing else could. But it had become too dark to admire anything but the lights and the contours of the city.

As if by some hidden signal the limousine drew up beside them in front of the church that housed Leonardo's *Last Supper*. Elena stood at the open door and waited for Bannigan to accept her invitation for dinner. She was smiling, sure of his answer.

Bannigan began to dance again, tapping his fingertips together. "Thanks but no thanks . . . maybe some other time the three of us can do it."

Fit me for a damn halo, Bannigan thought.

Elena thought only that this Georgio might even prove a challenge as well as a conquest. So much the better.

IN FARAWAY New York Carlatti jerked the strings of his puppets, and Elena danced. This time, though, his pleasure at controlling her was equalled by his annoyance. He had thought his secrets were doubly safe—buried twice in the closed vault of Monex and in the Swiss financial sanctum. But Marco Boni was taking a trip to Switzerland and, if Elena's information was correct, he was going for more than the fresh mountain air.

A change would be refreshing for Elena too. He smiled as he composed the cable to her, knowing how obedience grated on her. A few romantic days, strolling through the postcard-peaceful streets of Lugano, holding fast to the lawyer, would be a pleasant diversion. He pictured the idyllic scene in technicolor, allowing his mind to dwell on the erotic pictures of his own conjecture, before forcing his thoughts back to the question that nagged like the toothache he'd acquired from his compulsion for caramels. How had Boni found his way to Monex?

Carlatti's thoughts began to veer again. He was surrounded by ingrates. He was giving Marco Boni the most desirable woman in Italy and getting no gratitude in return—no relief. None of his best efforts for his friends, for Italy, had been appreciated, and now he was cast out, vilified, like a leper. This time he would have his revenge. While Elena was toying with Boni, his lawyers would move in.

He confided his plan to Immacolata. He'd begun to talk to her a few minutes each day, the way he used to, and to rely on her advice. She had never really left him. He saw that more clearly each day of his isolation. Donna tried to fill him with vitamins, but he refused to take them. With Immacolata beside him again, he had all the strength he needed. He reread the passages in Nietzsche on the superman and saw himself in the descriptions.

Marco Boni was no match for such a man.

Chapter Thirty-three

Lugano, Switzerland—a small city richly endowed with banks and foreigners, especially wealthy Italians who have crossed the border to take advantage of the more lenient Swiss regulations. Its population, a mere twenty thousand, gives no fair index of its importance, for its banks (approximately one for every four hundred citizens), not its people, give Lugano its international reputation.

Located at the southern end of the southernmost canton of Switzerland, Lugano is only a forty-minute drive from the center of Milan, and even less from Tremezzo. Boni could easily have made the trip in one day, but he elected to stay overnight. He told Bianca that he wasn't sure how long it would take to persuade the Swiss authorities to open the books on Dapro. There were other reasons as well. He had invited Elena to make the trip with him. He would be able to spend a whole night with her, his first, and she had surprised him by agreeing.

As discreet in public as she was unabashed in private, Elena insisted on going to Lugano alone. To avoid speculation or any taint of collusion, she arrived the day before. Coincidentally, she had business in

213

Lugano, too, although she didn't divulge its nature, and Boni didn't think to question her.

Boni had asked George to go too. His arguments were more persuasive than he realized. Bannigan could see a new country and keep Elena company while he was investigating Monex. Although her advice would be invaluable, he couldn't drag the president of Banco di Milano into the case too blatantly without appearing to compromise the professional integrity of both of them.

Whichever way one turned in Piazza della Riforma, the main square of Lugano, there was a bank. And all of them were open for business as usual, except one. The name MONEX was carved in granite above the steel gate that was drawn across the front entrance. Like so many Italian companies, it was a casualty of Carlatti's overreach.

Boni met the Swiss official on the steps. A large key unlocked the gate; then another, as impressive as a sommelier's, was fitted into the door. Metal grated. Hinges creaked. Doors groaned. The Swiss went in as if he were entering a tomb. His face was funereal. Boni followed. It had taken weeks of negotiations, formal appeals, petitions, arm twisting and persuasion to convince Swiss officials to open the vault. The Swiss guarded their banking secrets like the Soviets guarded their official lies.

Boni inhaled dust and followed the Swiss down into the bowels of the defunct bank. The vault loomed like a giant silver womb. The electricity had been disconnected, so they had to work by flashlight, sifting through stacks of documents and certificates. It would take weeks to sort through all the papers and examine them with care. For now, though, he was intent on finding one thing—the stock certificates for the holding company, Dapro.

The Swiss hovered over his shoulder, but Boni was too excited to be annoyed. Bruno Parente certainly knew where the bodies were buried. Hundreds of certificates, made out to a dozen different companies, spilled out onto the floor. Boni scrambled to collect them. He recognized every name. They were all subsidiaries, arms of Carlatti's empire that he was in the process of liquidating. Only instead of the shares being in Carlatti's name, they were held by the Vatican Bank, making the Istituto per le Opere di Religione the owner—at least on paper. He gathered them together but didn't put them back. The time had come for him to cross the Tiber.

They worked through the day, for twelve hours straight, examining each drawer. Just as he was losing hope, he stumbled on the Dapro certificates—tied together in a neat packet. Boni sat down on the floor of the vault and counted them carefully. Almost five thousand shares, enough to take control from the present directors, appoint his own board and open Dapro's books. In the morning he would come back and transfer the shares to another bank. Now, though, it was after hours, and he was in the mood to celebrate.

ELENA TORRE and George Bannigan wandered through the town. For once she was unguarded. She had left her bodyguards at home. He threaded his fingers through hers and they window-shopped at the fancy stores under the arcades of Via Nassa. It could have been Italy, Bannigan thought, or the set of an Italian village before life spilled into it: pastel buildings with arched windows, outdoor cafes with umbrella tables, palm trees and terraced vineyards, heaps of spaghetti and liters of wine. But Lugano was spotless and genteel—no shoving, no dirt-encrusted alleys, no graffiti. Even the weather was accommodating, balmy and mild although it was winter and Switzerland.

Elena had never been happier. She could have bought anything she wanted in the shops they looked in, but Bannigan pretended she was an ordinary girl. When he kissed her later in the park on the shore of Lake Maggiore, he changed that to extraordinary ordinary girl. And he knew then that he should not have come.

Boni found George and Elena drinking champagne in a cafe across the square. He sat down and took up Elena's glass, raising it in a toast. He should, he thought, drink to Bruno Parente, who had tipped him off, but in deference to her he refrained and proposed a toast instead to Dapro and Stefano Carlatti. "May they rest in peace."

"Hot damn." Bannigan cuffed him with a fist. "You mean you did it?"

Boni bowed as if he were on the stage of La Scala being feted with carnations. "Tomorrow I will deliver the kiss of death to Stefano Carlatti."

Elena laughed. "Immodesty becomes you. There's no need to ask how you're going to do it, I suppose?"

He gulped her wine. His face was flushed even before he drained the glass. "I can't tell you. But I will say one thing"—he raised her glass again—"Carlatti won't have Dapro this time tomorrow. The controlling shares will be in my own numbered account for safekeeping."

"In a great old movie called *The Third Man*, Orson Welles says the Swiss have had four hundred years of uninterrupted peace and all they have to show for it is the cuckoo clock," Bannigan said. "But he was wrong. They also have numbered accounts—slightly more ingenious, don't you think?"

Elena laughed again and touched his hand. Boni was too high to notice. "One day," she said, "I'm going to make you take me to Hollywood where your wonderful movies are made. I particularly like Bette Davis. But now I must go. Even on a perfect day like today, there is always business to attend to."

BONI WAS still excited when the three met for dinner in the hotel dining room several hours later. He had advised his superior, Mazeppa, of the cache and alerted his staff. Telexes were being sent to major banks throughout Europe, informing them that all future business with Dapro should be conducted through him. A press conference with the Swiss official was scheduled for the following afternoon to announce seizure of the Dapro shares.

The dinner was sumptuous, but Boni was too high to eat, and the others too preoccupied. Bannigan appeared strained, Elena brittle, but his success blinded Boni to their moods. He rattled on, talking about his plans. For the first time he could see the end of the reign of terror Carlatti had imposed on his family. The *manicotti,* the *ossobuco,* the artichoke hearts, the strawberries in a gossamer coccoon of *zabaglione* went back to the kitchen barely touched.

The maitre d' came over, a portrait of solicitude, to inquire if there had been something wrong with the meal.

"Each dish was exquisite," Elena told him. "The trouble is with our appetites, not your cuisine. They have been deflected by other things. . . ." She moved her hand in a graceful semicircular motion, indicating there was so much more better left unsaid.

Satisfied, the maitre d' withdrew and sent a vintage cognac to the table. Bannigan slid the stem through his fingers and cocked the snifter. The brandy glowed smooth and amber in the candlelight, like Elena's hair, he thought. He wanted to touch it, to feel it thick and smooth against his cheek. But she was Marco's girl. Her lips had been smooth and red and raised up to his, an invitation.

"To you." He raised his glass and clicked it against Boni's. Elena was rolling the cognac around the bottom of her glass, inhaling and sipping. Bannigan took too big a swallow. The fumes went up his nose and burned his throat.

Under the table her foot rubbed against his like a cat. "I'm going to retire and leave the two of you to continue the celebration."

Marco hesitated. He'd seen the way Bannigan looked at Elena. He didn't like to flaunt his good fortune, but it was his only chance to spend a whole night. "I'll go with you. . . ."

"No, Marco, it's early yet and Giorgio has never been to Switzerland before."

Bannigan's fingers rapped on the rough-hewn table. "Don't mind me." He looked directly at her with his winning half-smile. "I'm going to roam around for a while and try to find some music. I'll be up later."

Boni nodded and clapped him on the shoulder.

"*Va bene.*" Elena shrugged as if it meant nothing to her one way or another and motioned to Boni with a toss of her head. "You may as well come along, then. I'm not so tired after all, and evidently George can take care of himself."

To the victor belongs the spoils, Bannigan thought, and then said it.

"Tacitus, wasn't it?" Elena said.

"Would you believe Andrew Jackson?"

IT WAS after two when Bannigan went up to his room, moving stiff as a robot. There was no music to be found in Lugano, and too much wine. His head felt as if it would shatter at the slightest movement. He groped for the light. Both beds were turned down and untouched. A peppermint patty wrapped in gold foil lay on each pillow on top of a breakfast menu for room service. Bannigan swore softly under his breath when he saw Marco's empty bed, stringing together every expletive he'd ever heard in two languages. Friendship only goes so far at 2 a.m. with a stinging hangover in the making.

Bannigan promptly ate both peppermints, then lay down on the menu to wait. He'd had enough practice. All he'd done the whole damn evening was wait, and drink. The sky was lightening when he gave up and took an ice-cold shower, his father's prescription for everything—fever, irritability, hangovers and adolescent randiness. The first blast was brutal; then the body numbed, shriveled, turned blue and it didn't much matter any more.

Bannigan was just getting out of the shower, his teeth chattering in six-eight time when Marco came in and fell across the bed. "*Che donna,*" he groaned into the pillow. "I pray she will always be so tired." He knew Elena was passionate, sensual, capricious, tantalizing, but he had never known her to be so ferocious in her desires or insatiable in her demands. She'd kept him working all night. He had never even had a minute to telephone to Bianca.

* * *

ELENA WAS seated at a table set for two in front of a window with a view of the mountainside. A few intrepid tourists, probably Germans, she thought, were already riding the funicular up to the summit. She was wearing a yellow sweater and matching slacks, and Bannigan thought she looked like sunlight when she smiled up at him.

"Did you enjoy your evening?"

Elena laughed. "Marco isn't only a good friend, he's a good lover too." She smeared apricot jam on a croissant and bit into it.

"I wouldn't know." Bannigan sat down opposite her without waiting to be invited and ordered coffee, eggs and beefsteak, as if he'd worked up an enormous appetite in the night. She seemed so easy, untouched, for God's sake, and he felt so strained.

"Welcome to the real world," she told him. Apparently he was jealous. Was it possible he thought he loved her? Loved her . . . had anyone ever loved her except her father? Was there only lust, confused with love when one was too young to know better? Had she ever loved Peter Jenkins?

Bannigan watched each flicker of light, each shadow. She was too damn glorious for cynicism, he thought, although he wasn't surprised by it. She laughed too easily, too often. He would have to find out what all that was hiding.

ELENA WAS back in Milan when the newspaper accounts broke. Headlines screamed: "STALEMATE." She read every word. Just as Marco Boni had moved to seize the shares of Dapro, Stefano Carlatti had reached across three thousand miles to block him, helped by information she had provided. Lawyers went to court simultaneously in Geneva and Lugano to prove that the takeover was illegal. They argued that the shares were Carlatti's private property and, therefore, not subject to seizure. For a week front pages across Europe were plastered with head-and-shoulder photographs of Boni and Carlatti, until the shares were frozen by a court order, pending a hearing on the case.

* * *

IN CERVINO Parente read the reports datelined Lugano with a mixture of satisfaction and foreboding. Boni had followed up on his tip, and his move, if successful, would be devastating. But Carlatti's counter-stroke was diamond-sharp, the timing flawless and the cost astronomical. According to the film clip on the television news, Carlatti had hired a legal battalion to stop Boni. Parente had never met a lawyer who believed in charity, except from other people. He broke into a clammy sweat just thinking whom Carlatti would expect to pay for the attorneys' time and efforts, the two most expensive commodities in any market.

Chapter Thirty-four

BISHOP DESMOND fit Boni's image of an American better than Bannigan. Even when he was operational, Bannigan had been rather contained, self-conscious. Elena said that he'd blushed when they met.

"I'm glad you came to me, Marco," the Bishop said, offering instant intimacy. "So I can warn you. Carlatti can be ruthless when crossed—and I say that as a friend. He is a brilliant man, a financial genius in my opinion. That's his trouble. The classic case of Faustus. He came to believe he could do anything with impunity. An unfortunate delusion. We all suffer from delusions of grandeur to a certain extent, especially here in the Vatican." He laughed. "You can imagine, the weakness is endemic. You're lucky to work for Mazeppa. A remarkable man. His staying power alone is amazing. Just think how many governments you Italians have gone through since the war. It's incredible that the country still functions at all. But you didn't come all the way from Milan to talk politics. I'm betting you came to talk about power, or money. They seem to be about the same, don't you think?"

Boni shifted uncomfortably. It was one thing to confront an unscrupulous wheeler-dealer like Stefano Carlatti; it was quite another thing to sit in the Vatican and accuse a bishop as prepossessing as Joseph Desmond. "Actually," he cleared his throat self-consciously, "I want to talk about your relationship with Stefano Carlatti. As you know, we are in the process of liquidating whatever assets we can."

Desmond came around the desk and sat down in the chair beside Marco. "I'll be frank with you. The IOR is caught in a pretty embarrassing position, and I suppose I have no one to blame but myself. Americans are supposed to be such shrewd businessmen, but I'm the exception that proves the rule. A cigar?"

He opened a box of Havanas that sat at the edge of the desk and offered it to Boni. The Bishop was pleased that Marco took one. He paused to snip off the tips and strike a match. A magnanimous host and a comfortable man to be with, projecting warmth and sincerity. Boni was tempted to confide his own apprehensions, then caught himself. He had entered a business meeting, not a confessional, in spite of the cassock.

"If you can bear with me a few minutes, I'd like to fill in the background for you," the Bishop was saying. "When I took this job—more years ago than you can probably remember—I was still wet behind the ears. A decision had been made to pursue a new, more diversified policy for the IOR, and I was supposed to be at the forefront of it. Imagine, if you will, a captain who has never been at sea before charting a new course. That's how I felt. But the Holy Father trusted me, and I didn't want to disappoint him. I looked for someone to advise me and teach me—a tutor, you might say.

"Stefano Carlatti came highly recommended, and I had no reason to mistrust him. To be honest, the guy impressed me. His ideas were creative, innovative. He made banking exciting, if you can believe that. I followed his advice—too blindly, as I can see now. My father used to say ignorance is no excuse when he was taking his belt off to wallop us. But it is an explanation. After a few years Carlatti brought in Bruno Parente for his banking expertise. I imagine if you're investigating one, you must be sniffing at the other leg too." He waited, forcing Marco to reply.

"Parente has begun to cooperate, although reluctantly," Boni said. "But at some point we'll probably be forced to obtain a court order to look into the books of his Banco Bartolomeo."

"I value your discretion, Marco, and of course, anything I can do to help the investigation. . . ." Bishop Desmond's smile broadened, as though to cover his discomfort and embarrassment. Parente was not a strong man, and Desmond had granted more favors than he should have because of it, even providing letters of patronage—articles of faith from the Vatican to Parente. He had never questioned how they would be used, although he later came to suspect they were used to back bad loans—some possibly made to Carlatti himself. He did not want to know. A little knowledge was a dangerous thing.

He began to envision himself on a permanent retreat, and it did not sit well with him. A monk's cell was fine, even sobering and chastening for a week or two. Beyond that its charms were limited. Forty days in the desert were as much as Christ Himself could take. Desmond knew that his enemies in the Curia had begun to count the days he had left. He would be sent home and given a parish to administer. A consolation prize—as if raffle tickets, Sunday cake bakes and Friday night bingo could console him for the lost prestige and influence of the Vatican. He had, truth to tell, grown accustomed to marble. Pittsburgh was a steel town, gritty and down-to-earth. Rome existed on another plane, eternal. He did not look forward to his worst-case fantasy becoming reality. . . . "I have been hoping that Carlatti could cut his losses. Parente too." He turned to Boni with disarming candor. "A question of more than Christian charity, and they did serve their Church well, for the most part. . . ."

"Did Carlatti only advise you, Your Excellency, or did he use the IOR as a conduit, discreetly, of course?" Boni pressed.

The Bishop puffed on his cigar, sending halos of smoke heavenward. "I must remind you, Marco, that the Vatican is a sovereign state. We value and are entitled to our privacy. With due respect, its transactions are not subject to the scrutiny of the Italian state. I can't violate my Church's rights."

Boni admired the Bishop's smoke rings, thinking how impressed his children would be at such an astounding feat performed so effortlessly. "I knew, of course, that Carlatti advised the Vatican. He boasted freely of his influence, but I didn't uncover any questionable transactions until now. These stocks I discovered in a vault in Switzerland make the IOR, your Vatican bank, the owner of a string of small companies operated through Carlatti's holding company, Dapro. All the companies are bankrupt, making the Vatican ultimately responsible for their debts, which could run upward into the millions."

"As to these bogus stocks you dug up in Lugano—"

"Why do you say bogus?"

"Because they exist on paper only. Even their names—which incidentally I've never heard of before—sound phony. The IOR never invested in Carlatti's companies. We relied on him for advice only. Our investments have always been made independently. To put it bluntly, it looks like we've been had, Marco."

"Will the Vatican accept responsibility and honor the losses? As you say, Bishop Desmond, ignorance is no excuse."

The Bishop leaned over and placed a paternal arm around his shoulder. "You understand, that is not a decision I can make alone. I will have to take it under consideration, pass the information along, so to speak. But just between us, the climate here in the Vatican is . . . uneasy. It's not only the terror in Italy that has shaken the Church, but conditions in Eastern Europe too. A scandal now . . . if that's what we're talking about . . . could harm much more than the Vatican Bank."

BISHOP DESMOND called Boni back the following day. The answer had come from the highest authority, requesting time.

"It's good that I'm not a proud man," he said, greeting Boni at the door and leading him into the office, "because I have to ask for your understanding again. I am putting my own reputation and the Vatican Bank's in your hands. I admit I acted naïvely. I was young and ambitious for the Church. I should have questioned more, although I still would rather make a mistake on the side of trust than of suspicion."

"An honest mistake." Boni nodded. "We have all made them."

"I'm not asking a favor for myself, but for the Church. At the end of the month, Solidarity's representative is coming to the Vatican for an audience with the Pope, a historic moment. And with Solidarity gaining grass-root support each day and the invading forces poised on Poland's borders to crush it, the meeting between these two symbols of faith and freedom becomes even more significant. As you can imagine, the Polish and Soviet governments would like nothing better than to discredit it. You know how the Communists will seize on any opportunity to vilify us. All I ask is a little patience. You can help your Church, Marco, and a people seeking freedom, or you can, unintentionally, of course, help out the Kremlin. Personally, I don't see that there's a choice."

Chapter Thirty-five

I'M GOING to take a bath. I hope you don't mind waiting." Elena began to undress in the half-open bathroom door.

"I don't have much choice in the matter."

Bannigan leaned back and closed his eyes. He should have been trying to find out more about Lombardy Import-Export instead of waiting to escort Elena Torre to a business dinner sponsored by the leading industrialists of the city—a stand-in for Marco Boni. Boni was in Rome to pay a call at the Vatican Bank and he was here in Elena Torre's bedroom, not watching her undress. An unfair exchange, Bannigan thought.

As he waited for her, he tried to concentrate on the trail of lethal white powder he'd left across all those strange places. The sound of water rushing intruded and he imagined her balanced on one leg to test its temperature. . . . Concentrate, damn it. Presuming the TIR transport had carried morphine base from Sofia to Trieste, then the first question was: Where was it hidden? Two: Where was it transformed? Three . . . Bannigan lost his train of thought. The sudden quiet when the faucets were shut off distracted him. He opened his

226

eyes. Through the half-open door he could see Elena's clothes strewn on the floor where she'd stepped out of them. She began to hum.

"Giorgio, will you scrub my back?" Her voice was musical, or did all voices sound musical in the acoustical chamber of a tiled bathroom?

Bannigan shut his eyes again. She must have felt them boring through the wall. Three. . . . He imagined her afloat on a sea of soapsuds, bubbles clinging to every point—the jutting edges of her shoulder blades, the peaks of her nipples, the tip of her chin, the end of her nose. Bannigan's mind shut down on him, refused to consider the possibilities of anything except Elena Torre, and even from his uncomfortable vantage point, they seemed infinite. He wouldn't mind having his mouth washed in the soap bubbles that clung to her. Marco should never have trusted him as a stand-in. Had he run out of his capacity to resist?

He let his mind drift with her into white waters, waiting for the sound of the bath draining, some inner signal to steel himself again. It never came.

"I know what you want, Giorgio."

He opened his eyes reluctantly. She stood in front of him, a white satin robe clinging to her damp skin.

"I want, therefore I take. Is that what you mean?" He shook his head. Shook it again. To convince himself as well as her. "You're Marco's girl. Remember?"

"Giorgio." She leaned over him, placing a hand on each shoulder. "Marco is married. He goes home to his very nice wife and five very nice children every night . . . faithfully." She shrugged. "Yesterday there was Marco, and tomorrow? Maybe Marco again. But tonight?"

"What about your meeting?"

"We can go after, if you like."

"Marco said that you were the guest of honor. Aren't you supposed to give a speech?"

"It's not important. . . . At least not as important as you are right now."

The scent of lilac bubble-bath clung to her skin. He reached up and loosened her belt. The robe fell open, framing her nakedness. His eyes lingered along her slender figure, committing each contour to memory. She was so lovely. He reached up to touch her and felt the texture of her flesh—the smoothness of her throat, the velvet nipple, the tautness of her belly, the wiry triangle below.

"Sweet Jesus," he murmured against her skin, unaware of the inherent irony. She slipped the bathrobe off her shoulders. Pressing her down on the sofa, he began to kiss her shoulders, her breasts. His lips moved down, covering all of her, slowly, surely.

His curiosity was insatiable, even here. Especially here. His patience was maddening, his thoroughness excruciating.

"Please, Giorgio, I'm not a beggar. Don't shame me by making me one."

"What are you?" he murmured, as his lips followed the underside of her thigh.

"A woman. Nothing more."

"That may be too much." He slid up her body. Her legs locked around his waist and her hips thrust up to him, impatient, urgent. He made love to her in every way before he finally possessed her, holding nothing back.

When it was over he held her in the crook of his arm and watched the shadows flirt across her face. "Is that what you wanted from me?"

"It's what I was afraid of." She ran her finger down his chest, as smooth and hairless as a boy's.

"What do you mean? You Italians are so damned cryptic. I have to peel away a thousand veils to get to even the most trivial thing."

"It's a national trait." She caressed him, tracing elaborate designs around his navel. "We tend to look at everything through years of history, through theological conundrums, spiritual riddles, and mistrust. We are the masters of *chiaroscuro*, light and shadow. It's our invention."

"And we're the Ugly Americans? Too crude to understand the subtleties you thrive on?"

Elena laughed. "It is true. We prefer the subtleties to the facts. Food for the mind is not so different from food for the body. Ungarnished, it is dull, palatable at best. But presented with a delicate sauce, a subtle blend of herbs, a trace of wine, the possibilities are infinite and the interest is heightened."

He felt more in control now. "I only asked what you were afraid of. If I'd asked anything deeper you probably would have delivered the speech you're supposed to be giving right now. By the way, you're going to be late for it."

"I'm already late. I've missed the champagne reception, the *risotto con piselli* and probably the fish course as well. But I am the last to speak."

"In Italy do you always save the best for last?"

"You tell me."

"What do you mean?" Her nails were pink and pointed, like small dry tongues licking at him.

"Since I already talk too much for your taste, I will show you. Then you can answer for yourself." She moved across his body as she said it.

"You never told me what you were afraid of."

She kissed his face. "I was afraid that once would never be enough with you."

His body shifted on the bed, arranging itself to receive her. "You always take what you want, don't you?" There was no accusation in his tone, just a flat statement of fact.

"I suppose I do, although I've never thought much about it."

Bannigan closed his eyes. Her breasts brushed back and forth against his chest until his nipples were as hard as her own. "Then don't begin to think now, and I won't." His breathing came quick and shallow.

Elena laughed and reached down to kiss his face. Her hair brushed his cheeks, enclosed his face. His mouth was waiting, lips slightly parted, for her to reach it.

Now she would make him beg, take him as easily as he had taken her. Her nails teased. Her tongue slithered at every opening. Exhilarated by the quickness of his response, she slid down on him and felt the tremor in his body as she took possession at last.

PAPARAZZI SWARMED around the limousine that pulled up in front of the Hotel Principe e Savoia, where Elena had once refused Stefano Carlatti's too generous offer. She stepped out of the back seat in a kaleidescope of silver and laughing smiles. Flashbulbs exploded around her, catching her excitement. Sweeping up the tiers of chiffon that shimmered in the long skirt, she waved and surged forward against the press. Bannigan got out after her, his expression more contained, and walked a step behind her, like an afterthought. She turned and reached for his arm, drawing it against her so that he could feel the warmth of her body. Laughing, she stood on tiptoe and whispered something in his ear that produced a half-smile. Liveried attendants bowed and held open the hotel doors. After her speech she would take Giorgio home with her again. She bowed at the entrance to the ballroom, accepting the applause that greeted her arrival as her natural right. Then alone, she mounted the dais, thinking how he would explore her again with his agonizing thoroughness.

She would insist, and she was sure he could not refuse her now.

Marco and Giorgio—two policemen now in her thrall. A comforting thought.

Chapter Thirty-six

WILL YOU tell Marco?" Bannigan exhaled and watched his breath smoke. It was the coldest day since he'd been in Italy, and he wasn't prepared for it.

"Will you?" Elena was bundled in sable, as casually as if it were down.

He shook his head.

"Why? Am I so shameful you are embarrassed to admit that you made love to me?"

"Not you. I'm the shameful one."

"Because you wanted a woman?"

He shook his head, blew on his hands and stamped his feet. He was frozen to the core. For the fourth straight day, he had staked out Lombardy Import-Export and hadn't come up with anything except crates of olive oil. No wonder Lacrisso had never spent a day in jail. He ran a clean operation. One of the cleanest Bannigan had ever seen. If it weren't for Dante and the beating he'd narrowly escaped, he'd be inclined to write off Lacrisso's company as a dead end. If he could only get into the warehouse. . . . He had been studying it all this day, trying to convince himself there was a way to get in short of nitroglycerine. A windowless rectangle, smooth walls without details to double as footholds, and guard dogs, pit bulls with a lean and hungry look.

He looked at Elena. "Because Marco is my friend and I wanted his woman," he answered her. "I still do."

"Good." She leaned into him, radiant even now after a full day at the bank. "I can think of better ways for you to warm your hands," she said, slipping her arm through his. Her limousine coasted behind them.

"Why are we walking when I'm freezing?" He let his teeth chatter.

"I thought you preferred it, and it's only another block."

The *corso* was crowded with early diners, late shoppers, workers hurrying home, an occasional face standing out from the blur, like the magnified detail from a painting. He admired Elena's reflection in the store windows as they passed. Without the paparazzi surrounding her she strolled unrecognized.

In Milan the time between seven-thirty and nine-thirty, the end of the work day and start of the dinner hour, was the liveliest. The cafes filled with noise and discussion on every topic—the state of the nation, the production at La Scala, the mysteries of Italo Calvino, the wildcat inflation, the fashions of Giancarlo Ferre, the new challenger to Basile Armani, Missoni, Fendi and the rest. In the days of Dior and Chanel, Paris had been the epicenter of fashion, but the locus had changed, although the French refused to admit it. The shapes, the textures, the colors—the fashion excitement was coming out of Milan now.

They pushed into the crowded cafe where Marco waited. Elena slid into the banquette beside him. Dropping her furs over her shoulders, she leaned over so that he could kiss her on each cheek.

"I missed you," he said with the kisses. "Did George take good care of you?"

"Good enough." She laughed and squeezed his hand. A reassurance, a promise, a lie freely given and gratefully, hopefully accepted.

Bannigan sat down opposite them. "How was Rome, Marco? Did you absolve the Vatican or are you holding out for a strict penance?"

"I'm not sure yet. Do you know the head of the bank is an American bishop—from Pittsburgh, Pennsylvania."

"Unless his name is Carnegie, he's come a long way for sure. I can't imagine he'd be anxious to be sent home soon."

"He was very . . . direct. I like Americans—you are so straightforward."

"Even when we lie." Bannigan pulled his chair closer to crowd out the din. In Milan talk was almost as important as industry, and the noise level in the cafe was somewhere between loud and louder. "What did my compatriot have to say for himself?"

Boni fumbled for Elena's hand under the table and held it in both of his. "The situation in the Vatican is complicated, especially at this time." He leaned across the table as if to bring Bannigan even closer into his confidence. "The Bishop admitted that he'd made mistakes in his dealings with Carlatti . . . Parente, too. He was too trusting, too naïve."

"Innocent mistakes, I suppose?"

"Yes. But with dangerous repercussions."

Elena's glance shifted back and forth between them, occasionally turning away to glance over the room. She didn't attempt to join in their conversation and she barely sipped the *Negroni* Bannigan had ordered. He didn't accept that she only drank champagne. Even when she told him, he thought she was joking. It was like only eating white truffles, he thought, or chocolate mousse.

"Not only for the Church but for the people of Poland," Boni was saying.

"Now you've lost me." Bannigan's attention kept drifting over to Elena. She was too quiet, too reserved. He wanted to read her mind, to know everything that she kept hidden from him.

"At the end of the month the head of Solidarity is going to Rome to have a private audience with the Pope. Solidarity is already so strong in Poland that many believe the Soviets may be planning an invasion, and this meeting will show the world that the union is not afraid, even with foreign troops on its doorstep. The Communists will seize on anything to discredit the meeting."

"What better than a scandal over the Vatican's finances." Like most of the city's power class, Elena was a Christian Democrat and resolutely anti-communist. "In this country, too, the Communists would be so happy they would declare a holiday."

Boni was nodding. "Exactly. Under the circumstances, I agreed to wait until after the meeting. Then I will go to Rome again."

"So you allowed the American bishop a grace period?"

Boni dropped his voice to little more than a whisper. "The Bishop didn't say so directly, but I understood that the request came from the Pope himself. How could I refuse?"

"I wonder if the grace period will be extended until finally it becomes a saving grace for the IOR." Bannigan wasn't sure he believed in a God who had a kingdom, let alone a Vicar, on earth. He put Boni on the defensive.

"Coming back from Rome I made a decision. I'm going to put everything I've found on tape—even this business with the Vatican. Then I can concentrate on finishing my work, and if anything should happen to me, at least the investigation won't suffer." He thought Elena's hand stiffened, but maybe he was holding it too tightly.

"Now that you've got God on your side, I'd think you'd stop worrying so much." Bannigan was mostly teasing but Boni was deadly serious.

"I admit I am preoccupied with Carlatti—and maybe I am worrying too much about his threats, but I want you to promise me something, George. If anything does happen to me, you take the tapes. They'll be safer with the Americans. It's hard to know who to trust here. Carlatti has bought so many."

"You Italians really go for drama. Must be something in the blood. What about you, Elena? Are you preoccupied too?"

He felt the toe of her shoe slip behind his knee. "A person with an obsession will stop at nothing."

* * *

BANNIGAN WAS humming "Satisfaction" as he pushed his way out of the cafe and by Elena's bodyguard, who was clogging the door with his intimidating bulk. He stopped at a butcher shop and bought five pounds of liver and the knife the butcher used to slice it with, then headed north to find out for himself just how pure Lacrisso's olive oil really was.

He circled behind the warehouse so that he was upwind from the dogs that padded back and forth behind the wire fence. The pit bulls were squatter, thicker and much uglier than Dobermans, but he didn't even want to guess which breed was more vicious. He counted three of them. Creeping up to the fence, he sliced a V in the wire, just enough to push himself through. He waited in a crouch to see if the dogs had sensed him yet. The stillness of the night was absolute, as if the world had come to an abrupt end.

He dropped a piece of liver at the opening and squeezed through, running across the yard toward the trucks lined up as neatly as dominoes. He only had to cover a few feet but it might as well have been a marathon. The bulls tore around the building before he'd gone a stride, howling their intention. The bloody liver did attract one of them, and without breaking stride Bannigan pulled out a second slice and threw it over his shoulder. A second dog stopped to feast. Now, inches from a truck, Bannigan tossed the rest of the liver behind him as far as he could and lunged for the door handle. But the first dog had wolfed down the meat in two bites and returned to the chase. It leaped at Bannigan and caught his heel, ripping off the sole of his shoe. Bannigan dove into the cab and twisted around to pull it shut, the bull right behind. It came down on top of him, its front paws pinning him down on the seat, its jaws inches from his jugular, closing in for the kill. Bannigan yelled and brought the butcher knife up with all his strength. Entrails gushed over his hands, and the animal collapsed on his chest. The other two dogs howled and leaped at the door. Struggling to sit up, Bannigan pushed the carcass toward the open door, using it as a shield. The smell of fresh blood drove the other bulls crazy, and they leaped at the body as Bannigan heaved it out as far as he could. Pulling the door shut, he started the truck, backed it up, and before the two bulls could look up from their feast he'd gunned the accelerator and run over them, then backed up and done it again.

The absolute stillness returned to the yard of Lombardy Import-Export. Wiping his hands and knife on the seat cushions, Bannigan swung down from the cab. Dog hairs matted in the blood that drenched him from the neck down. He wondered what the Italians gave for breaking and entry with intent to kill three bulldogs as he went to work on the back door. Surprisingly, the lock was easy to pick. The dogs had been considered protection enough.

Inside, the warehouse was cold. Concrete floor, walls, even the ceiling. It was lower than he'd expected. He peered around, orienting himself. Wooden platforms stacked with crates. Idle fork-lifts. Tin gallon cans waiting to be boxed. He pulled up the plastic seal of one, spilled the liquid over his finger and licked it. Olive oil, one hundred percent *pura*, as Marco had said. He tested a second and a third. All he needed was a little vinegar and a tomato. Trash barrels overflowed with broken crockery. He picked up half a cup, then tensed and turned around, sensing someone watching him. No movement, no sound except the faintest click. He strained. It sounded like a telephone receiver being lifted. He moved toward the glass enclosure at the far corner of the warehouse, knowing he should have checked it out first. An old night guard could have been sleeping. His hand closed around the knife in his belt. Flattening himself against the glass wall, he inched along until he was close enough to kick open the door.

And found himself staring directly at two men in white coats, one of them pointing a submachine gun in the vicinity of his abdomen, the other just putting down the phone. His gun hung from his free hand. All three momentarily froze as if their scene had been freeze-cut, then came to life together. The butcher knife flashed through the door. The carbine stuttered, one of the volleys catching Bannigan in the shoulder. The men in white obviously weren't marksmen, Bannigan thought. He turned and ran for the door, the V in the fence.

He thought he heard an animal whimper as he squeezed through, or maybe it was himself. It was only a flesh wound, but it hurt like hell. He started back to the city, avoiding the highway. He didn't know whom the men in white had called and he was in no shape to hang around and find out.

He considered hitching, then thought better of it. No one in his right mind would pick up a hiker with a slug in his shoulder and a wardrobe of blood. With luck he'd make it back to his *pensione* by dawn. He tried to think and fit the pieces together as he trudged along. The men in the lab coats had to be chemists; no wonder they hadn't chased him. But what were they doing in a warehouse with submachine guns, and why were all the dishes smashed? He tried *not* to think how Elena and Marco were spending the evening.

Chapter Thirty-seven

Elena smiled up at him from his Louis XV desk, framed against the arched entrance to La Scala. Her shoulders were wrapped in sable, her hand rested on Marco Boni's arm. The color in the photograph was so clear Carlatti could see the gold of her necklace and the blue glass of the stones just visible above the fur. He wondered if she wore it as a penance or as a goad to herself to give an inspired performance. Marco Boni was at her side. From the expression on his face, he looked as if he'd been struck by a thunderbolt, as if he couldn't believe his good fortune.

Carlatti took out a second picture and spread it on the desk. Elena looked even more radiant than before. The paparazzi had caught her rushing out of her limousine in a swirl of silver chiffon. A tall blond man was at her side. When Carlatti examined the picture through his magnifying glass, he could see that she was clutching the American's hand. Maybe it was the glasses, but he appeared to be preoccupied, remote, as if he had removed himself from the picture, and the woman.

Carlatti laid the two pictures side by side so that the edges of the photographs met. He'd clipped them both from *Gente*. Elena Torre was as popular as a movie star with the paparazzi, and scarcely an issue of the magazine appeared that didn't contain at least one picture of her. Although the man in the second photograph wasn't identified, Carlatti had learned who he was. So had Pietro Lacrisso.

He took out the message he'd received from Elena that morning and reread it.

It seemed he had succeeded in frightening Marco Boni, but not scaring him off. Fear had made Boni even more dangerous. Instead of getting off the case, the ridiculous lawyer was putting everything he'd uncovered during his investigation on tapes, so that the evidence could not be destroyed with him.

Carlatti opened a fresh box of caramels and began stuffing them into his mouth. A line of sticky spittle drooled onto the lapel of his dressing gown, disgusting him. He considered himself a patient man. He'd tried to quiet Boni with money, lust, intimidation. Nothing had worked. Boni was too stubborn—a slow learner. A family man should be more reasonable. He removed the offensive dressing gown and called to Donna to bring a fresh one. More decisive measures were required.

Chapter Thirty-eight

Is your girl very young?"

"What?"

"Your girl in America. I assume you have one."

Bannigan nodded, preoccupied, and ran his tongue over the reed and his fingers down the shiny tube of Mister Antoine Sax's demented invention. "Maybe too young." His shoulder still ached.

Elena shook her head. There was a sadness in the motion and in her eyes. "No, I am too old."

He took the scales down breathily. "You'll never be too old."

She laughed. "You were learning the alphabet when I was learning to make love. That's how old I am . . . forty-four, and you?"

"Thirty-three." He knew he should have lied, but he didn't—the least he could do for Marco. "Do you know there's a song named for you? It's called 'Maria Elena.' "

"My name is Elena Maria."

"That's close enough." He began to pick out the tune on his sax. Did Ben Webster start this way? The great tenor sax Ben Webster breathed heavily and out the other end came music. Then there were

Lester Young and Coleman Hawkins. He stopped to adjust a sticky valve.

"It's beautiful," she said.

"When it's played right, almost as beautiful as you."

She lay back, wanting him—and wanting him to make her believe it was true. Her sadness clung to her like a perfume. It had come over her like a sudden mist, somewhere on the road between Milan and her villa at Tremezzo that hugged the shore of Lake Como, the mountains rising behind it like protective arms. She'd planned an idyllic weekend for them, and she was spoiling it herself. . . . She hadn't been able to convince Marco the tapes would be a waste of his time. She'd tried, but it had been difficult not to be too obvious, not to provoke questions about why she was against it. She was sorry, oh yes, she was sorry, but there *were* priorities, or rather a priority, and he had to be served. . . .

"I have a son, you know, at the university."

"I know. Marco told me."

"One day he will join me at the bank."

"What if he doesn't want to?"

"He *will* want to. He is a Torre." Her determination was glacial, inescapable as her family's destiny. She bore her son like the stigmata, accepting his weakness, and paying any price for his wantonness because he was the last of the line. This time, though, the terms had been set by Stefano Carlatti, and the cost was being carved out of her heart.

BANNIGAN SAT fingering the valves of his saxophone, staring across the lake through the French windows. He thought of his own mother, lean and brown, with the leathery skin of a country club wife. When he remembered her, he thought of her throaty down-to-earth voice ordering another Manhattan on the rocks with a maraschino cherry, or he thought of her long legs splayed over pom-pom socks, a putter angled just in front of them. Where was she now? At the club in

Santa Clara, driving across the fairway, or had she followed her caddy into the rough at the twelfth hole? He could imagine his mother having sex, but not making love. She had five children, which of course proved nothing.

Below them the lake stretched like a cliché—clear as glass, winter-blue. Beyond, the promontory of Bellagio rose into amethyst mist. The nasal squawk of the ferryboat horns and the honk of gulls called across the water over the pleading bells of San Giacomo. There was no glint, no shimmer in the harsh white light. In summer it would gleam off the Romanesque spire of the church, off the tiled roofs of Bellagio and the lemony-yellow walls of the Grand Hotel Villa Serbelloni, a time when flowers cascaded along the lake's edge; now the banks were masked with green.

"Over there is Bellagio," Elena said, pointing across the water, "where there is a hotel that ranks with the Danieli in Venice and the Excelsior in Naples as one of the truly great hotels in the world. The Villa Serbelloni." She reached up and traced the trajectory of her desire down his body. "Tonight we'll take the motor launch across the lake and have dinner there in the old-fashioned gilded dining room. It's only across the water, but it is like going back in time to an era when manners were gracious and dinner dress *de rigeur.*"

He blew a discordant note through the sax. "I feel like a kept man." Also something of a rat.

"Don't worry, Giorgio, I won't keep you long." Her skin was smooth and golden. A dark brown mole just below the navel. A single stretch mark across the left hip, the only sign of age or of maternity. He knew he would never really possess her, yet he wanted to leave some imprint. All her son had left was the single stretch mark . . . and her husband, her other lovers, Marco? Had they made any mark at all?

"Over there . . ." Elena was waving in a vague northerly direction ". . . is the village of Varenna and Villa Monastero. It was a convent once but the nuns were driven out in the sixteenth century, a punishment for their alleged immorality."

George laid his sax down beside her. "You look pretty gloomy. Are you sure this is what you want?"

Elena leaned on her elbows and lifted up so that he could pull down her slacks. But her sadness suffused even their lovemaking and he withdrew leaving her dissatisfied for the first time, his tenderness only deepening her melancholy. She needed Marco's boisterous athletics to drive away the gloom. Marco . . . Carlatti . . . her son . . . a terrible triangle with no escape for her.

Bannigan began to play her song again, alternately picking out the tune, then singing the words. She heard it as if from a distance, scraps of melody drifting into her consciousness. She saw his face in the same oblique way, the trace of a smile just showing a glimpse of small even teeth, the pale curious eyes like question marks. He always seemed to be waiting for her to tell him something. And of course she could not.

He reached over and stroked her throat with the backs of his fingers as he sang. It didn't matter. Marco's presence intruded like an ache, blunting her desire, feeding her depression.

Stefano Carlatti was patient only as long as it served his purposes. Since Lugano, it no longer did. Now he was thirsting for vengeance, forgiving nothing. Almost anything seemed benign compared to Carlatti's methods of retribution.

Elena hugged herself. The sky was darkening too quickly. She must try, risk something. . . . "You are Marco's friend. You should make him give up this investigation—for his own good."

George stopped playing and looked down at her. He could see the faint traces of lines spreading out from the corners of her eyes and the feather-thin circles that ringed her neck. "Usually you laugh a lot, Elena, and today you're all sad and gloomy. What's up?"

"I am talking about Marco."

"How come you know so much about it you'd want him to give it up?"

She met his eyes steadily. "Marco has told me how frightened his wife and children are."

"Did he tell you I killed a man who'd been beating him up?"

"I am serious—"

"So am I. I pushed the guy over the highest catwalk on the cathedral. That didn't make Marco stop." His fingers played around her jaw. "Were you by any chance thinking about him when we made love just now?"

Elena shook her head. "Of course not. I am worried for him, that's all. I would be for you too, if I thought you were in danger."

"Would you?" He gathered her up in his arms and kissed her with an urgent thrust of lips and tongue. "I can't imagine you losing sleep about anyone as insignificant as George Bannigan. My family tree is a dentist and a golfer. We haven't even got a coat of arms." His lips returned to hers, drawn back by a desire that kept mounting. "Tell me what the hell you're hiding behind your laughter and sadness?" He carved the words into her lips.

She'd risked enough. "That I love you, Giorgio," she whispered, slipping her arms around his neck.

He laughed and pushed her down across his lap, wanting her more because he knew that she lied. He stripped her. The excitement was not in the pleasure of exposing each hidden part but in having all of her naked beneath his hands. She lay across his knees, head thrust back, and let him have her body. His hands and his lips and his tongue took possession of her, bringing her flesh alive until the desire to take him into herself was so strong that she began to tremble out of control.

Only then did he let her undress him, pleased when she swore at a stubborn button.

"What are you thinking about now?" His voice was quiet.

"I want you, Giorgio." She pulled him over her, blocking out everything with the sweet, sweaty redolence of their sex. In the rough, unrestrained lovemaking even the threat of Stefano Carlatti was forgotten.

Chapter Thirty-nine

THE BOOTS of the armed guards knocked on the inlaid marble floors of the Banco di Milano. The beam of their flashlights roamed across the empty desks. German shepherds padded beside the guards, sniffing the stones for an excuse to attack. It was the last round of the evening. The sun would rise in an hour but it wouldn't matter. A chill fog wrapped the city, insulating it from any warmth or light. Other than the guards, the only sound in the baroque banking house was the whirr of a tape-recorder upstairs in the president's private office.

Marco Boni lit his last cigarette and aimed the crumpled pack at the wastebasket beside the desk. It was a navy leather octagon embossed with gold, as elegant as everything else in the office except the woman who normally occupied it. Boni looked over at the couch where Elena slept, curled up under his suit jacket, and thought of the first time they had made love, high above the Straits of Messina. Each time was perfect, and the next even better.

Inhaling deeply, he began to read again. By the time he reached the final page of his voluminous file his voice was cracked and rasping. He clicked off the tape recorder, removed the cassette, and marked it: "The Case of the Bank of Italy vs. Stefano Carlatti, #47." He stacked it on top of the other forty-six and ground out the cigarette. Three years of digging as meticulously as an archaeologist, three years of his life—an obsession—compressed in a pile of plastic rectangles. The threats were empty now. His work was safe. He had Elena to thank for that. Putting the cassette back in the machine, he added an official note of thanks to Elena Maria Torre, president of the Banco di Milano, for permitting him the use of her office for the tapings. He watched her sleep as he spoke, keeping his voice low so as not to disturb her.

In repose she looked as vulnerable as his daughter Francesca, only fairer, a golden girl, his golden girl. Stray curls like ripples of gold clung to her cheek, and the skin beneath was flushed with sleep. Her lips were parted, emitting the faintest whistle. It made him smile to think that she snored, even so slightly. The three years had changed his life. Bianca had borne him two more babies, and Elena had made him faithful, after a fashion. He only lusted for two women now instead of all women. He wasn't sure if it was an improvement. If forced to choose between Bianca and Elena . . . he pushed the impossible thought aside.

He got up and walked over to the window, rubbing the back of his neck to work out the cramps earned from hours hunched over the tape recorder. From such a distance the gilded copper Madonnina atop the Duomo seemed sculpted of solid gold. He thought of the night he spent by its spire with Bannigan, who had saved his life. Butch Cassidy and the Sundance Kid.

The bells of the cathedral rang out, a vibrant reminder to obey the second commandment: Remember to keep holy the Sabbath. From the couch Elena watched him, rubbing the sleep from her eyes. "Are you tired, Marco? I can send one of the guards out to bring back some breakfast for us. Then you can go on."

"I'm going out myself." Boni laughed. "I'm finished, Elena." He pointed to the cassettes stacked on her desk. "Forty-seven tapes. Will you keep them in your safe for me?"

"I told you I would." She sat up, unfolding her body from the position of sleep. His jacket slipped off her shoulders as she smoothed her hair. "I must look like a disaster."

"You've never looked more beautiful."

She laughed. "You always say that, Marco."

"And always it's true."

"Do I look respectable enough to go out to breakfast with you? That's not the same as looking beautiful."

Marco turned away. He hated to refuse her anything. "Maybe tomorrow we could have breakfast together if you like."

"Where are you going now?" There was no trace of disappointment in her voice. "My car is outside so I can drop you off."

"You left your chauffeur sitting out there all night?"

"I didn't know how late you'd be."

Marco sighed. "I'm going home to take my wife and children to Sunday mass as soon as you lock these things up."

"And on the seventh day Boni rested. I never knew you were so devout, or such an admirable husband and father."

"You know I'm not, so don't mock me." He was losing his voice, the little left was a rasping croak. "And it's not devoutness, it's selfishness. I'm hoping to bribe God. I need somebody's protection."

Elena pulled his jacket around her although the temperature in the office hadn't changed. "More calls?"

He shook his head wearily. "Worse. A letter bomb exploded when Bianca opened the door yesterday. We were lucky. Only her leg was burned."

"That's why you were in such a hurry to finish taping?"

"They're just trying to frighten me. I keep telling myself, Carlatti is a thief, but a killer too?" He shrugged and tried to joke. "Maybe when George hears the tapes I'll be a voice from the grave."

She said nothing. She couldn't.

"Promise me that you will give them to him, Elena, if anything happens to me."

"You don't have to suspect everyone." She tossed aside his jacket.

"You can give them to him yourself if you don't trust me. Tomorrow evening at seven-thirty. I told him to meet me here."

"I've trusted you with all my secrets, Elena." He moved closer, as if he was going to take her in his arms, then stopped. "Why did you tell him to come here?"

She stretched. "So I could take him home and make love to him, why else? Your Bannigan is very handsome."

Marco grabbed her wrist and pulled her up against him. The sharpness of his jealousy surprised him. "For once you'll be disappointed, Elena."

"Are you so sure? You go home to your wife. Why shouldn't I go home to Giorgio?"

"Because I love you, and George is my friend."

She reached up and ran her fingers through his hair, combing back the curls. "You make it sound so simple."

"It is. George wants you, Elena. A man would have to be a eunuch not to. I've seen the way he watches you, but he'll never go any further."

"Can you be so sure?"

Over her shoulder he saw the spires of the Duomo melding into a gray blanket of sky. "Friendship between two men is different than between two women."

She broke away from him.

"What's the matter?"

"You're too innocent, Marco. Tomorrow I should teach you the meaning of friendship."

"WHERE HAVE you been, Marco?" Bianca had been sick with worry. Now that she saw he was safe, she was angry.

"Working." He went to kiss her.

She turned her face away and picked a golden hair off his jacket as if it were a leech. "All night?" He had never stayed away from her bed all night before.

"I'm sorry. I should have called but I was afraid to wake the children. How are they?"

She shrugged. "Do you care?"

"You know I do." She'd never questioned him before, either his loyalty or his love.

"What are you going to do now? Sleep? Or do you want breakfast?"

"I thought I would go to mass with you."

Before Bianca could answer, Francesca rushed out of the bedroom and threw herself into her father's arms. "Will you really come, *babbo?*"

"If you want." He picked her up and hugged her so tight she screamed. "Are your brothers ready?"

"Almost. Will you button me?" She turned her back on him so that he could fasten her best Sunday dress and tie the sash.

Bianca watched him for a moment; then she went to get the babies ready. Her mistrust was spilling over all of their lives. After church, when the breakfast was finished and the children were playing, she would show him the picture that she had cut out of the magazine. She hoped it wasn't too late.

Marco came and stood in the doorway. He wanted to tell her that he loved her, but Bianca pretended not to notice him. He watched her dress the babies, admiring her sure, efficient motions. By quarter to nine she had all the children lined up at the door.

The Boni family hurried down Via Boccaccio on their way to nine o'clock mass at Santa Maria delle Grazie, their parish church and a tourist attraction.

Francesca and the two older boys ran ahead, followed by Marco carrying his youngest daughter. Bianca had the baby. Just as they started out the door, he spit up on her dress. By the time she cleaned it and started out again, the others were almost a block ahead.

"*Aspettami,* Marco," she called, hurrying to catch up. "Wait for me."

Turning back to answer her, Marco did not see the two men who pushed past the older children. Francesca stopped skipping and stared after them, suspicious of everyone now. The boys, who had been imitating her, pestered her to go on, but she hushed them. The men drew within fifteen feet of her father and stopped. She saw the stock of a gun and ran back screaming to protect him.

Startled, Marco turned back into the face of two muzzles. Instinctively he doubled over to protect the child in his arms. As he did, bullets riddled his neck and burst open his skull. Francesca fainted as her father's face blew apart in front of her. He fell forward, still clutching his youngest daughter. The child died moments later, suffocated by the force of his embrace. Though she clawed desperately at his bloodied body, Bianca could not pry the little girl from his arms.

Chapter Forty

M ARCO BONI is dead."

Carlatti did not care for her tone. "It is too late for you to be offended . . . after blackmail, extortion, seduction, spying. A question of pragmatism."

"You never mentioned murder—"

"Are you lonesome without your lover, Elena?" His voice was like dirty fingers touching her. He had never dared call her Elena before. His behavior toward her had always been correct, even respectful. "There is always the American, George Bannigan I think his name is. Surely you can convince him to comfort you?"

Elena shifted the phone to her other ear and rolled over on her side so that she could consider her body in the mirror as she talked. She could afford to take his abuse now. "You made a mistake. You killed Marco for nothing. He didn't have the tapes. But I do. I will tell you, Carlatti, they are devastating." She kept her voice low, intimate. "You will have to live several lives to serve out the prison sentences you will receive when I make them public. And I will, you have my word on that as a Torre. Unless, of course, I receive my necklace and the protection it will give my son from you. I will give you forty-eight hours of grace, and not a moment more. Enjoy them, Carlatti, because they could be your last."

CARLATTI'S GILDED cage was closing in on him. The supreme control he had shown to the world—and particularly to his enemies—was giving way. He talked aloud to Immacolata as he paced, pulling at his hair and gesturing extravagantly.

Hearing his excited voice, Donna rushed in and found him alone. He banished her like a servant and went on ranting, cursing the enemies who still persecuted him . . . cursing his nemesis whose scorn had been his downfall and, damn her, could still destroy him.

Chapter Forty-one

THE FUNERAL of Marco Boni and his two-year-old daughter passed all but unnoticed. It came on the same day that a *carabinieri* general was gunned down in Rome and a magistrate was crippled in Milan by bullets fired into his knees. In the fabric of terror that spread over the nation, the burial of one unfortunate bank lawyer seemed incidental.

The cemetery was in the northern sector of the city, close enough to the train tracks to hear the cars streak by, a more mundane departure. Bannigan walked all the way through the bone-chilling January morning—his own *Via Dolorosa*—to stand at the gravesite. The two coffins, one small and white, the other long with a glossy brown finish, were placed side by side and lowered into the same pit. The priest, a raincoat pulled over his lace surplice, rained holy water on the boxes.

"Deliver him, O Lord, from everlasting death on that day of terror when the heavens and the earth will be shaken as Thou dost come to judge the world by fire."

For the family huddled behind him the new year had ended

abruptly. The children, too stunned to cry, circled their mother, each clinging to some part of her clothing for comfort. Only Francesca stood apart, so straight she might crack, her face as white as the smaller coffin.

"That day will be a day of wrath, of misery, and of ruin. A day of grandeur and great horror. . . ."

Bannigan counted a dozen family members besides Bianca. A black lace mantilla was draped over her hair, which was drawn back in a bun too severe for her face. She wore it like a punishment, he thought. Her shoulders, her head, even her eyes were cast down in sorrow, like a *pietà*. There were few mourners besides the family. Only Bannigan, a cluster of four men, Marco's young assistants, who looked around continuously as if wondering which of them would be next, and an older man who stood slightly apart, his black raincoat buttoned to the neck, his hat in his hand.

"I am the resurrection and the life. He who believes in Me even if he die, shall live, and whoever lives and believes in Me shall not die forever."

Ugo Mazeppa murmured, "Amen," and turned away, pulling his hat straight down to the tops of his large ears. Bianca picked up a handful of dirt in her bare hands and sprayed it over the open grave.

Bannigan caught up to Mazeppa at the line of waiting cars. Like the rest of the funeral and burial, they were being paid for by the Bank of Italy. Mazeppa had made the arrangements personally. A duty to a loyal employee or an act of contrition to ease his own conscience. Bannigan introduced himself. Mazeppa mumbled something Bannigan couldn't catch and shuffled forward.

Bannigan persisted. "I'm an American agent investigating the case of Stefano Carlatti. Marco and I were working together."

Mazeppa stopped reluctantly. "A funeral is not a place to discuss business. If you would like to call my office and make an appointment. . . ."

Bannigan held back his anger. "I have something for you . . . Marco Boni's last will and testament, you might call it. As you know, his death wasn't exactly unexpected. He anticipated they'd try to shut him up."

The old man shivered in the cold. "Marco didn't tell me. He should have confided his plans—"

"You knew his life had been threatened before—his wife and children badly frightened."

"We do not know yet if his death was the result of his work or something else . . . a random attack, so common these days—"

"I know. I was with him when he was attacked the first time."

"These cases sometimes become unpleasant. A difficult job. I would have relieved him willingly but he insisted on going on with it."

"After he came back from Rome the last time he decided to put everything he knew about Carlatti on tape."

The furrows from Mazeppa's nose to the corners of his mouth were like trenches; the cheeks sagged on either side of them. His body, once compact, sagged too, the flesh slack with age, only the mind still firm. "Where are the tapes now?" His eyes were half-shut, creating a deceptive impression of somnolence.

Bannigan rocked on the balls of his feet. "He asked me to make sure you received them in the event that something happened—"

"Yes, yes." Mazeppa cut him off. "I could bring them back with me to Rome today."

"Since we're investigating Carlatti too, his drug connections, we'd like to share the tapes. . . . International cooperation would be helpful to have on the record if you decide to ask for extradition."

Mazeppa's eyes opened a fraction wider and fixed on him like a suspicious father's. "What are your intentions?"

Bannigan pushed up the bridge of his glasses. "I thought I'd take them to Rome myself, to the American Embassy, and have a copy made for us, then hand over the originals to you. You said to call for an appointment when I get to Rome. . . ."

Bianca came up to them, her family fanning out behind her. She must have been a lovely bride, Bannigan thought. Her tears flowed soundlessly, like the holy water.

"Mi dispiace, signora." "I am sorry" sounded insufficient in any language, Bannigan thought. *"Sono un amico di Marco."*

"Americano. The policeman. You promised to help my husband."

"I tried. I guess not enough—"

"He is not responsible, *signora."* Mazeppa surprised him, coming to his rescue.

Even in her sorrow, Bianca was deferential in front of her husband's employer, *un grand signore.* She had her own pride and dignity, but also a deeply ingrained respect.

Mazeppa was full of praise for Marco. "He died the way he lived, with courage. You should be proud to be his widow." He had spent the ride from Rome choosing those exact words to express his condolences. He had made the trip that morning, leaving the Eternal City before dawn. "His death will be investigated, and whoever is responsible—"

"I know who murdered Marco." Bianca's grief took over. "Stefano Carlatti."

He passed over that for now. "We all feel a measure of guilt, *signora."*

Bianca's dark eyes opened wide, and she looked from one man to the other. Yes . . . guilt . . . she would carry the burden of her own guilt with her for the rest of her life. "I was angry with him, I turned away from his embrace, refused his kiss. I had never done that before. He died without my love. In the ten years we were married I never turned away from him. Never. . . ." It was as if somehow her coldness to him at the end had sent him to his death.

Mazeppa patted her hand, a kindly grandfather. "You shouldn't blame yourself. None of us is responsible. . . ."

BANNIGAN LOOKED back one last time. The grave of Marco Boni and his daughter looked like a fresh wound in a bed of hoary grass and gray stones. Bianca had pressed him to come back to her home after the funeral, but he declined, afraid that he might start to cry.

Chapter Forty-two

BANNIGAN SANK against her breasts and let the tears come. "Was Marco in love with you?"

Elena stroked his hair. It was silky and fine, the texture as different from Marco's as the man. "He loved you, Giorgio. He valued friends more than lovers."

"You didn't answer my question."

"I know."

"What will you do now?"

"What do you mean?"

"Without Marco."

She loved his innocence. "I'll go on, as I always have." She kissed the top of his head, the crest of his forehead. "Stay with me, Giorgio, for the whole night. We'll lie in bed and hold each other. You're not the only one who needs comforting, you know."

She lifted his glasses to kiss his eyelids, then her lips moved across his cheek, along the bridge of his nose to his mouth. He opened her blouse, lifting her breasts over the edge of her slip. The points of lace scratched against the nipples. He took them in his mouth, seeking . . . giving . . . consolation and sustenance.

257

Inexplicably he remembered Zenah. He hadn't thought of her in weeks. She'd saved his life so that he could end up this way, end up here in Elena's juices?

He stood up and began to undress. Elena slid her skirt over her hips and began to roll down her stockings. When he was naked she came to him in her slip and held her arms up. Reaching under the hem, he inched it up, a deliberate ascent over her thighs, the swell of her hips, the curve of her waist, the slope of her breasts. As each configuration was exposed, like a relief, she brushed it against him. Their hands never touched, only their bodies. Bannigan was the first to give in.

The first time was fast and relentless—a kind of exorcism. The next, all-consuming. She held him in the darkness that had gathered unnoticed, still caressing his body in the residue of their lovemaking.

"Why the hell am I here, Elena, a California beach bum, mediocre sax player and God knows what else—I'm not sure myself anymore—instead of a thousand other men?"

She stroked him, her fingers sticky with his sweat and semen. "Is there someplace else you would rather be?"

"No."

"Then that's an answer."

"And Marco . . . ?"

Her fingers toyed with him for a moment before she answered. "He was here for other reasons, Giorgio. They don't matter now."

He tried to see her face but her head was curled against his chest and she refused to lift it.

"Do you have the tapes he left for me here?"

She let him go and pulled the sheet between them. "Tapes?"

Bannigan tensed beside her. "Marco told me he was putting everything he had on Carlatti on tape . . . in your office. They're still there, aren't they?"

Elena closed her eyes, abruptly shutting him out of her life. Going on with her own. The necklace had been delivered while Bannigan was at the funeral. She'd already arranged with her jeweler to examine it in the morning. After that . . . ? She hadn't yet decided whether to turn the tapes over to Carlatti, wash her hands of the whole distasteful business, or perhaps hold them for further protection . . . ? Bannigan didn't fit into either plan. . . .

"Well . . . are they in your office?"

She opened her eyes again. He had sat up and was crouching over her. Elena shrugged. "Why would I have some tapes from Marco? He was my lover, not my business partner."

He leaned down and kissed her. "Don't make me hurt you, Elena."

"Would you?"

She started to slide out of bed but he slipped his arm under her and pulled her back against him. "Only if I have to. I want those tapes. I gave Marco my word if anything happened to him I'd get them to Washington. Maybe then we'll be able to get Carlatti on two continents for this."

"You're so sure it was Carlatti? What about your American justice?"

"Innocent until proved guilty? Tell that to Marco Boni. The tapes, Elena. . . ."

"Yes . . . well, perhaps I should keep them. You fly back to Washington, then I will send them to you."

"I can't leave now, even if I trusted you enough. I still have unfinished business. At least I think I do."

"Don't be a fool. Marco is dead and you're alive. I want you to stay that way." She tried to persuade him, beginning with her lips, and she almost succeeded.

THE NEXT morning at eight-thirty they took the elevator to the underground garage where Elena's bulletproof chauffeured Mercedes waited with the engine running. They were flanked by her personal bodyguard. Instead of following the usual route to Banco di Milano, the car detoured to the northeast and stopped across the street from the Hotel Garibaldi, a modest *pensione* a few blocks from the railroad station. Bannigan went into the hotel alone and came out a few minutes later carrying his saxophone in its well-traveled black leather case. The car then proceeded to the bank, where they went upstairs to Elena's office.

Bannigan looked around the room, efficient and at the same time elegant. He had never considered Elena in that way before, but now he realized that she was both. The safe stood at the far end in the corner. He went to it and waited, wordlessly, for her to open it.

"You don't know what you're doing, George," she said, realizing now it was useless to try and save him.

His only answer was to wait for her to open the safe. The morning streamed in the windows with the blinding clarity of winter light. Four piles of cassettes were stacked one beside the other. Bannigan stooped down to examine them. His knuckles grazed something hard and cold. He picked it up. The light reflected off the blue stones like starbursts. His hands closed around them and he stood up.

"What's this doing in with Marco's tapes?"

Elena turned away from him. "It's not *with* the tapes. It is the Torre necklace, an heirloom that has been in my family since the Renaissance. The jeweler is coming for it today. To clean it."

Bannigan held it so tightly the stones cut into his fingers. Marco's words came back to him: "There was one transaction—harmless enough, as I remember. Carlatti bought a piece of jewelry from Pietro Lacrisso. It must have been for something very special. . . ." Somewhere, stuffed in a pocket, he had a Xerox of the transaction that one of Marco's assistants had made for him. He remembered now the description: "A sapphire and gold necklace dating from the Renaissance. . . ." A coincidence? Something much worse? He didn't want to face that, the implicit connection with Carlatti. . . .

Bannigan dropped the necklace back into the safe as if it were poisonous. "You would never have bothered with Marco for himself, would you, Elena?" His voice was so low she almost didn't hear him.

"Boni. . . ." She said his name as if she'd forgotten him already. "He was a good lover and a good man, but too easy." She leaned against the window frame and smiled. "I could make him feel powerful, or foolish, as if his trousers were too short. Not like you."

"You were Marco's girl, for Christ's sake. He was nuts about you. I thought you—"

"And you are hopelessly American . . . so naïve." She threw up her hands in exasperation. "I am no one's *girl*. I was a wife, briefly, and I am a daughter, a mother, a woman with responsibilities to preserve a heritage, interests. Mine and many others. You are rootless, no ties to place or history. We live in time here. Our lives have a context, a continuity, which we must respect—even sometimes die a little for."

He looked at her. "Did you know he was going to be killed? Did you set him up? How did they know he was going to mass? He probably hadn't been to church in months. Why this Sunday?"

"Now I am a murderer too, as well as heartless, cruel, conniving."

"I didn't say that. I asked you how they knew he was going to church. He came from your bed, and went out to get killed. A damn short road—"

"Not my bed, Giorgio. My office. He could have been watched. It's not so unusual. You forget, he trusted me. I have these tapes to prove it."

Bannigan turned his back on her and began to take them out in sequential order, counting each one. He was meticulous, a man discharging a sacred duty. Elena didn't offer to help, believing as he took them that he was earning himself a death sentence.

"What are you going to do with them?" she asked as she locked the safe again and watched him put them in the instrument case. "Will you try to take them to Washington?"

"I'm not sure yet." The office felt cold. Bannigan zipped up his jacket and tucked the case under his arm. "I need time to think."

She devoured him with her eyes. "Call me, Giorgio, so I won't worry."

He went up to her, and for a moment Elena thought he would kiss her. Instead he brushed her lips with the back of his hand and quickly left her.

* * *

A CUSTOM Jaguar was parked in front of the bank when Bannigan went out. On another day he might have stopped to admire it. Now he scarcely noticed it, or the young man who was getting out of it. Even without Lacrisso's description, Lucco Torre would have recognized his mother's latest lover from the photograph in *Gente*. That was how he had kept up on her activities ever since she'd made him get out of her house.

Lucco hesitated, then followed Bannigan, hating him on sight for his closeness to his mother. It was more than the physical intimacy that he resented. Although Lacrisso had made his request sound innocent enough, Lucco felt sordid, like a procurer. He didn't like to hear his mother's affairs discussed by strangers. He remembered Dante's threats. At least Lacrisso spoke like a gentleman, regardless of what he really was, and his request was impossible to refuse.

Bannigan was easy to follow even in the morning crowd. His blond hair, his height and the specially shaped case he carried made him conspicuous. Lucco trailed behind him at a comfortable distance. In exchange for arranging a meeting with this George Bannigan, Lacrisso would return the Torre necklace. Bannigan stopped in front of the Hertz rent-a-car office and went in. Lucco followed, reluctant to let the American out of his sight. He vividly imagined his mother's happiness, and her forgiveness.

Bannigan was at the desk. He wanted a car that he could drive to Rome and leave there. Lucco stood in line behind him, and when his turn came inquired about monthly rental rates, pretending he was planning a trip through France. By the time he had finished, Bannigan was at the public telephone placing a transatlantic call. Lucco went to the next phone and listened. The call took a long time to go through, and Lucco was getting nervous waiting. Finally Bannigan began to speak, delivering his message clearly and impersonally, as if he was talking to a machine. "Len, I'm leaving for Rome. Will stay at Pensione Isa. Check the diplomatic pouch tomorrow."

Lucco waited until a car was brought around for Bannigan, then called and gave his own report. Lacrisso sounded pleased, until he asked for his payment. "You want the necklace? Ask your mother for it." He laughed and hung up.

Chapter Forty-three

Len Hindle looked around the Milan airport as he waited for his call to go through. It could have been any city in any country—brightly colored walls, plastic furniture—but it was Milan. Hindle smiled to himself thinking how surprised Bannigan would be when he showed up at the door of the Hotel Garibaldi.

"Hattie? Are you there? Well, I made it." He hadn't been in Italy since '44 and he was looking forward to the vacation, even if it was a working one.

Her voice came through as clearly as if she was talking through her intercom at the office. He'd expected to wake her up. Instead she sounded as if she'd been waiting up for his call. "Are you sitting down, Len?"

"What the hell time is it over there?" He didn't want to hear her say you'd better catch the next plane home. Not this time.

"Too early. Listen, Len. You've missed George. He left a message on your line an hour ago—make that an hour and a half."

He imagined Hattie checking the log. "I should have had him meet me," he muttered.

"I'll read it to you." Hattie proceeded efficiently as if she hadn't heard his complaint. She rarely admitted to hearing them. "What do you think?"

"How the hell do I know. I'll get on the next plane to Rome and find the sonofabitch."

"Give him my love, Len. . . . I hope he's not in trouble again."

IT WAS a brilliant day in Rome, bright blue and defiant. Hindle half-expected to see sandbags and seas of uniforms as he rode in from Fiumicino. The beachheads of Anzio were only a few kilometers to the south. Bloody beaches. Half his company never got beyond them. He leaned back and looked out at the remains of the ancient aqueduct. It was good to be on terra firma again. Washington–New York. New York–Milan. Milan–Rome. If he never flew again it would be too soon. He should take the boat back, if they still sailed. The beautiful Italian liners, Leonardo, Raffaelo, white and majestic as swans, were beached now, casualties, like the bodies at Anzio. There was an American cemetery in the next town, Nettuno, green and white and perfectly symmetrical. An Elysian field with row after row of plain white crosses stretching as far as the eye could see. He would visit that too, show Bannigan what war was really about.

The city was coming into focus, sacred domes and triumphal arches, and sounding over all of it was the rush of pure water. What could you think about a city that produced such wonderful food and such terrible drivers. Hindle rolled down the taxi window and craned his neck out, taking it all in. He was anxious to see Rome again, and George Bannigan, and it didn't even matter that the cab driver was getting ready to fleece him.

The driver pulled up at a modest hotel. Hindle paid the outrageous fare without flinching, and even added a tip, glad just to be there finally. In the foyer the manager approached, oozing apologies. The pensione was full, but if he could come back tomorrow there would be more rooms available.

Hindle, a large man, could be insistent when he chose, but after checking the registrations and finding no American by the name of George Bannigan, he could feel the manager becoming suspicious. Hindle found himself out on the street again, with his valise in his hand and no place to go. He wandered down a couple of blocks, thinking that the city had seemed friendlier in '44, and ordered a Coke at a stand-up bar, then bought a nougat bar from the cashier and started back, watching for Bannigan. After all, he had to show up sometime, unless there was another Pensione Isa in Rome.

Later, Hindle would remember that he had stopped and put down his valise so that he could unwrap the candy when he glimpsed Bannigan a block ahead, but at the time events seemed to collide pell-mell, leaving nothing certain but the confusion. . . . Bannigan loping along, black saxophone case under his left arm, right hand in his pocket . . . "George," Hindle boomed out, started to wave, in the distance could see two men coming toward the *pensione* from the opposite direction but never gave them a second thought . . . Bannigan beginning to turn . . . the men coming toward them opening fire . . . Bannigan turning, his Beretta drawn . . . must have kicked one of the gunmen because Hindle had heard a cry and saw a man stagger . . . Bannigan had never had a chance to shoot again . . . a moment later he jerked back a step, clutching at his chest, black case thudding to the ground just before he did. . . .

Hindle started to run then, not that there was anything he could do; the two men were instantly gone, probably in a car. He stopped, looked down at his feet. If he moved forward an inch, the toes of his shoes would touch Bannigan's blond hair. The bullet that had opened his chest had exited through his back, making a hole the size of a quarter. Hindle picked up Bannigan's saxophone case and started walking as fast as he could without being conspicuous, and in the confusion of the shooting passed unnoticed.

If he'd kept his big mouth shut . . . if. . . . He hailed the first cab he found. Walking away from the body of George Bannigan

was the toughest thing he'd ever done, but he knew how suspicious
foreign cops could be, and he couldn't even have described the assas-
sins, except to say that they both had black hair.

Ah, Bannigan. God*damn.*

Chapter Forty-four

THE AMERICAN Embassy in Rome—a rose-colored villa located at the foot of Via Veneto, where the avenue curves in like an ankle to form Piazza Barberini. Leonard Hindle's oversized body was crumpled in an easy chair in a second-floor anteroom, his oversized feet propped up on a straight-backed chair he had pulled in front of him. His mouth hung open. Jet lag had finally caught up with him, and he was snoring loud enough to wake the dead. In a morgue across the city the corpse of George Bannigan was being subjected to a battery of forensic tests that would do little to answer the questions surrounding his death.

Hindle had refused the ambassador's offer of more comfortable quarters, preferring to wait outside the door of the room where the preliminary report was being prepared. When it was finished, he would fly back to the States with the body in a special army plane. So much for his working vacation. It never failed, except this time was the worst.

If he'd called Bannigan home after that damned memorial service, or even if he'd come over sooner himself when he first sensed trouble, it might all have been different. The last eighteen hours had been agonizing. What he'd gotten out of them was Bannigan's old saxophone case, and he'd only picked that up out of sentiment—to give to Hattie. The Irish and the Italians treasured relics of their dead. Leave it to Hattie. He still wasn't sure what had made him open it in the cab, except that it had seemed unnaturally heavy. Now a joint force of American and Italian technicians were closeted in the soundproof room behind him, listening to a saxophone case loaded with cassettes labeled, "Carlatti 1, 2, 3. . . ."

Gradually he became aware of a firm hand jolting him awake. Though exhausted, he was grateful to be relieved of the horror of sleep. His eyes had closed on the bullet that exploded in Bannigan's chest, and he had watched the body jerk and stutter like a film clip replayed over and over at every speed. He blinked now in confusion, trying to shake off the disorienting fragments of sleep . . . bloody scraps of flesh were spliced across the faces staring down at him.

"Sorry to have to wake you like this, Len, but we'd like to get this business cleared up as quickly as we can. I know you feel the same." Although they'd never met until ninety minutes before, the ambassador called him Len, to show, he supposed, that they were in a sticky business together. He rubbed his eyes, blotting out the faces, and forced himself to stand up.

"This is the Italian interior minister," the ambassador was saying, introducing the face beside his. "He'd like you to go over the whole incident, as much of it as you know."

Hindle nodded.

"We'll talk in the office across the hall." The ambassador took his arm as if he were an invalid. "I've asked the CIA bureau chief to join us too. You may know him, Len. Sturges Grahame."

Hindle didn't know him personally but he recognized Grahame the moment he saw him draped against the arm of a chair in the empty office.

"Sorry about your man." Grahame shook hands. "I met Brannigan once. . . ."

"Bannigan. George Bannigan." Hindle's correction was angry, but it passed over Grahame.

"He struck me, frankly, as a disturbed sort. Came to me with some story about a Bulgarian connection." He had the bad taste to smile as he said it.

Hindle moved in as if he might devour Grahame with a snap of his teeth. "Bannigan was one of my very best. He might have been too smart for his own good, too zealous, too committed. But that's *all*, Grahame. I always send the nuts who come in wanting to be agents over to Langley. They fit in better there."

"Every agent is a valued government servant," the ambassador cut in with the smoothness that had earned him his job. "In this case, regrettably, we may not be able to make our appreciation known publicly. But you will be glad to know, Len, that the deaths of Bannigan and the Italian investigator who made the tapes you found have not been for nothing. Of course it will take weeks, even months to transcribe and translate all of them, but our people judge that there is enough to nail Stefano Carlatti in both Europe and the U.S. The minister and I have agreed to cooperate fully."

"A formal letter of thanks will be sent from my government to yours," the minister said cordially.

"We also intend to draft a joint letter of thanks to Elena Maria Torre, president of the Banco di Milano, who allowed Boni the use of her private office for the taping. She belongs to one of the finest families in Italy," the ambassador said.

You scratch my back, I'll scratch yours, Hindle thought, but he wasn't going to let them bury Bannigan with a couple of letters. "What does she have to do with the Carlatti case?"

"Elena Torre is the leading businesswoman in Italy, and a highly respected banker." The warning in the ambassador's voice made Grahame smile.

"We will make inquiries, discreetly, of course, Signore Hindle," said the minister. "Marco Boni was a married man with five children, and the woman in addition to being very successful and of a most prominent family, is very beautiful." The minister was being worldly, and expected Hindle would be the same about the matter. "I am sure she will cooperate. In view of the complications, we would like to treat this case as quietly, as diplomatically as possible. So many nations, so many conflicts of interest are involved—your government, my own, the Vatican, perhaps even the Kremlin—who can say? The least public attention, the better for all concerned."

The three men were looking at Hindle, waiting for his agreement.

Hindle looked from the ambassador to the minister. It was two o'clock in the morning but their faces were clean-shaven, their suits unwrinkled. Marco Boni and George Bannigan had been professionals, killed in the line of duty. It went with the job, even if it wasn't spelled out in any job description. Their lives were disposable. These were the rules of the so-called game.

And it was a little late in the game for him to start getting holier-than-thou about the rules.

The others took his silence for assent. They sat down in a circle of chairs.

"The first problem is that we didn't know your Bannigan was operating within our country," the minister said. "And you, yourself—"

"I'm here on vacation, if you can believe that," Hindle corrected. "I'm having trouble believing it myself."

"Why don't you begin with your arrival in Italy, Len, and bring us up to the time you came to me here at the embassy," the ambassador coached. "You arrived at the Rome airport at—"

"Actually I flew into Milan this morning. I was going to look up George, ask him to show me the sights. I never got to see anything but the airport."

"You will come back, Signore Hindle, I'm sure," the minister told him. "But now you have just landed in Milan. . . ."

"The first thing I do whenever I arrive any place is call my secretary and check in with her. Even though it was some godawful hour at home I telephoned to Hattie. . . ." He began his narration as if it were already a tired story. And it was, because he could see in their faces that they were in the process of composing a more acceptable one.

"Unfortunately George didn't keep in as close touch as I'd have liked the past few weeks. So your guesses are as good as mine. I'll probably spend every night for the next twelve months speculating about what happened today. Right now, as I see it, there are two possibilities. First, Bannigan's investigation of the flow of southwest Asian drugs brought him back full circle to Stefano Carlatti, whom he'd been investigating in New York. He sensibly joined forces with the local investigator, Marco Boni. At some point, probably realizing he'd become a target, Boni entrusted the tapes to Bannigan. When Boni was killed, Bannigan came to Rome to deliver the tapes to the embassy for safekeeping."

"Very reasonable." The ambassador was grateful for good non-controversial answers. Good diplomacy.

"It is," Hindle agreed, "except that it leaves unanswered whether George Bannigan was silenced because he knew too much about the drug smuggling set-up or because someone wanted the tapes enough to kill for them. Or both." Hindle looked from one man to the next. "There's one other question. To me . . . I suppose because I knew George so well . . . it's the hardest of all to figure. Where is his saxophone? It was his prize possession, and I know he wouldn't entrust it to just anyone."

The ambassador shrugged off the question as an irrelevance. "It's probably back at the *pensione* with his luggage. I'll have it sent over here so you can take it back with you or dispose of it as you like."

"Thanks a lot," Hindle muttered.

HE WAS still muttering to himself an hour later when he opened Bannigan's duffel bag. It was depressing to go through the remains of someone's life. At least he was alone to perform the squalid act. He turned the duffel over. The remains were always so pathetic, and Bannigan's were no exception: toilet articles, clothes and a bundle wrapped in corrugated paper. Hindle nicked his thumb on a chip of broken saucer trying to open it. Swearing, he tore off a piece of the paper to wrap around the cut. Billows of white powder flew over everything. Bannigan's hunch had been more than crockery.

Chapter Forty-five

E LENA TORRE went home alone after work and lingered in the tub, soaping herself in continuous circular motions, the way she used to soap Lucco when she took him into the tub with her. She couldn't remember anymore when she'd stopped bringing him into the bath, or when he had become his father's son. The one time she had consented to see her husband between her discovery of his infidelity and their annulment, Peter Jenkins had quoted Pope to her: "To err is human, to forgive, divine." She had learned otherwise.

To forgive wasn't divine—only necessary sometimes. The time had now come to forgive her son. With the proper inducements Lucco might be persuaded to take his place at the bank, where, as the Torre heir, he belonged. Elena got out and wrapped herself in a long terrycloth robe that had been warming on a heated towel rack. She could be very persuasive when it suited her purpose.

The evening dress she was wearing that night to the charity ball to benefit the city's orphans was laid out on her bed. A simple black velvet with long leg-o'-mutton sleeves, a wide skirt and a square neck that would show off to its full advantage the priceless necklace that every generation of Torre women had worn.

Flicking on the television, Elena watched the evening news as she dressed. She had missed the first minute or two but was just in time to see the camera zoom back to the street scene where a bloodied body lay face down on the cobblestones. The reporter's voice chattered on: "One man lies dead tonight, his identity as yet unknown, in what appears to have been a terrorist attack." Elena stepped into the black velvet, unable to turn away from the morbid scene. An ambulance sped up behind the reporter as he talked, forcing him to pause until the siren quieted. "All we know at this point is that gunfire was exchanged between the unknown victim behind me and two assailants who escaped."

Elena was fastening the necklace at her throat when medics lifted up the body to place it on a stretcher. She stared at the screen and found herself devouring once again the familiar, even features of George Bannigan. A white sheet was drawn over his bruised face. She studied the picture, searching for the black saxophone case in the street. There was nothing on the cobblestones, except his blood.

"We will bring you an update on the story as soon as we have more information," the reporter was saying. Elena turned the television off and sat down at her dressing table to arrange her face for her son. Lucco would be arriving in an hour to escort her to the ball. If poor Giorgio hadn't been so foolish she would be dressing for him now. Or undressing. They would have made love at least once before the dance, and then again when she brought him home. He liked her to undress him and fondle him as if there was no man in the world she wanted more. For a while that much had been true.

She also had wanted to make him forget everything except her— to make him lose himself in her desire, her body, the way Marco had. But she always felt as if he held back a part of himself from her. In the end, he'd walked away as if she'd been any woman. He hadn't walked away from Marco Boni, even after Marco was dead. Elena couldn't trust a man who put another man before her. Especially not after the betrayal of Peter Jenkins.

* * *

LUCCO LED her in a waltz by Strauss. The ball was very formal, very proper, and her son was a graceful dancer, holding her as if her flesh had changed to porcelain.

"Did you notice what I'm wearing, Lucco?" Their eyes were level. Her dancing slippers made them the same height.

"The necklace. . . ."

"I've been waiting for you to admire it. I thought at least you'd be surprised to see me wearing it again. I put it on just for you."

"That was kind of you, *mamma,*" he said, not knowing if it was, or if it was cruel. "But I'm not surprised."

Elena waited for him to go on, studying him. She'd thought his father was the most beautiful man she'd ever seen, but Lucco surpassed him. It was his curse to be exquisite, and a man.

"I was going to get the necklace back for you," he was saying. "But when the time came to collect it I was told to look in your jewelry box. I couldn't admit that you don't even permit me in your house."

"How did you plan to get it?" The thought of Lucco going up against Stefano Carlatti was like the fable of the elephant and the ant. Still, he was young yet, and she had hope.

"It's not important. . . . I did a favor for a man. How did you get it?" He threw the question back at her.

She turned her eyes away from him and let her body meld with the music. Lucco felt her breath against his ear, then the whispered words. "I paid for it . . . a very high price." She touched his cheek with her fingertip and smiled at him. "I have my necklace back, Lucco. Now I want my son."

He had not seen her since the day she struck him, and the excitement of being with her again was almost more than he could control.

LATER THAT night Elena returned to her office, the cold stones now warm around her neck. Her arrival upset the normal routine. Lights flicked on. Guards snapped to attention. Dogs snarled. Sending them off with a wave of her hand, she brushed by them and went upstairs alone.

In the sanctuary of her office, she locked the door and pulled the drapes closed. Then, turning on a single lamp, she turned the combination of the safe that she alone knew. She stepped back as the door opened and stared at the silver horn that gleamed in the single light.

Elena took out the saxophone and touched it as if it possessed life. In the morning Lucco would begin to work at the bank. It had been his choice—she only showed him the way. She held the cool metal against her cheek for a moment, then she brought it to her lips and tried to pick out the notes to "Marie Elena," the song Bannigan had played for her.

Chapter Forty-six

E XCEPT FOR the marshals who waited like footmen, the air-conditioned room was as serene as the expanse of sky that spread over Central Park and spilled through the wall of windows across Fifth Avenue. Leonard Hindle watched from the door as long, slender fingers chose a fresh sheet of origami paper and began to fold it, each move precise, each crease exact. When he was finished, Carlatti stood up with the same apparent calm and motioned to the marshals, indicating his readiness. They clapped handcuffs on his wrists to escort him to JFK Airport where an Alitalia jet waited to bring him back to Italy to stand trial for the murder of Marco Boni.

The extradition proceedings had dragged on for six months. Hindle had hoped to nail Carlatti for Bannigan's murder as well, but the circumstances surrounding it were still nearly as vague as they had been when he was killed. And no one else, on either side of the Atlantic, seemed too interested in clarifying the case. He bit into his cigar stub, glad that somebody at least was getting Carlatti.

One of the marshals picked up a calfskin valise packed with the only worldly goods that Carlatti still cherished—his Nietzsche books, his origami papers and his stash of caramels. He had arrived in Milan the first time with nothing but a single dark blue suit and prospered. He would, he swore, again.

Carlatti brushed past Hindle as if he were part of the furniture. His vow to Immacolata made him eager to return. He was never lonely now or even nauseous. He conversed with her each day, feeding on her dreams as he had when he was a boy. Her faith in him was absolute.

Alone in the hotel suite, Hindle took one last look at the leased elegance that Carlatti at last was exchanging for a prison cell—unless he somehow managed to buy his way out of that too. But maybe I've gotten too cynical, he thought. The origami that Carlatti had been fashioning so meticulously was a blue square with a single crease that had been folded and refolded, creating nothing so far as he could see.

Hindle closed the door and took the shuttle back to Washington. When the trial got started in Milan, he'd have to fly back to testify. At the same time, he'd check on the new DEA investigator who had replaced Bannigan in Milan. He was working with the Italian police to penetrate Lombardy Import-Export. Now that they knew how the morphine base was getting through from Bulgaria, they were trying to locate the processing laboratory before they went after Lacrisso.

Even that was cold comfort. Hindle was still lying awake nights counting sheep and trying to figure out what had become of Bannigan's saxophone. Everybody except Hattie thought he was nuts to carry on so about a horn.

ANNA STIRRED and turned over on her side as Parente opened the curtain a crack. He froze, afraid of waking her. The Matterhorn rose through the bedroom window, its white summit lost in the morning mist. He'd seen the pictures of Carlatti on the television news the night before, being led from his New York hotel in handcuffs. It was only a matter of time before he would be led away too. Even the thought of prison was claustrophobic. He would lose his mind in a cell . . . his dignity. He couldn't save his bank or himself, any more than he could count on Carlatti's gratitude to protect him. They had agreed to use each other, and Parente had learned that Don Stefano was not a man who made idle promises.

Parente hesitated as he began to dress, then pulled on the woolen knickers that still fit him after thirty years of non-use. Not much dignity in knickers, but he wanted to be convincing for Anna and the children. He had taken out private Swiss accounts for them so that they could settle on any gold coast in the world they liked. It was his only legacy. Nothing was left to Banco Bartolomeo except the Renaissance building. The transfusions of cash to Carlatti had bled it dry. Carlatti was like a hemophiliac. No amount was enough.

And Parente could not hide the losses anymore. Bishop Desmond was calling in his letters of comfort, and the board of directors had scheduled a special meeting on Monday morning without consulting him first. He buckled the knickers over the tops of the thick gray knee-socks and began to lace the heavy boots, for once not concerned with the scuffs they would make on the hardwood floor. When he was a boy he had climbed all over the Alps, attempting more and more difficult approaches requiring increasingly demanding techniques. But none of them came close to the size, the danger or the grandeur of the Matterhorn. Although he had grown up at its foot, he had never challenged it before.

He strapped on the leather belt and checked his equipment. Claws, crampons, picks, spikes, pitons, ax and rope—all in pristine condition. He slipped the tools in the belt and looped the rope. He lingered at the foot of the bed. Anna's breathing was blessedly even. He did not kiss her. He did not even touch her, just the blanket that covered her, afraid to awaken her, even more afraid to weaken himself.

The Matterhorn rises 14,780 feet into thin air, the jagged configuration of its rock-hewn horn the result of some long-forgotten glacier. The morning was chill. Dew still clung on the air and shimmered on the first flowers of spring, the season of life. Although he didn't whistle, the dogs bounded up to him and bumped against him, wanting to feel his hand on their heads. The bodyguards crowded behind them, their presence reminding him of the reptile, Gattino. Parente dismissed them and got into his Mercedes. The dogs wedged in the back seat. They loved car trips.

The Matterhorn had always been an inescapable fact of his existence. He'd been born in its shadow. He drove up from the foot, as close as he could to the dangerous southeast wall; then, leaving the keys in the car, he started the strenuous trudge before the final feat. The dogs clambered around him as he climbed.

Although it took him a while to regain the rhythm—he had been physically idle so long—the ascent was liberating. He was where he loved to be the most. He thought of a lifetime in jail. Courage, or cowardice, drove him higher. He could have been a figure like Elena Torre, he thought, a person of honor and respect, if someone had delivered him from the evil of Stefano Carlatti. Or if he'd been older when Carlatti had first tempted him. . . . But then he reminded himself that wisdom didn't come with age, it came with hindsight. His mistake had been trying to climb too high, too circuitously. A mountaineer should know that the *direttissimo* was the best, the most satisfying—the straight-line ascent from foot to peak with no traverses, no ways around.

He looked up. The mist had dissipated. The peak of the Matterhorn stood out, a rugged, uneven pyramid, splendid in its isolation and majesty. Behind it the sky opened and closed like a contest of wills, puffed-up pockets of white and brilliant blue patches fighting for pre-eminence, first the one then the other crowding each other out.

He stopped and clamped spikes onto his boots. Just ahead a sheer wall of rock rose two thousand feet. The dogs, panting and straining, followed as far as they could. He could hear their urgent barking as he began to scale the stony face. He climbed steadily, alone against the rock-hard world, as in a way he had always been. He drove in a pick and heard a rumble over his head. A shower of rocks pelted down. Although he swung out to avoid them, several ricocheted against his shoulder. The ascent demanded his total concentration. At first he was tentative but he gained confidence the higher he climbed. Wedging pitons into the wall, he hooked the rope over the circular heads of the iron pegs and looped it around his waist so that he could lean out from the rock to search for footholds.

The wind was punishing the higher he climbed. The ice thickened. He was only a fraction of the way to the summit, yet the rarefied air burned his throat. He dug his spikes into the glassy wall and looked down. His boots disappeared in vapors of clouds like the feet of saints in cheap plaster statues. His eyes smarted. He had been a hero once on the Russian steppes. Maybe he would be again, at least in his family's eyes.

He drove in the next spike and pulled himself up to it without fastening the rope. His heel found the foothold. For a moment he held on, knowing that the ascent is always easier than coming down. Overhead the sky pushed back clouds of cotton. He wondered if Bishop Desmond would say the funeral mass or if he would already be on permanent retreat. His foot slipped out, fastening onto emptiness, and his body began the quick, suffocating descent.

Chapter Forty-seven

DONNA CARLATTI sat in the cramped prison room and wept. Her husband didn't notice. In five days he would go on trial—a public spectacle—Don Stefano who had contributed so much to so many. She had spent a week in Rome with a list of those who had received his generosity—a beggar, pleading for help. Not a single person would stand up for him publicly, although privately many expressed sorrow, some even outrage.

Carlatti preened, a proud man again. He boasted aloud of the take-overs he was planning with Parente and Desmond. Donna had told him that the banker was dead and the Bishop disgraced. It made no difference. He was in the grip of his delusions. The trial would vindicate him and restore his honor. His grandmother would be proud. He didn't need his wife to comfort him any longer. Immacolata was with him.

He stuffed his face with caramels, ignoring the sticky spittle that seeped down his chin. His tie and shirt were spotted; he thought his dress impeccable. "Women will bow and men will tip their hats when they hear the name Carlatti," he assured his grandmother.

Donna could not bear to have the world see him like this—exposed, defenseless. The doctor in New York had given her sedatives for him. Even when she lied and said they were vitamins, he refused to take them. She had brought them home with her, still hopeful.

Donna had never questioned whether she loved Stefano Carlatti. He was her husband, and she had devoted her life to him. His disgrace was her own. She mopped at her tears with a handkerchief she had sewn herself and reached for his hand. He evaded her.

"I brought you more caramels. I'll leave them here on the table for you." She gathered herself up. "Don't forget them, Stefano."

BIANCA BONI looked constantly from side to side, as if, once inside the prison, she was afraid she would never be allowed to leave. She needed to see, face to face, the man who had kept his vow to make her a widow and her children orphans. Once the trial began, judges, lawyers, reporters would make it impersonal. She had no faith in its outcome.

"Bianca Boni." She had to repeat her name three times for the guard, she was so nervous. Since Marco's death, she'd been taking sedatives to get through each day.

He checked his list. "Boni." The name sounded familiar but he could not place it, and only authorized visitors were allowed to see Stefano Carlatti.

Bianca had wanted to look at Carlatti, even touch him, to focus her hatred on more than a photograph or a remote figure. Marco had said he was a man, not so different from other men with a sweet tooth, especially for caramels. She didn't really believe it, but she had brought a box with her as a kind of test to see if he were a mere mortal rather than the legend she'd heard about.

She took the box out of her string bag and pushed it at the guard. "For Carlatti," she murmured. What else, after all, could she do with them? If she brought the candies home her children would want them. She didn't let them eat sweets—especially caramels.

* * *

THE LIMOUSINE slipped soundlessly up to the prison door, cloaked in the fog of night. The warden, a man who understood the value of discretion, escorted the visitor to the receiving room where the prisoner had been led just moments before.

Carlatti stared at her blankly. She was dressed darkly, enshrouded like a nun, a veil lowered over her face. Her eyes gleamed through it like a cat's.

"Elena Torre." He reached out to embrace her but she shrank back from his touch. His fingers were sticky, his nails implanted with dark moons. "I have been waiting for you. You received my call and came running, as I knew you would. How could you resist? As I once tried to tell you, together we will conquer not only Milan, not only Italy, but Europe . . . the world. You know my grandmother, Immacolata. . . . The three of us will be the new triumvirate."

Elena did not lift her veil. She was shocked by the change in Carlatti. With his trial just days away, she had grown too apprehensive to stay away. She knew the value of his word as a gentleman. But instead of calming her fears, the visit upset her. He could say anything. It was impossible to do business with him. "I was hoping we would settle our differences to our mutual self-interest, but now—" she stopped herself. There was no point in trying to explain. "Here." She handed him a small bag. "I brought you something, a peace offering. I remember you said caramels were your favorite."

"Why have you come here?" Carlatti turned on her in a rare moment of lucidity. "Do you think you can buy my silence with a few candies? I, Don Stefano Carlatti?"

Elena backed away. "They were made at Dolcetta especially for you."

THE DAY after receiving the three modest presents, Carlatti lay down on his prison cot for a siesta. The candies were at his elbow where he could reach for them even if his eyes grew heavy, cramming handfuls into his mouth at a time—a habit he had acquired in his solitude. When the guard brought his dinner five hours later, he was still sleeping. In the morning, when his breakfast was brought in, his body had already begun to stiffen. An autopsy revealed that his death was due to an overdose of caramels laced with sedatives. Although a total of six pounds of candies had been received, only a handful was left.

All three boxes of caramels had been opened and emptied into a large coffee tin that one of the guards admitted giving to Carlatti for a price. One could conjecture that Carlatti wanted to possess *something* in quantity, even if it was only candies. Conjecture about the caramels was more difficult. There was no way to distinguish which had come in which box, and so there was no way to determine which of the three women had brought the lethal sweets. On questioning, all three professed innocence, although each did make a small confession.

Donna Carlatti, reticent and self-deprecating while her husband lived, spoke out forcefully to the prosecutors, defending her husband as a man of great genius and even greater passions. But she did admit a certain relief that he would not be subjected to the humiliation of a public trial and the prospect of a future confined in a miserable prison cell. She was confident that death, for him, had been no more painful than the stomach cramps and nausea he had suffered throughout his life.

Bianca Boni's hair had turned gray since Marco's death, and she no longer wore it down around her shoulders like a girl. Her dress was the widow's black that Immacolata Carlatti had worn for so many years. After crossing herself and prefacing her remarks with requests to the Almighty for forgiveness, she confessed that she was happy a murderer had been brought to justice, one way or another. For her children their father's death was an irredeemable loss. For herself she was content that Stefano Carlatti had paid for her husband's cruel murder.

Elena Torre expressed surprise but no grief when she received the prosecutor in her office. She met his questions with scorn, angry that her visit had been revealed. "How is it possible to grieve for a man like that, who spent his life destroying others?" she said. Her son Lucco hovered behind her chair uncertainly. She reached back and touched his hand. "At last Stefano Carlatti has received his just deserts." For a moment the prosecutor thought that her eyes glinted with amusement, or maybe it was just the sun bouncing off the gilded Madonnina that was playing tricks on him.

Chapter Forty-eight

S TEFANO CARLATTI was laid to rest beside his grandmother on a slope of the Monti Peloritani that hung over the port of Messina. Ferries and fishing skiffs slid in and out of the harbor below, combing the deep Straits. The funeral was a private affair. No one except the family chose to attend.

In Milan, Elena marked the event with a bottle of Roederer Cristal. The champagne was sweating in a silver bucket beside a bowl of fresh caviar. Edith Piaf was singing *"Je ne regrette rien."* She hummed along with the music. The letter she had received from the government commending her for assisting Marco Boni in his investigation was in a silver frame on her office wall. Bannigan's sax was still in the safe. She was considering taking lessons, although she knew her best talents were not musical.

Without Parente and Carlatti, her Banco di Milano was quickly regaining its preeminent position and, with the proper inducements, Lucco might even be persuaded to find a suitable girl. When he did, she would name him a vice-president of the bank. Elena was radiant when she contemplated that moment. The Torres, as always, had survived. She popped the cork and poured herself a glass. She had planned a private celebration—just for Lucco and herself—but he had telephoned to say that he was bringing a friend. Elena tried to imagine herself as a mother-in-law, and thought instead of Carlatti in the high Sicilian cemetery, cold even with the sun beating down on his stiff corpse. Christ died to set us free—and so, unintentionally, had Carlatti. . . . As long as he'd been alive she had been afraid. Elena swallowed the Cristal and turned to greet Lucco and his friend, sure that her son would not disappoint her again. Her smile evaporated.

Lucco mumbled the introductions, his voice strained and apologetic. He did not know how to refuse a man like Pietro Lacrisso when he demanded a favor.

"I should offer my condolences on this day when Stefano Carlatti is being buried." Lacrisso was most courteous.

"Why to me?" Elena felt suddenly fragile, vulnerable. At the slightest pressure she would crack. "Carlatti was merely a business acquaintance."

"Then we have something in common . . . besides Lucco here." Lacrisso's glance lingered like a caress over the beaten silver ice bucket, the antique china, the curved mirror, the oriental rug. He was clearly an appreciative man. "You have many beautiful things, but none more beautiful, I think, than the Torre necklace."

"You will have a chance to see it at first hand very soon." Elena smiled her indulgence, wondering why her son had brought such a man to her home. She knew Lacrisso by name and reputation. "I am donating the necklace to the museum, where it will be displayed with a text explaining its history." It wasn't so much that she mistrusted Lucco; she felt the necklace would be safer out of temptation, and it held too many memories for her ever to wear again with pleasure.

"Not its complete history, I trust," Lacrisso was saying.

"What? Why not?"

Lucco sat apart from them, pressed into himself—hands, knees, ankles so tight they seemed glued together. His pills, as his mother had discovered, were at the bank. He'd found that he could work better with her after he'd swallowed a couple of Seconals.

"With all respect"—Lacrisso helped himself to the caviar—"Stefano Carlatti received the Torre necklace from me . . . an accommodation I have regretted from time to time in the past, but not, I think, in the future."

Elena looked at her son. His face was all the confirmation she needed. "Pour some more wine for your guest, Lucco, and perhaps he will tell me why you brought him here today."

"Don Stefano was a clever man, whose death has left a void difficult to fill. He is already missed by many, but I tell you frankly, none more so than the Commission in his native Sicily. You are a northerner, but I trust you know of the Commission." Lacrisso licked a black egg from his index finger. "It is looking for a new financier, but there are none with both power *and* honor—other, of course, than yourself."

The crystal flute trembled slightly in her hand, causing the champagne to lap at the sides of the glass. Elena brought it to her lips to steady it, and considered Lacrisso over the rim. Carlatti's death, it seemed, had not been an ending but an overture. Piaf was wailing *"La Vie en Rose."*

"And if I refuse?"

Lacrisso looked from mother to son and back. "Can you, and your esteemed family, Elena Torre, afford to do that?"

She put down her champagne glass. Her celebration was over.